About Rod

Roderick Clyne is a journalist and television producer. He was born in Edinburgh but grew up in London, and worked on magazines and morning, evening and weekly newspapers until switching to television production. He was deputy editor of *Labour Weekly*, the party's official newspaper, and worked on the *Guardian* financial desk for 11 years. He was a researcher on Channel 4's *A Week in Politics* and LWT's *Weekend World*, and producer for Tyne Tees Television's *Face The Press*, then a producer/director for the Central Office of Information. After all this, he decided to see something of the world, but only got as far as Singapore where he married and joined the local all-news radio station. This is his first novel.

The
IMPERIAL
FATHERS

RODERICK CLYNE

LION CITY

Book design by Peter Langdon

ISBN 978-981-18-4866-7 (paperback)
ISBN 978-981-18-4867-4 (ebook)

Lion City Publishing
29 West Coast Crescent #11-30
Singapore 128049

for Gina

Preface

There were no social media in 1956, when opinions were filtered by the newspapers and television. The people who ran the country still expected obedience and deference, and were shocked when they did not always get it. The glory days of the British Empire were over, they had probably ended even by the time of the first world war, let alone the second, except that the patrician class tried to ignore the tiresome truth, carrying out a series of squalid rearguard actions, of which the Suez campaign was the culmination. The people who ran Britain had made the mistake of believing their own propaganda, as in the *Daily Sketch* headline: **Let The Cry-babies Howl! It's GREAT Britain Again!** This was an echo of the old music-hall song: "We don't want to fight, but by jingo, if we do, we've got the men, we've got the guns, we've got the money, too." But this time they didn't have the money. After the Suez invasion the pound came under so much pressure that the Government had to go cap-in-hand to the International Monetary Fund, and the US vetoed any help. As Vice-President Richard Nixon explained: "We couldn't on one hand, complain about the Soviets intervening in Hungary and, on the other hand, approve of the British and the French picking that particular time to intervene against Nasser." So there was what was politely called a ceasefire, followed by an ignominious withdrawal.

The inheritor of Britain's tarnished glory was not the Soviet empire, which was experiencing its own humiliation.

Membership of Communist parties worldwide had soared during and immediately after the second world war, in which Soviet Communists were depicted as "the bravest of the brave". After the war these new Communists believed the future was bound-up with socialism, what they called "historic inevitability". Theirs was the alternative to the unemployment and misery offered by capitalism, and this provided a feeling of worth, dignity and self-confidence. But if the main cause for the popularity of Communism in Britain was the Soviet Union, the actions of the Soviet Union became Communism's nemesis. After Hungary was invaded by Russian troops, how could people condemn Britain over Suez and accept that Hungarians had no right to make their own choices? Members left the Communist Party of Great Britain as fast as the flow of refugees fled Hungary. Around the world, it became clear that a country going Communist was to be treated like the loss of innocence, which once lost may not be regained.

The seeds of the subsequent disintegration of the Soviet Union and its satellite states were sown in the fields and streets of Hungary in 1956. In the same way as the British ruling class had not woken up to the fact that the days of their imperial power were over, the fate of the Soviet Union was already sealed, its rulers merely carrying on like dead men walking – for another 35 years.

This tale is told here as the people involved would have experienced it, largely through newspaper headlines. The headlines are all genuine, published on the date stated in the newspapers named. The exceptions are when the headlines refer to one of the fictional characters. There were no newspapers called *Daily Tribune*, or *Forward!* It follows that the people associated with these papers, the Ross and the Farnsworth families and their employees, are also fictional, as is the boxer George Crawford. Similarly, there was no nightly ITV current affairs show called *As It Happens*, Associated-Rediffusion television did not have a controller of programmes called Howard Hay, and there was no Communist Party official called Sørensen. Printing unions really were organised in the manner depicted, and the senior elected official at each paper really was called the Imperial Father of the Federated Chapels, the title doubtless owing something to a working class view that imperialism was actually quite good, at least for the imperialists.

R. C.
September 2022

Contents

1

Wednesday 25th July 1956

By far the best parties were in aid of charity, Lady Farnsworth told Jessica. "That way you can keep the lower orders out in a way you do not seem to be able to do anywhere else these days."

They were queueing up for a glass of punch at the only brightly lit part of the cavernous ballroom. Lady Farnsworth was wearing a sequinned calf-length gown that chinked as she walked. She told Jessica she liked the sound it made. Jessica wondered whether it reminded Her Ladyship of the chink of money jingling in Lord Farnsworth's pockets.

A ball such as this, Lady Farnsworth said, had to have a purpose. "It is no use in these post-war days merely enjoying yourself, it looks so frivolous. You need a theme." Lady Farnsworth's theme was Anti-Vivisection[1]. Thousands of defenceless animals worldwide were being tortured to death by the Communists. It was the task of the ball to set them free.

It was so important for everyone to have a group to belong to — even several overlapping groups, she said. That was another reason why they were all there that night. "We are here for Anti-Vivisection but also because we are all of one class and because we are all friends. We spend time with each other; we visit each other's houses, both in town and in the country; we marry each other and we attend each other's weddings and baptisms and funerals. Our families might appear to be rivals in business — like my husband and your father — but there is more that binds us together than divides us, even though your father *is* a foreigner. We belong together, you know."

The hired-in celebrities did not belong, apparently; they were there, not by right, but to provide something to look at; as the Victorians exhibited exotic animals or children with two heads, so the charity balls invited sportsmen, actors and famous explorers. "We are the real people, not them," said Lady Farnsworth. "The only reason they are famous is because my husband's newspapers decide to make them so. It helps divert attention, dear."

Jessica responded to the snobbish lecture in the way she was supposed to, by staying quiet and nodding her head in apparent agreement, although she tried to avoid to looking directly at Lady Farnsworth, revolted by the way her ladyship's facial hairs protruded through her thick powder. Instead, Jessica gazed at the ritual of making the punch. Each of the waiters, most of whom appeared to be Continental and who were surprisingly dextrous, had before him an enormous silver tureen, so large that it would have been difficult even for a tall man to encircle one with his arms. Just behind the waiters were stacked cardboard crates, each holding a dozen bottles of rum. All around them were half-gallon tins of fruit juice and there were basket upon basket of exotic fruits, such as oranges and bananas, imported from distant colonies.

One waiter caught Jessica's eye. Grinning all the while, and without turning round, he reached behind himself with both arms and picked up a bottle of rum in each hand. Changing his grip on the bottle necks as he brought them forward, he spun them both in the air and caught them, tops downward, as they fell toward the tureen. With a flick of the thumbs, he opened each bottle and let the contents fall with a jerking rush into the bowl. The contents of tins of fruit juice, each perforated with two triangular holes, followed two at a time. Then came the oranges and bananas, each peeled and chopped in seconds. Still without saying anything, the waiter took a cut-glass half-pint mug, half filled it with a ladleful of punch and topped it up with a practised swoosh from a soda siphon. He held the glass by its body and, with a slight inclination of his upper body that people could interpret as a bow if they wished, extended the glass, handle first, toward Lady Farnsworth. She took it without saying anything, and moved away.

Then it was Jessica's turn. She said to the waiter, quietly, so as not to be noticed by Lady Farnsworth: "No soda in mine, please. Just fill it up."

The pair moved back to their companions at a table beside the dance floor. It was not just to get a stronger drink than the one she would have been offered at table that had made Jessica suffer the minutes queueing up with her self-appointed chaperone; it was also to give her a few moments' respite from the strained company of her escort of the evening, the scion of the publishing family, the Hon Lear Farnsworth[2].

Lear was as awkward with her as she was with him. Jessica was sure that he would not have been pursuing her so much of late off his own bat; he would have chosen someone who shared more of his interests. He was doubtless acting on instructions from his family, not very successfully.

Jessica considered trying, yet again, to look at his good points. It was not as if he looked bad. Tallish, he had a slight stoop, but otherwise wore his uniform[3] rather well. It was a silly conceit for a second lieutenant, especially for one who was only a National Service officer[4]. He had just finished his two years and was now on Zed Reserve, to be called on only at times of national emergency. Dashing he might be, but handsome he was not. He did not make up for it with natural charm: he was maladroit, and tried too hard, especially when his mother was looking. As she was tonight.

Jessica was wearing a strapless evening gown, tightly held in at the waist and falling only just below the knee. It was in oyster duchess satin with sparkling embroidery and she wore it with a bright red satin stole and a four-stringed pearl necklace. The dress and Jessica's dark Marcel-waved hair showed off an expanse of unmarked pale skin on her long neck. The whole outfit, except the pearls, came from Marshall & Snelgrove[5]. Lady Farnsworth told her it made her look most elegant, but Jessica felt a fraud. She would far rather have been wearing tapered pants and a Continental sweater, or even a pencil skirt. She felt horribly out of place among people she did not trust and was not attracted to.

The conversation was of little interest to her. Lear and his friends could only talk sports. The young subaltern[6] had only been back in London for a few days, after the return of his regiment from Cyprus. He had travelled a bit, including a spell on garrison duty in the Suez canal zone, but he did not know much about abroad, he admitted. He was a civilian now, anyway. "We run our own show out there," he told Jessica. "Don't have to mix with the natives too much."

Lear's vapid chums were just like him. No point in trying to encourage any of those.

Lady Farnsworth had insisted on sitting next to Jessica, planning to have a long talk about the future. This misbalanced the seating arrangement at the round table, so she had to have two young men sitting together. She had put Lear on Jessica's other side. Beyond him sat Jeremy Keenleyside, an old school friend of Lear's and a keen cricketer. Beside Lady Farnsworth sat another of Lear's school-friends, Giles Hope-Jones, who had brought his sister, a rather sweet but strangely silent girl called Camilla.

Lear tried talking about the Fourth Test against Australia, starting the next day at Old Trafford[7], but Jessica showed no interest. He tried that day's International Horse Show, the racing at Kempton Park, polo at Cowdray and even prospects for the forthcoming shooting season, but received only the most correct responses. Jessica was experimenting with a way of showing private disdain by being especially formally polite and correct. Lear was a fine target, and was already beginning to stutter under the strain, but his mother did not appear to notice when the technique was used on her.

Jessica was similarly brutal to the boy when they were together on the dance floor. The band restricted itself mainly to old stuff from the inter-war years and before, but occasionally accepted a request for something more modern, but by altering the tempo they somehow managed to make anything sound old-fashioned. They even managed to turn one of that season's surprise hits, *Stompin' at the Savoy*[8], which should have been their theme tune, into something that sounded traditional.

Lear was a reasonably competent dancer but, by anticipating his moves, Jessica managed to get him to tread on her feet several times. "Sorry!" he said the first time, and "I'm terribly sorry!" on the second and third. "Don't mention it," Jessica replied each time — so Lear said nothing on the fourth and fifth occasion. He just looked increasingly disheartened. Overcome by embarrassment at his apparent clumsiness, Lear took Jessica on to the floor only twice. Neither Jeremy or Giles managed more than once, which rather prevented Jeremy dancing too often with Camilla.

Every so often, Jessica left for the ladies' room and most times Lady Farnsworth accompanied her, talking variously about her love for charity, what a splendid couple Lear and Jessica made and what a splendid idea it would be for the heirs of two newspaper families to get married. Each time, on the way back, Jessica managed to get her glass refilled. Gradually, the trips to the ladies' that had started out as an excuse for going to the bar became necessary in their own right.

In one of the periodic reprieves from the band there was a charity auction. A return voyage to South Africa via Ascension and St Helena on the Union Castle line's Rhodesia Castle[9], a pair of Majestic First-class tickets to any destination on a Super B.O.A.C. Constellation, with soft-as-mist Slumberette seats, and a compartment on the Golden Arrow train to Paris were all sold at great ostentation for many times their retail value. "Remember," said the celebrity auctioneer, this time the Himalayan explorer, "it's all for charity, but that doesn't mean we shouldn't have a good time as well."

Microphone in hand, he walked up and down coaxing increasingly large bids for a week's shooting out of increasingly large men. At his elbow was a young lady who appeared to know the names of most people in the room. As a hand was raised she whispered in the explorer's ear and he was able to greet the bidder by name and with a merry quip. "£500 from you, Sir Jephcote — and I thought you had your own grouse moor already."

It was not the possibility of owning a grossly overpriced Swiss wristwatch that made Jessica decide to bid for the next lot. It wasn't just that she had had far too much to drink and decided to give up being on her best behaviour and to draw attention to herself. She wasn't bidding for the Rolex but for the auctioneer, George Crawford, former light-heavyweight boxing champion of the Commonwealth.

No chinless wonder, he. He looked like someone more given to doing than to talking, and Jessica was sure that when he did talk there would be no stutter.

Nor was there. Crawford's words jolted Jessica awake and quite shocked many of her fellow ball-goers. He had a marked accent, which Jessica assumed was Glasgwegian, but he spoke clearly and was easy enough to understand. It was a welcome change from supercilious drawls, stammers and lisps.

"Ladies and gentlemen," Crawford started. "You all know why you're here." Nothing controversial so far.

"Some of you are here to meet friends. Some of you are here to have a dance and meet the opposite sex." There was an intake of breath from some of the tables around the empty dance floor. There were certain things one just should not say. What daring!

Crawford had stage presence. There was no fear there, as he developed his speech with carefully constructed dramatic pauses, engaging the eyes of individual members of the audience as he moved around. "Others of you have come to be seen on the social circuit.

"Others," and here he seemed to look directly into Jessica's eyes, "are here merely because they were invited, didn't really want to come and are anxious to get away as soon as they can." There was a murmur from the audience, many of whom felt that they ought to accept this as a joke even though they suspected it might well not have been fully intended as such.

"But I'll bet," Crawford continued in a lower voice, calculated to increase dramatic impact, "that very few of you have come to support Anti-Vivisection." This caused a few shouts of protest — including a yelp from Lady Farnsworth. Then Crawford goaded his audience even more. "*I* certainly haven't come here for that. I've come here because they've paid me." There were more angry shouts. One man called out: "This is intolerable!"

Crawford continued, unabashed: "You've paid, or had paid for you, ten guineas a head to come to a party where there isn't even any proper food — just what they call 'canapés' — and they've *paid me* twenty-five guineas to come here to speak to you." At this, the man who had earlier shouted "Intolerable!" made to get up and confront Crawford. A lady pulled him back to his seat, to which he returned with a show of reluctance.

"Brave man, that," remarked Crawford in an aside, before asking his audience — or asking Jessica individually, she felt: "Why do you think the organisers feel I'm worth more than double what any of you are?"

He supplied his own answer before any heckler could get a chance. "It's because *they* won't have to pay me: you will." He had got the audience's attention.

"One of you is going to pay a fortune for this watch, which, I might add, didn't cost Anti-Vivisection anything because it was donated free by the makers. And that's why the first bid I accept will have to be for at least £100 . . ." He advanced on the man who had got up to attack him: ". . . if any of you can afford to, that is." The man reluctantly and grudgingly raised his hand.

The young lady who appeared by Crawford's elbow whispered in his ear. Crawford announced: "£100 bid by Viscount Tolpuddle — shouldn't you be at home evicting your tenants, Sir?"

The antagonistic approach appeared to be succeeding far better than the explorer's obsequious cajoling. Crawford strode up and down between bidders like an enraged man-eater seeking its next prey. After the bidding had reached £600, Jessica, already sitting bolt upright, edged forward in her seat to make a bid. Lady Farnsworth grabbed her arm and hissed: "Don't make a fool of yourself, girl. Don't draw attention to yourself. Ladies are not supposed to bid. Leave it to the men. If you must, get Lear to bid for you."

Jessica shook herself free from Lady Farnsworth's clutches. She leapt up, her hand in the air. Crawford stopped pacing, turned toward her and raised one eyebrow. Everyone, it seemed, turned to look at her. "One thousand pounds," she said, in a faltering tone, already regretting it. She had no money at all, and even if she had, there would have been better uses for it. You could buy a new Ford for just over £413 12s, including purchase tax.

The assistant whispered to Crawford once more. He said: "That's obviously a winning bid. Sold, for one thousand pounds, to Miss Ross, obviously a young lady with more money than sense."

He then said: "I think I've earned my fee for tonight."

Jessica fell flat to the floor, her fall only partly broken by Lear's outstretched arm. "Gosh," said Lear.

Jessica was soon sitting at the table again, although in a rather stunned silence, wondering what she had done and why she had done it and what her father, who would have to pay the bill, would say. £1,000 was more than most people's income for a whole year[10].

Everyone else at the table was talking with apparent animation about the merits or otherwise of the orchestra, which had just started up again, about the rowing season — about anything except Jessica's indiscretion. After a few minutes of this, Crawford himself moved over to the table, carrying a spare chair with him, and asked Jessica: "I hope you don't mind if someone from the servants' quarters sits down in your presence?"

Jessica did not reply, so Crawford sat down and looked closely at her. "Are you still in shock?" he asked.

Jessica did not reply because, in truth, she really was still in a state of shock. That and the alcohol, although she had made the first step to sobering up by realising that she had indeed had far too much to drink. She did turn her head round in Crawford's direction, hoping to indicate that, while she was not up to speaking, she was not ignoring him. He said: "When I saw you go down like that it certainly took me back a week or two. I've been a boxer, you know. Not that I managed to knock many people out. I do hope you're not hurt. I just had to come and say 'sorry'."

Jessica nodded slowly and still said nothing, so Crawford kept talking. Nobody else at the table had spoken to him, although most were listening by now. He kept talking. "I meant it when I said it was like being in the ring again. You don't really look on your opponent as a person while you're fighting, just as a target and as something that might hit you. The audience was there to put on a show for. That's what it was like tonight — the audience was there to perform for but they, you, were also the target, something that really had to be hit. I just didn't expect to see a knock-out."

Jessica was someone who tended to cover her shyness with aggression, something for which she was constantly reproaching herself but did not know how to cure. "Don't flatter yourself," she said. "You didn't knock me out. I was just tripped."

The words were somehow involuntary. Far from wanting to drive him away, what she wanted was for this self-composed man to stay beside her and to keep talking in that reassuring and soothing manner. Which, rather to her surprise, he did. He turned to his other side and spoke to Lear: "I hope it wasn't you who tripped Miss Ross."

"I did no such thing," said Lear, trapped between contradicting a lady and antagonising a crazed and violent Scotsman who was also a hero of the Noble Art.

"We were all rooting for you in that latest fight," Lear said. "I think it was a crying shame that you lost. We all thought it was absolutely terrible, especially to see the title go out of England." Crawford raised one eyebrow. "I mean Britain," said Lear, his stutter returning once more.

Gradually, Jeremy and Giles joined in the conversation. If Lear was talking to the man it was obviously all right for them to do so too. They wanted to know lots of things. Jeremy asked, did he think the judges were biased? Giles asked, what did Crawford think the chances were of Canada's James J. Parker beating the 40-year-old American negro Archie Moore for the world heavyweight title the next day[11]. Jeremy asked, how many knockouts had Crawford scored? Lear asked, didn't Crawford think the army life was jolly good for bringing on boxing talent?

In a few minutes, Crawford appeared to have been accepted by the group. He answered the questions — No, he was not bitter in defeat; all boxers had to retire sometime, even Archie Moore — although he was at even-money[12] to beat Parker for the title and £16,500 purse; he had seen enough punch-drunk old boxers to want to get out while he still had all his marbles; it wasn't a career he would wish on anyone but if you had been brought up as he had you would be grateful of any way out; and so on.

Camilla remained quiet, smiling sweetly and with every outward sign of polite interest in the proceedings. Lady Farnsworth said nothing, either. Wasn't it marvellous to see the young people enjoying themselves?

Jessica, who had spent the earlier part of the evening privately sneering at Lear and his sports-mad pals, now felt jealous of them. It had been supposedly for her sake that Crawford had visited the table but she was losing him to this bunch of hearties. She listened while they chatted away, although it was not so much a conversation as a question-and-answer session. Crawford responded with a sentence or so to each one in the way he might have answered the queries of a group of sports reporters after a title fight or as a visiting policeman might have talked to a class of schoolchildren asking him about his job.

As with schoolchildren, his questioners fairly soon lost interest and returned to talking among themselves. Crawford was about to get up and go, when Jessica took hold of him by the upper arm and said: "I'm sorry, I shouldn't have spoken to you like that, earlier. I was embarrassed and shy. I didn't want to admit that I'd made a fool of myself." Crawford sat down in the chair again, turned back toward Jessica and smiled.

She said: "Tell me about the Glasgow slums, Mr Crawford."

"I'm called George," he said. "I'm not from Glasgow, you know, I'm from Dundee, but even Glasgow's not all like *No Mean City*[13]. We Scots are not just a bunch of razor-gangs killing each other for the sake of half a crown[14]. Besides, almost all the tenements[15] have gone, now. It's all slum-clearance programmes and housing schemes.

"They're pulling down thousands a week. Soon everyone in Dundee and Glasgow will be living in modern flats in proper housing schemes run by the city council, not in crowded tenements run by rackrenting landlords. It's a tremendous social advance."

It was a strange speech, thought Jessica. She could not help herself from picking it to pieces, even though she knew as she did so that it was not the sort of way you were supposed to act in ballrooms. She realised that people resented it when you could not indulge in small-talk. But she did not know how to. So she said: "You say with one voice that there was, is, no violent squalor. Then you tell me how it's all being put right and how the new Glasgow will be a safer, happier and healthier place. How do you reconcile the two contradictory statements?"

George appeared to be no more fazed by this strange way of speaking than he had been by Lear's earlier questions. He said that he supposed the truth was that in most Scotsmen there was a romantic as well as an idealist. In the cities, they rather liked the idea of there being razor gangs[16]; it made them feel special, that, if they couldn't be richer, or prettier, than everyone else then at least they could be poorer and uglier. In each city, whatever they were going to do they wanted to do best, even if the only thing they were doing was being Glasgow. After all, he said, Glasgow was world champion at being Glasgow.

Jessica was rather surprised at getting George's full attention, and to find him talking in the same way as books were written rather than on the superficial level at which Lear and his friends were so accomplished. She explained to George, and in doing so explained to herself something she had not understood before, how difficult she found it to make small talk, how she had been brought up, partly in Switzerland, partly in America, but never at the type of English school to which everyone else at the ball seemed to have attended. Most of her knowledge and understanding of life, such as it was, came from books, she said. By and large, she preferred them to people, especially these people, she said, with a sweep of her hand. In the end, Jessica found herself telling her life story, such as it was. George appeared happy to listen.

The pair of them talked together for a long time. Rather too long. So long that it began to be noticed by other people. Not only had Jessica made a fool of herself over the watch auction and then by falling over, now she was making a fool of herself again, with a Scotch prize-fighter. What on earth could Lear Farnsworth see in the girl?

Something had to be done. Lady Farnsworth eventually interrupted them: "Jessica, I'm afraid we've stayed far longer than we should have. Lear has to get up early to re-join his regiment. Our car is outside." Then, in the instructional tone of voice she used for addressing people of a certain class, she said: "Mr Crawford: Miss Ross is leaving now."

"Oh no I'm not," said Jessica. "Just when I'm beginning to enjoy myself."

George said: "I think Miss Ross is suffering from concussion. It's a delayed reaction to her fall. I'll see that she gets home." As much as Lady Farnsworth, George had a manner of speaking in a way that assumed there need be no discussion.

Lady Farnsworth, evidently not wishing to add a public argument to the indignities the family had suffered that night, left Jessica to her fate. No one could say that she had not tried to put her on the right path.

Lear, his dress uniform looking slightly more comfortable after a few hours of wearing it, held Jessica at correct regulation distance, kissed her once on the left cheek, and said: "Goodnight Jessica." So that only she could hear, he said: "For God's sake don't do anything silly." He then left with his mother. Jessica was grateful to him for saying the words so privately. Almost as if he cared.

The band played a staid and mangled version of the current hit *The One o'Clock Jump*[17]. After Lady Farnsworth, her son and the rest of their party had gone, George said: "I think she might be right, you know. Perhaps you ought to go home now. I'll fetch your coat."

"But I want to go home with you," said Jessica.

"Don't be silly. You hardly know me. Pick on someone of your own class," George told her.

"Didn't you understand what I've been telling you? I'm totally unlike them. I don't think like them, I don't understand them; my father has kept me away from people like that. I don't like them and they don't like me. I want to be with you."

"Now I know you're drunk," said George, as he helped her to her feet. Indeed, she was unsteady on her feet as she and her boxer went to collect their coats. Jessica's was a full-length, 25½-guinea model coat in Furleen Nylon Beaver, by Astraka.

They left the party, which appeared to be breaking up anyway. It had been one of the season's few days without rain, the hottest day since the previous August, reaching 79°F[18] in central London. Outside it was still mild. Even though it was almost 2 in the morning, the photographers from the newspaper gossip columns were waiting. Some bulbs flashed and shutters clunked, and Jessica, even though she was holding tightly on to her boxer's arm, stumbled and almost fell. George caught her, both his hands around her waist. More flashbulbs.

"Lay off it," shouted George. "No pictures."

Another flash. "Stop it, you bastards," said George, with his right arm steadying Jessica and his left index finger raised in warning. Another flashbulb went off in his face. None of the photographers could be seen behind the blinding lights of their flashguns but George selected a point six inches to the left of the latest flash and two feet beneath it, let go of Jessica for a moment, and swung a firm blow with his right fist.

There was a sickening thud as the blow smacked home in the photographer's stomach, a crash as his heavy camera and flashgun fell and smashed to bits on the pavement and a second thud as their owner followed them. He said nothing and did not move.

"Gosh," said Jessica.

George lifted her in his arms and ran off down the street to where he could see a waiting taxi.

All but one of the photographers gave chase.

2

Jessica woke up in her bed with the first truly awful hangover she had ever had. On quite a few occasions, particularly during illicit evening escapes from her Swiss finishing school[1], she had had far too much to drink, but each time she had felt only slightly muddle-headed in the morning. She had assumed hangovers were only for men, of for older people, or the poor. Now she knew differently; hangovers were truly as awful as their advance publicity. Perhaps, previously she had had the drinks to have fun whereas last night's intake had been in order to escape from the fearful Farnsworths, mother and son.

She rolled over on to her back, then pushed her back a few inches off the sheets by edging her elbows up the bed, kicked at the bedclothes until they loosened, put her feet on the bedside mat and very slowly stood up. There was just enough light coming in to the room for her to see that she was wearing her Terylene night-dress, which rather surprised her as she could not remember putting it on. Indeed, for the past few weeks she had been going to bed naked, fancying it tremendously grown-up and daring.

She walked, carefully, over to the window and rearranged the hang of the curtains so they let in a bright but narrow beam of light. She winced, walked over to her dressing table, sat down, looked at her face with its smeared and sorry make-up and winced again.

As Jessica examined the blotched residue from the previous night, there came from outside her room the thumping sound of angry footsteps. There was a crash as her bedroom door was hurled open and smashed against the wall. The proprietor strode in, threw a newspaper on to the bed, grabbed the curtain cord and pulled it firmly. Light shone into the room. Jessica winced yet again. The proprietor turned to her. He shouted: "What in God's name are you doing to me? Don't lie: just tell me!"

Jessica always thought of the man as "the proprietor" — someone who owned her in the same way as he owned his newspapers — and avoided using the name Father, let alone Daddy. She turned slowly toward the proprietor, away from the mirror, and hung her head slowly down in a gesture of submission. "I've got a headache," she said.

"I'm not surprised," said the proprietor, in a slightly less angry tone. "Mrs Burgess tells me you didn't get home till half past two. You were incapable. A taxi driver rang the bell and the pair of them had to get you out of the cab and upstairs. You had no money at all and Mrs Burgess had to pay your fare. You were in such a bad state that she had to take your clothes off and put you to bed as if you were a two-year-old, not 22."

Jessica looked at the proprietor in a manner she hoped appeared duly contrite. She started to dab cold-cream on her face with a ball of cotton wool.

"Don't you know that you mean all in the world to me?" said the proprietor, sitting down on the edge of the bed, still facing Jessica. She said nothing. "You're all I have — your mother's gone. You are all I have to live for. As it is, my heart could kill me any day. I've done everything for you. I've tried to protect you from the evil and nastiness of the world. I ve got you everything you could want — and *this* is how you repay your father."

The hangdog look had not spared her the proprietorial lecture, Jessica realised. So she said what she wanted to: "You're not my father; you never were. You're just pretending. Do you expect me to be grateful for all you've done for me? Well, I' m not."

"No," said the proprietor. "I don't expect gratitude — but sometimes I hope for love."

There was a pause, after which the proprietor said something he had said many times before: "After all, it shows love to adopt someone. More love than if you were my natural daughter."

He sighed, and then said: "Now, to get you in the mood for apologising, I am going to get Mrs Burgess here so you can say 'Sorry' to her for the trouble you caused last night. After that, there is another apology for you to make, which you won't enjoy, either." Jessica looked a bit perplexed but decided not to ask about the second penance.

"Oh yes," said the proprietor, "and you're going to have repay her the taxi fare. She's not a rich woman, I don't pay her a lot for being housekeeper, so it's unfair for you to expect her to subsidise your flighty escapade."

"I can't pay her — I don't have any money. You never give me enough," said Jessica.

"If you don't have any money, why did you bid at a charity auction? *I'm* not going to pay for that watch. I only support charities I agree with. Besides, if you wanted a watch you should have bought one when you were in Switzerland."

This shocked Jessica. She had rather assumed that the proprietor was going to rescue her from her silly gesture of the night before. "How do you know about the watch?" she asked. "Have you had your spies out following me, like you did in Switzerland?"

The proprietor shook his head, and said: "Who needs spies, when you've got journalists? They come cheaper."

He stood up, walked to the door and said: "Mrs Burgess, you can come in now." She had evidently been standing there, just outside, all along. Mrs Burgess, was a tallish, slim lady of about 35, with auburn hair in a loose perm and wearing a well tailored blue suit. She walked in, stood in front of Jessica and tilted her head to her right, slightly, with an almost playful smile, waiting for Jessica to speak.

The proprietor cued her: "Jessica has something to say to you." To Jessica he said: "You evidently feel pretty ashamed of what you did yesterday. There is no need to cover up that perfectly natural and extremely justified feeling with a display of bravado. Just tell Mrs Burgess you're sorry."

"I'm sorry, Elizabeth," said Jessica. "I'm sorry for causing you so much trouble. I know you and Mr Ross have better things to do at night than look after me."

The proprietor rose his right hand across his body and took a step forward as if to strike her. As Jessica shrank back in anticipation of the blow, Mrs Burgess put a restraining arm out toward the proprietor and said: "Don't you both think there's been enough punching?"

"Maybe so," said the proprietor. Mrs Burgess smiled at them both and left the room.

The proprietor picked up from the bed the copy of the London *Evening Standard* that he had thrown down when he came in. The front page was about the long-running car strike: **SIT-DOWN PICKETS STOP LORRY — They defy mounted police**[2].

Opening the paper as he moved from the bed to the dressing table the proprietor sat down beside Jessica on the padded bench, which was not really large enough for two people. He opened the paper, smoothed it out, put his left arm around Jessica and pointed to a printed item with his right index finger.

He said: "What do you think about that? Pretty damning? It's Beaverbrook, of course. Out to get me. He doesn't want Lord Farnsworth and me to get together. I'm going to sue."

Jessica read the item, once, and then again, more slowly.

THE BOSS'S DAUGHTER

THE LONDONER is pleased to welcome the fun-loving Jessica Ross to the capital's social scene. Her father, Otto Ross, the bombastic, Hungarian-born proprietor of the Daily Tribune, has managed to keep the talented 21-year-old's lively sense of fun a secret from Society until now that she has completed her education, in Switzerland. What a début!

The carefree newspaper heiress danced the night away, at yesterday's Savoy Hotel charity ball, in the arms of that young blood of the sports field, the Hon Lear Farnsworth, a member of an even more distinguished newspaper family. Do we hear wedding bells linking the two dynasties?

Miss Ross can hardly have failed to notice the hours flitting by — she bid a munificent 1,000 guineas for a diamond-encrusted wristwatch in the charity's auction.

The night ended not altogether happily for Miss Ross as, while she was leaving, just before dawn today, she witnessed the unfortunate injury of a photographer from her father's own paper, who was hurt in a mêlée trying to gain the attention of one of the party's star guests, the noted pugilist George Crawford.

"It's not true," Jessica said. "I'm 22, not 21. It was £1,000 not 1,000 guineas[3]. I hardly danced at all with Lear and I certainly don't intend marrying him."

The proprietor hugged her tightly. "My angel," he said, kissing her still-smeared face, "I'll make them pay for it. I've had lawyers going over this. I've told them to sue for thousands, possibly millions. 'Bombastic,' indeed! And the Farnsworths 'more distinguished' than me — preposterous: the Farnsworths are idiots. I think we've really got Beaverbrook on the suggestion that I have kept you a prisoner.

"Nevertheless, if I were you, I wouldn't say you don't intend to marry young Farnsworth, even if he does come from a long line of dunces. A marriage to him could turn out to be most advantageous to you, especially if I decide to say that you won't get any more money out of me unless you do."

Jessica stiffened. Before she could say anything, the proprietor let go of her, rose and said: "Get dressed now. After that, get Mrs Burgess to make you a lunch, or is it breakfast? I also recommend two aspirins and a pint of milk. I'll call for you in one hour. Put on suitable clothes for visiting the sick: it's time for your second apology of the day, and I expect it to be made with more grace than your last effort."

He left behind him, as presumably intended, a shocked young woman. She looked in her wardrobes, trying to imagine the most inappropriate dress to wear for visiting the sick but, bearing in mind the awful threat of forced marriage to a congenital moron, decided to attempt to humour the proprietor, at least in certain areas. She selected a white, dirndl dress, with tight-fitting bodice and a full skirt and took out a pair of three-inch-heeled sandals, red to match the lipstick she intended wearing.

Before she had a chance to wash, put on fresh make-up or start dressing, let alone try the aspirin-and-milk treatment, the telephone bell went. Mrs Burgess shouted up the stairs: "It's a young gentleman for you, Jessica."

Jessica, still in her night-dress at lunchtime, went out to the landing to pick up the extension. She hoped it was George, even though Mrs Burgess's words of introduction belied the possibility. George was not particularly young and was not a gentleman[4]. She wanted it to be George. She remembered wanting to give him the ex-directory telephone number but somehow could not recall whether she had managed to. She answered brightly: "Jessica!"

"Hello, Jessica! It's Lear!"

"Oh," she said, noticeably less brightly.

"I just thought I ought to phone to see how you were, after last night. Did you get home all right?"

"The fact that I'm speaking to you demonstrates that I got home all right," she said. Then she reproached herself. She could not help treating Lear in this fashion, even though, especially though, he might have to be a future husband, if the proprietor had his way. There was something about the boy that irritated her, but she checked herself: "No, I'm sorry Lear, I didn't mean that. I was only joking, I didn't mean to be nasty. It's been pretty beastly here. Have you seen the *Evening Standard*? It's thrown the proprietor into one of his furious moods."

For the first time since she had met him, Lear sounded almost intelligent. "Yes, it's sent the old man, BF[5] — that's what we call him, Baron Farnsworth — pretty spare. He sees the hand of Beaverbrook at work. What do you think of the 'wedding bells' bit?"

"I felt it a bit precipitate," said Jessica, tact for once overcoming her. "But something else, Lear. The proprietor's so furious he won't pay the £1,000 I bid in the auction."

"Don't worry about that," said Lear. "I'll cough up. It will've been worth it just for the look on mother's face. It was a picture:

she's pretty set on you, you know, but I don't think she always approves of absolutely everything you do.

"Look, Jessica, there's some hoo-ha[6] overseas and it seems I've got to go back to the regiment pretty soon, but why don't you come with me to the cinema tonight? I know you're a bit of a brain-box and like foreign things, so we could see a foreign film."

A further evening with Lear was not what Jessica would have liked. She might even have preferred to have been locked in a padded cell with a strangler, but there did appear to be £1,000 linked with the offer. She forced herself to be enthusiastic: "Lear, that would be marvellous. Perhaps you could pick me up this evening. I'm in a terrible rush now — I've got to go out with the proprietor on some horrible errand. And, thanks for the cash, you saved my life."

She went back into her room; one problem over, even if it did store up another for the future. Mrs Burgess stopped listening at the bottom of the stairs and left to instruct the cook on preparing a lunch tray for Jessica, leaving the telephone switched through to the landing extension. Thus it was that when the phone rang again, it was Jessica herself who answered: "HAMpstead 3404."[7]

The urgent voice at the other end was speaking almost in a whisper: "Thank God it's you, Jessica. This is George Crawford."

"George!" said Jessica, breathily, trying to communicate ecstatic joy without alerting Mrs Burgess.

George said: "You've got to help me. I was going to phone you anyway, but now I *have* to."

"I'll do anything on earth for you," said the excited Jessica.

George asked: "How's your photographer? Is he still alive? I suspect that if he dies they'll want to try me for murder. I've got to have a witness to clear me."

"I think it's him the proprietor is making me visit in hospital," Jessica whispered. "He's coming for me any moment. He'll kill me if he finds I'm not ready. I'll see you tomorrow: 3 o'clock outside Swann & Edgar's[8]."

He would not have killed her, but Jessica did not dare to add to the proprietor's anger of that day. She forgot that she was feeling quite ill, and managed to sort out her hair, clean her face and put her clothes on in time. There was no time for anything to eat but she was just being issued with her aspirin by Mrs Burgess when the proprietor's chauffeur came to collect her.

Walking out to the car, the chauffeur's umbrella protecting her from the rain, Jessica finished drinking a glass of milk. In the back of the large, black Humber Pullman touring limousine, on the way from Avenue Road, Regent's Park, to the Charing Cross Hospital, the proprietor said he was going to tell Jessica some important facts of life. It was time, he said, as they drove south, pausing for long periods at traffic lights and for policemen on point duty[9], for her to know more about newspapers.

Things in the newspaper business were not doing that well. Competition was intense, which meant only extraordinarily strong papers could sell enough, or charge enough for advertising, to make a long-term profit. There had to be larger groups for the whole business to survive into the next generation. The Beaverbrook group[10] was by far the strongest, entire unto itself, and immune, for the time being, from takeover. There were various other, weaker, publishers, some of whom recognised their weakness and others, such as the Farnsworths, who did not. It was Jessica's task to take over the Farnsworth empire by using non-boardroom means.

Jessica sat glumly, taking in the horrific instructions, and thinking despairingly about how to get out of the mess. If only George would appear and beat the proprietor to a pulp.

In thinking about newspapers, said the proprietor, who often gave the appearance of believing it was a waste of time to think about much else, the first task was to forget any notions about journalism. The newspaper trade operated on two levels, politics and business, and it was difficult to say where the one started and the other ended. Take the scurrilous attack in the *Evening Standard*; that was primarily business but it had political undertones.

The proprietor said Jessica would be pleased to know that she, too, was taking a libel action in the matter. Her writ had been served not half an hour previously. It claimed damages for falsely asserting, by the use of the words "fun-loving" and "lively sense of fun" that she had been intoxicated, by the use of the words "danced the night away . . . in the arms of that young blood of the sports field, the Hon Lear Farnsworth," that she was a woman of loose morals, and, basest of all, that she had stood idly by while one of her father's employees had been beaten senseless, possibly even killed, whereas, in truth, she had agreed to be a prominent witness in the trial of the poor man's assailant, one George Crawford.

That was going too far, felt Jessica. "Oh no, I'm not!" she said. "That man got everything that was coming to him. Mr Crawford was only trying to protect me. He warned them not to take pictures. Besides, he's more of a man than you'll ever be, he's so good, and strong, and so real..."

The proprietor hurriedly tapped on the glass and said to the chauffeur: "Fibbins, stop the car and get out at that telephone box. Call the hospital and tell them I'm coming."

He gave the man fourpence[11], remarking to Jessica: "Can't have him hearing everything. All the drivers are Union members."

When they were alone, the proprietor said: "I don't know what your dear mother would think about you now. We brought you up to be so good and pure. Now you have fallen into the hands of street thugs and ne'er-do-wells. I'll tell you this — we are just about to get to the hospital. I want you to come in and see Monty Evans, the photographer, tell him how you saw everything and will stand witness against his evil attacker. If you don't, the police will doubtless link your name with Crawford's in a charge of conspiracy to commit a murderous assault."

"You wouldn't do that to your own daughter!" wheedled Jessica, snuggling closer to the proprietor.

"Why is it that I have to threaten you before you show me any love?" he asked, as Fibbins got back into the driving seat.

When the car eventually drew up at the pavement outside the hospital[12], there was a thin man in a brown suit waiting. He opened the car door and, as Fibbins jumped out and stood by for the proprietor, said: "Hello, Sir. My name is Ollerenshaw. I'm the hospital secretary. I'll show you to the ward where your man is."

"Ward?" said the proprietor. "Why isn't he in a private room? I won't have my staff dying in a ward full of other people. Get him to a private room."

"I'm not sure that that would be wise, Sir, even though I'm sure he's not going to die. I'll have to ask Matron whether he's well enough to be moved — besides, I don't think there are any private rooms available at the moment."

"Don't argue," said the proprietor. "Just do it. But take us to him first; you can move him later."

They walked along corridors of polished linoleum, between echoing green walls, up stairs, along more corridors smelling of ether and carbolic. Somehow, wherever the proprietor went there was always someone to open doors for him, even here where the egalitarian National Health Service was not in his direct employ. It's not subservience that makes them do it, you know, the proprietor used to say. It's because they like me. I just have that effect on people. Jessica always wondered whether he actually believed that.

In the hospital it was Ollerenshaw who scuttled speedily along the corridors in order to be present at each pair of swing doors before the proprietor. He went through each and held the left one open by standing against it, supporting the right one with a hand extended across the corridor, high enough for the proprietor to walk underneath without stooping or pausing. Ollerenshaw then let the doors swing. Jessica, walking a pace and a half behind the proprietor, was just able to catch them without injury, as the hospital secretary, attempting to make it look as if this was just a natural courtesy extended to all visitors, walked fast enough to overtake the proprietor before the next set of swing doors. The sequence continued until they entered through the wide doors of a general surgical ward (male), to where Monty Evans, staff photographer, in a room with a dozen or so other patients, was regaining consciousness after an operation.

There were screens available for putting between the beds but they were not in use. Sister, apparently, believed they were untidy. Sister said to the proprietor: "And who might you be to come barging on to my ward without so much as a by-your-leave? Don't you know patients may not have visitors except during Visiting Hour, and certainly never until the day following surgery?"

The proprietor just ignored her, somehow immediately locating his staff member's bed without needing to be told which it was. Sister was beckoned aside by Ollerenshaw for a whispered conversation. There was great interest among Monty Evans's fellow patients, watching what would happen to the important-looking interloper who had dared defy Sister on her own ward. The proprietor's glamorously demure companion was also worth staring at. Monty Evans himself was not yet sufficiently conscious to appreciate the dramatic events. He was lying, chest downward, under one cotton sheet, with no pillow, his head turned left, in the direction of the entrance to the ward. It was, apparently, hospital practice to have all recovering operants laid so their faces could be seen from the door.

Monty Evans was wearing a hospital gown, tied like a straitjacket at the back. The upper part of his head was swathed in a long crêpe bandage like a turban. A nurse was stroking his left, uppermost, cheek and was whispering in his ear as the effects of the general anæsthetic wore off.

His first words were: "Don't stop, I like it."

Then: "Oh my God! I feel terrible. Get me a whisky."

Sister, who was still some feet away, looked like she was arguing in angry whispers with Ollerenshaw.

The proprietor heard Monty Evans's first words and called to the hospital secretary: "He says he's feeling terribly ill. Get him shifted immediately."

The photographer heard the voice of his proprietor, a man for whom employees had every reason to feel most worried about meeting. This had the effect of bringing him rapidly back to consciousness, while making him feel most ill indeed. "I'm all right, Sir. Honest!" he said.

"Oh no you're not, Evans," said the proprietor. "You've been the subject of a murderous attack. You are lucky to be alive. But do not worry; the *Tribune* will see you all right. Put your trust in me. There will be no expense spared. We are going to get you a private room."

Monty Evans contorted his face in an expression that could have been that of gratitude, as his boss went on: "We are all desperately concerned about you. My daughter especially."

Here he beckoned to Jessica to come to the bedside. "She witnessed the attack on you and she has come here to give you sympathy."

Jessica looked at Evans. A shifty-looking little man, she felt. Somehow pathetic in the worried way he looked at the proprietor with eyes just visible below the swath of bandage. On this man's words lay her future. She moved closer and, edging the nurse out of the way, looked beseechingly into the frightened man's eyes. Please don't let him say that he was attacked, unprovokedly, by George.

"Just one thing before we move you," said the proprietor. "Tell us the name of the man who attacked you." Monty Evans was in a tricky position. His proprietor, a man whom he had feared for years but had never before had the ill luck to meet, demanded that he should name names, and his daughter seemed most distressed by it all.

Any employee of the great man would happily finger anyone the proprietor wanted him to, especially when his job, possibly even his life, depended on it. The trouble was, the proprietor had failed to tell Evans who he wanted named. The attack had left the photographer without any memory of it.

The patient began to look even more ill, and he fainted. By now there was a small cluster of people around the bed. The proprietor, Jessica, Ollerenshaw, Sister and, recently arrived, a white-coated doctor, and a man in a suit and yellow bow-tie who turned out to be consultant surgeon.

"You see how ill he is. He must be moved," said the proprietor.

"That is precisely why he must stay where he is," said the consultant.

He explained how the photographer had been carried in to casualty the previous night by his fellow snappers, apparently suffering from a fractured skull after falling over.

"We know these Fleet Street types," said the consultant. "Always getting drunk and falling over. Nothing much to worry about, so they cleaned up the head wound and put him to bed to sleep it off. It was only several hours later that they realised he was almost dead, bleeding to death from internal injuries. We opened him up and took out his ruptured spleen. He's lucky to be alive.

He's had several units of blood and I wouldn't recommend moving him anywhere until he's had time to stabilise."

"Besides," said Ollerenshaw, "there's no private room left in the hospital."

"Then," said the proprietor, "we must find a hospital which *will* take him. If you people can't tell the difference between a man dying from loss of blood and a case of concussion you are obviously not to be trusted.

"Jessica: go and get Fibbins. We're taking this man to the King Edward VII Hospital for Officers[13]. If there's no space there, we'll take him to the Royal Masonic[14] — they won't be able to refuse me. I want him to die in a place that befits one of my staff."

"You," he said, pointing to the nurse. "Find his clothes. We're taking him to the car."

To the company in general, he said: "I hate hospitals. They remind me that I'm close to death myself. I'm not a well man."

Evidently realising that there appeared little point trying to reason with the proprietor, the consultant changed his tack. "It so happens I have good contacts at both those hospitals," he said. "I didn't realise you were on the square[15]. I think I can guarantee good treatment for you. I take it you will require me to take charge of his case? On a fee basis of course."

3

That night, in the dark, stone labyrinth of the building, there was much work to be done. On the editorial floor there was the Shock Issue, **DEATH OF A DREAM — How Eden Has Murdered the NHS**, to prepare. It was what the proprietor wanted. Readers aren't worried about foreign affairs, he told his editor. "What they want," he said, "is something that affects them and their families: something like a shock issue on the death of a dream — how Eden is killing off the Health Service. Let the others witter on about the doings of tin-pot African dictators and we'll see who's right when we get the circulation figures. Not that I'm giving you an instruction as such, of course. You're the journalist: you do as you see best. It's up to you to provide the creativity." Given this licence, the editor was able to demonstrate his independence by using the word **Murdered**, rather than "killing off".

The page was filled with stories of people waiting weeks for operations and with case studies of hard-pressed hospital staff. One featured the complaint of a doctor, saying: "I am married with a child and get £745 a year. We can afford only the plainest types of food, margarine instead of butter and no cakes for tea."

Several floors below where these strategic decisions were made and acted upon, in a small cubby-hole of an office, open on one side to the corridor of which it had once been part, sat Jim Anstruther, the Imperial Father of the Federated Unions of the newspaper[1]. He was on a chair with a partly torn canvas seat attached to the continuous piece of metal tubing which formed the body of the chair, shaped, when looked at from the side, rather like a lower-case Greek delta, or a printer's "delete" mark[2]. The chair's construction made it difficult to tilt it back and balance with one's feet on the desk, but that is what the Imperial Father was having to do, so that the light from the one low-powered electric light bulb fell on the newspaper he was reading. There was also a cantilevered desk lamp bolted to the green linoleum-covered desk, but the bulb in that was no longer working and the Imperial Father had been waiting for a month for a maintenance electrician to be allocated to change it.

It was one of those irritating things. You couldn't change the bulb yourself, because that would be breaking union demarcation lines[3], but management had failed to provide an electrician when called on to do so. On the other hand it might be a useful complaint to add when the Imperial Father next needed some excuses for the next strike over management's attacks on trade union rights.

In fact, the whole office was an attack on trade union rights. There was he, the elected official looking after hundreds of workers and all he had to help him do the job was a chair and a desk without drawers in a corridor with inadequate lighting. There was no dial on the telephone, so you had to lift up the handset and wait sometimes five minutes before the operator would get your number. The filing cabinet had no lock on it. He had to look after the union while working in a part of the building which shook and rumbled so much when the presses were running that you couldn't even hear yourself think.

He kept reading the papers, tomorrow's editions which had just been delivered, both the one he and his colleagues worked on and the papers the management called "the opposition" but toward which the print workers were traditionally far less hostile. It was always their own employer the men hated and Jim's continuing regret was that he had so far failed to instil in them any great loathing for employers in general.

The *Tribune*'s front page, as he knew from seeing it printed, was one of the proprietor's pet Shock Issues again, although almost all of the others led on Egypt's nationalisation of the Suez canal. Most of the papers were similar to each other in their outrage and affronted patriotism. The Farnsworth paper, *Forward!*, was, as usual, the winner in crypto-fascist posturing.

HITLER-STYLE RAID ON
OUR LINK WITH EMPIRE

The Imperial Father turned to the *Daily Express* and found it outdone in the patriotism stakes with a mere

NASSER GRABS SUEZ CANAL

The *Times*, on its centre news page, had a single-column, four deck headline:

EGYPT SEIZES
SUEZ CANAL

«»

NATIONALIZATION DECREE

«»

REVENUE TO PAY
FOR HIGH DAM

«»

Jim mentally set aside the front-page news for later reading, and turned to a few of the other stories.

In the *Tribune,* the nationalisation of the Suez Canal was relegated to pages 2 and 3. The only story on the front page apart from the NHS special, was a rather shocking item:

BOXING HERO
CRAWFORD IN
'ATTEMPT ON
THE LIFE OF
OUR MONTY'

Jim read:

A police dragnet was last night closing in on former Commonwealth light-heavyweight champion George Crawford, 28, wanted for questioning in connection with a murderous attack on award-winning photographer Monty Evans.

Police said that Crawford, who is unmarried, did not return home to his lodgings in Holborn, London, after the attack, which took place outside a Society charity ball at the Savoy Hotel in the early hours of yesterday.

Meanwhile, the victim is fighting for his life in a London private hospital under the care of a team of expert doctors instructed by proprietor Otto Ross.

Mr Ross said: "Monty — famous for his Coronation Day picture 'Her Raining Majesty' — is one of the world's greatest photographers. To think that such a man cannot go about his legitimate business in the streets of our capital city without being set on is an appalling comment on the lawlessness of our times.

"Monty has spoken to me at length about the incident and, believe me, we shall not rest until the assailant concerned is punished with the full vigour of our laws."

Eyewitnesses said that Crawford was leaving the ball when he set on the photographer, who was engaged in taking pictures of the charitable efforts of the sporting hero. He is said to have hit out without provocation and then to have run off alone.

At his London home, his landlady said of the handsome Scots-born boxer: "The police have come round looking for him several times but I haven't seen **- Turn to page 4**.

Inside some of the other papers there was a similar story, except that there was no suggestion of attempted murder. Only *Forward!* named the charity in whose favour the ball had been held. Neither it nor any of the other papers named the photographer involved, except the *Times*, which called him Mr Montague Evans, and none of them said he worked for the *Tribune*. No one else reported that Crawford ran off alone, some saying that he ran off with "a mystery girl" or "an unidentified young lady". In the *Express*, on page 5, William Hickey[4] had a blurred but identifiable picture of the fateful blow but Jessica did not appear in it, even though she must have been standing directly behind Crawford at the time.

Oh dear, thought Jim, folding the newspapers up into a bundle to take home with him; young Crawford was always a one for getting into scrapes.

It didn't feel like a night where he would be needed. No great crisis had arisen that day and everything appeared to be going smoothly enough, without any hint of an exploitable grievance, so it was time for Jim to go home. He took his leather coat from its peg and put it over an arm. He was not a man for hats, which he thought of as being the mark of the bourgeois and of the servant.

He set out on a circuitous route to leave the building; through the case room[5], where all the clatter of the Linotypes[6] had stopped, past the stone, where there were no pages being made up, through his own department, the foundry[7], where the stereotypers had ceased their task for the night. There were still a few people left in each department, often sitting at their machines reading books and smoking hand-rolled cigarettes or in small groups, playing cards held in their ink-stained fingers. The proprietor was evidently happy with the first editions of his paper. It didn't look as though there would be any more editorial changes tonight.

Not wanting to spare the time for a long conversation with anyone, Jim skirted the proof-readers' room, but he had a word, frequently mock-aggressive, for most of the men as he passed through: "Good night, Bill, you old bugger." "Hello Fred — you still here? I thought you'd died years ago!" "Strewth, Arthur. You look like you've lost a shilling and found sixpence. What's the problem? Wife not left you yet?"

Jim descended into the thundering print hall and walked between the lines of the two giant presses humming and clanking as they spewed out almost a dozen Shock Issues a second for the packers to bundle up and send off to the railway stations. There were machine-minders in the press hall but there was nothing much for them to do, not so long as everything was running smoothly. Jim made a thumbs-up gesture to them rather than attempt being heard over the rumbling roar of the presses. He walked on into the packing hall, where at last people really were working; he followed the line that a bundle of newspapers was taking along the conveyor belt, via a roller incline to where they were being labelled and thrown into the back of one of several vans with running engines.

"This lot for Blackfriars?[8]" he asked. After a nodded answer, Jim walked around the front of the van, reached up, opened the passenger door and climbed in. He rolled his coat up, placed it on a stack of newspapers, sat down, turned to the driver and said: "Better go now, Bert. I don't want to miss my train home."

After the two-minute drive to the station, the Imperial Father got out and jumped into a Second Class carriage in the train to Bromley North. It was the same carriage as had last month been called Third Class[9]. The same grime on the windows and a similar quantity of flattened cigarette ends and uncollected rubbish on the floor. Nothing else had been changed, just the name. That was Tory prosperity for you.

The Imperial Father's own father had first moved the family to Bromley on coming to London in search of work before the war. The town was more respectable than the areas that some other print workers lived in and it was a popular choice, being served by the Blackfriars railway line, which was convenient for Fleet Street and had trains that ran all the way through the night. He spent the journey reading some more of the papers, marking passages for further attention.

At Bromley North he got off, shewed[10] his season ticket and collected his motor-cycle combination[11] from its place in front of the station. He put on his coat, took a sparking plug[12] out of his pocket and screwed it into place with the tube-wrench he took from under the single seat of the Swallow Tudor sidecar. He connected the cable to the plug, disconnected the parking light from its battery[13], turned on the fuel supply, adjusted the mixture, stood up, and jumped on the starting pedal. Unusually, the 498cc engine of the Matchless G9[14] started first time. It was only two years old, but already it was showing signs of age. The trouble was, he rarely had time to work on it.

Jim swung his leg over the saddle and drove off through the night-time drizzle, down Widmore Road and round the corner to his newly built council house.

He arrived home well after 1am, bumped the motor cycle and sidecar over the kerb and parked on the paved area he had laid out in the front garden. He did not bother to take out a sparking plug this time, but just let himself quietly into the house by the front door. Upstairs, he undressed on the landing and went into the bedroom without turning on the light. As he expected, Sheilagh was already in bed and asleep. That was how it normally was, these days.

When he woke at half past seven, Sheilagh was already up. Jim came downstairs in his dressing gown to a breakfast of streaky bacon, a fried egg, bread and marge[15], Keiller's marmalade[16] and milky tea. Sheilagh was finishing her breakfast, standing up, before hurrying out for the 15-minute walk to Bickley Station, the train to London and her job as a typist at union headquarters. She was dark-haired. It was naturally wavy but she wore it short. She had pale skin which at this time of year, despite the appalling weather, came out in a ridge of freckles over the bridge of her nose, only partly obscured by a pair of light-rimmed spectacles. She was wearing a loose, cream, open-necked blouse above a tight-waisted navy-blue skirt, just below the knee, light-tan Bear Brand long-life stockings and medium-height court shoes.

"Look at this rubbish," said Jim, putting down on the Formica[17] table-top some of the newspapers he had brought home with him. "Things are hotting up, aren't they? This Suez business looks like developing. It's the collapse of capitalism. Before you know it, we'll even have socialism in this country."

Sheilagh looked at him. "As you know, I can talk about the collapse of capitalism with the best of them, but isn't it time to look at something that is collapsing rather closer to home? Does the impending arrival of socialism mean you'll be home early today, or late again?"

"Could be either way," said Jim. "It looks like being one of those big news days when they'll try for a long print run to put on extra sales. That could mean I'll be late. But it could be that they're not willing to pay for it — then I might be early."

As he was saying this, Sheilagh was hurriedly putting on her princess-line summer mac and looking around her for something. "We've got to talk, Jim," she said, picking up her handbag and moving out of the kitchen into the entrance passage.

He nodded and did his best to smile although realising that a man in his dressing gown is not obviously in control of a situation. He followed her into the passage as she continued: "I haven't seen you for more than five minutes at breakfast-time for weeks. Something's going very wrong." She stood on the threshold with the door open and kissed him on the cheek. As she hurried off down the road to the station, Jim shook his head slowly for the benefit of anyone watching, closed the door and went back upstairs to bed. He did not manage to go to sleep again.

Instead, he mused. About Sheilagh, about the impending collapse of capitalism as presaged by the Suez crisis, and about the day ahead at the *Tribune*. Sheilagh was quite right — as people, they were turning into what others already believed them to be: a married couple. They had not set out to become seen as man and wife living a settled existence together, but it appeared to have happened that way.

He had met her, or she had met him, they never could agree which, in the pub after a Communist Party meeting. This was how most of Jim's sexual experiences had started. The Party was an unbeatable organisation for facilitating meetings between willing partners, or that is what Jim had found.

If he had been feeling uncharitable toward his own motives he could even say that that was one of the reasons why he remained active in the Party. Someone such as he, who had been elected a borough councillor within days of his 21st birthday and who was still only 32, constantly fending off pressure to sit on the Party's District Committee or even the Executive[18], and who was already holding high union office, was an object of desire for a certain type of woman. Especially as he was demonstrably working class — not something all his Party comrades, particularly the women comrades, could claim.

Most comrades had come to the Party during the war, as Jim had, almost as a way of saying thank you to Uncle Joe[19] for everything that he was doing against Hitler. It was only afterwards that they began to learn what the Party stood for, or believed it stood it for. Some comrades went to classes on the labour theory of value[20], some studied Marxist philosophy, others, particularly the women comrades, attended reading groups analysing such works as Engels's *Origins of the Family, Private Property, and the State*. From each according to his or her bent[21].

Jim had started sleeping with Sheilagh, who was a couple of years younger than him, on a casual basis, when and where they could, which was not as often as they would have liked. They spent weekends away at the seaside when they would book in at guest houses registering in the names of revolutionary hero-figures in front of suspicious landladies. Their first time had been under the names Mrs and Mrs Marx, then Mr and Mrs Engels. By the time they had booked in as Mr and Mrs Karl and Sophie Liebknecht[22], Jim had been offered the council house due to him by traditional venality after his brief period as a councillor. Sheilagh had started staying the night more and more often until the day they both realised that she lived there.

Nowadays she was there rather more of the time than Jim, what with the union, the Party and his job. Things were indeed coming to a crisis, you didn't have to be a Marxist to see that. Something was bound to happen soon. That, Jim's lessons had shown him, was the way with crises; nothing ever stood still.

No chance of sleeping, he realised. He felt sure that something big was going to happen today. He wondered what it was.

He collected the *Daily Worker*[23] from the doormat where Sheilagh had left it on her way out. It was the only paper he did not get to see at work and it was also part of his duty as Party member to get it at home. Sheilagh was wary of taking the paper with her to work as she did not want her colleagues to know she was a Communist. The *Worker* was still leading on the BMC car strike, not having caught up with the news from Suez. There was nothing else in it that caught his eye that day.

He tried a bit of desultory filing of the union papers he did not care to keep in the filing cabinet with the broken lock. He gave up after a few minutes, took out a Biro[24] and a leather-bound minute book to write up some union business, but instead of writing as intended he did the washing-up, pondering on what he was going to do about Sheilagh. It did not look as though he was going to get anything constructive done that morning, so he gave up trying and went upstairs to get dressed.

Slacks, a shirt and pullover, his windcheater and brown brogues. He took his father's old hickory-shafted golf clubs out of the understairs cupboard, dusted off their leather bag with a cloth from the kitchen, loaded them into the sidecar, locked the front door, started up and rode off to the nine-hole municipal golf course. For once that month, the rain was holding off.

Arriving at the golf course he found it unusually empty for half-past nine. There were no other partnerless golfers waiting around the greenkeeper's shed for a game, so he paid for his round, teed off and, much to his surprise, for he generally found that he played badly when in an edgy mood, hit a good, strong, long shot straight down the first fairway. A good start: something big really was going to happen today.

Playing on his own, he could walk faster and did not have to concentrate on his companions. Because he was playing well, with a fair distance between strokes, Jim was able to put himself in a better frame of mind for whatever it was that was going to happen later on. The first two holes he par-foured. He was rapidly approaching a rather slow-moving pair in front of him. The two were just moving off the third green when he approached the tee. It was a short hole, followed by a very long one. Jim would catch up soon and would face having either to dawdle on behind them, be waved through by them or be invited to join.

It was a dreadful shock when he recognised Gudger, his predecessor as Imperial Father of the *Tribune* Federated Chapels and now night manager at the same paper. Class traitor if ever there was one — and not a very pleasant man, either. Jim did not welcome the prospect of being asked to join him for the remainder of the round, but on the other hand he did not intend letting Gudger deter him from playing on his own golf course.

As Gudger and his partner walked back to the fourth tee they had to pass near to where Jim was teeing up for the third, using his father's old mashie[25]. Jim was so taken aback by seeing Gudger, whom he had never before thought of as having a life outside the *Tribune*, that he did not even glance at his companion.

"Morning, Gudger," said the Imperial Father in a mock-cheerful tone. "What are you doing on my golf course?"

Gudger, who had spent most of the working hours of his adult life in newspaper press halls, was profoundly deaf. He looked at the Imperial Father as he was being greeted. Although everyone knew he was deaf, Gudger rarely admitted to it, consequently frequently appearing to be rude, a characteristic that he had come to play on. "Hello, Anstruther," he said. "Here! I bet you miss!"

Jim looked back at the ball, adjusted his stance, took a firm grip of the club, tried to control his anger, made a forceful swing, and hit the ball. Unfortunately, not in the right place. It skittered and bounced along the turf more like a billiard ball on the baize. It rolled to a stop in a small clump of stunted buttercups scarcely 60 yards from its starting place.

Gudger and his companion said nothing, but resumed their walk to the fourth tee, Gudger with slightly more spring in his step than earlier. Jim calmed himself by raising a quizzical eyebrow, found his tee, which had gone almost as far as the ball, put the mashie in the bag and moved on. Reaching the spot where his ball lay, he looked at its lie, picked the niblick[26] out of his bag, took a firm stance and forced himself to concentrate on getting the ball out of the rough. This time it was a fine golf shot. The ball rose high out of the rough and went considerably further than could have been expected. It tumbled out of the sky on to the near edge of the green, trickled onward in a meandering path but in the general direction of the pin. Then it disappeared. It must have gone in. One of the best golf shots in Jim's life. He looked round to see whether Gudger and his pal were still watching, but if they had been they made no sign of it.

Jim told himself that he would not have wanted congratulating by the likes of Gudger, anyway. He walked up to the green, collected his ball from the hole and moved on to the fourth. Both Gudger and his pal appeared to have lost balls in the undergrowth and were paying no attention to him, so Jim played on, taking extreme care not to join them in the rough.

"D'you need any help?" he called as he drew up parallel to the place where the two golfers were scrabbling around. Gudger heard nothing, so said nothing, which suited the Imperial Father fine, but Gudger's companion said: "That's no way to treat a friend of mine, Stan."

To Jim, he called out: "Did you see where they went? Mine's a Dunlop[27]."

Gudger's companion was far from being a friend; he was Eric Durkin, cigar-smoking, Jaguar-driving greengrocer and borough alderman[28], Tory through and through, when he was not describing himself as Progressive Ratepayer[29] for council purposes.

Gudger, pausing in the fruitless search for his ball, looked at Jim as he walked up to him. Durkin was standing a few paces beyond Gudger and thus in full and open view of Jim although not of Gudger himself. The alderman was noisily and ostentatiously pushing at the undergrowth with a booted foot. He made no attempt to conceal from his former council opponent his action in taking a fresh ball from a trouser pocket and dropping it on the piece of ground he had trodden flat.

"I've found my ball, Stan," he said. "We're never going to find yours. Why don't you give up and drop another? We'll get our Red Scotch[30] comrade here to join us, to see how real gentlemen play. Sixpence a hole all right for you, Anstruther?"

Gudger said nothing. Deaf people grow used to unexpected and unexplained things happening around them.

"I'll join you if you like," said the Imperial Father, "but I won't play golf for money. It's not what the game's about."

"Always said the Scotch were tight," said Durkin, as Jim reluctantly tagged along.

As they played the remaining holes, Jim was for once glad that it was only a nine-hole course. He studied the alderman's behaviour, and Gudger's. Durkin was determined to win. He made sudden noises when either of the other two was addressing the ball, he extended exaggerated sympathy whenever anyone played a less-than-perfect shot, which was most of the time. And Jim believed that as well as miraculously finding his own ball earlier the alderman had also hidden Gudger's ball by treading it into the soil.

In contrast, Gudger's aim appeared to be merely to manage somehow to complete the round. He made no sign of acknowledging Durkin's attempts to put him off but was nevertheless more and more flustered as he lost hole after hole. The harder and more aggressively he attacked the ball the shorter it appeared to go and the more frequently he had to hack at it. His face became redder, he puffed furiously and struggled for breath which he then wasted by swearing loudly and often. He spoke largely to the ball, his clubs, the elements and God but not at all to Jim.

The alderman, however, made a point of talking to the new arrival, even when not necessary to put him off his stroke. "Fine asset to the municipality, this golf course. Good thing we stood together on this one . . . what do you think of Stan? . . . reckon we'll make a golfer out of him? . . . he's thinking of moving to these parts . . . coming up in the world . . . it's a great place . . . but then you know that, what with having been on the council . . . local councils are all about being of service to the local people, I always say . . . such a pity when they try to bring party politics into it, don't you think? . . . you did the right thing, standing as an Independent . . . you got a lot done for the people . . . and don't forget we fixed you up with a council house . . . you just messed things up by waving that big, red flag of yours and going on about communism and socialism and the rights of man and all that claptrap . . . you made a right, blithering idiot of yourself, if you don't mind me saying so ... lost a lot of friends that way ... didn't know what side your bread was buttered on ... could have done with a lively lad like you ... you'd have had to give up the politics, mind ... you can get a great deal of respect within the borough, being on the council ... it's good for business, too, of course ... you could have been a councillor for life ... we would have made sure no one stood against you if you gave up all that Red stuff ... could have become an alderman yourself, eventually ... mayor, even. Now that's a fine post ... have you ever considered joining the Conservative Party? Of course, you'd have to call yourself a Progressive Ratepayer at election time."

"I thought you were going to ask me to join the Masons, the way you were going on," said Jim.

"Oh no, it's early days for that," said Durkin. "Besides, what makes you think we're Masons?"

"I was only making a joke," said Jim. "Not an application."

"Never joke about the Masons, there are specific punishments laid down for infidels, sceptics and unbelievers," said the alderman, as they reached the final hole. "Masonic charity is the royalty of virtues. All that we send into the lives of others comes back into our own."

When he holed his final putt, Durkin told Gudger: "That's four and sixpence you owe me."

As they had been going round, Jim was thinking about how he should play the rest of the day. He got back on the Matchless, rode home, changed into his *Tribune* clothes, and left again for the station. He bought the three evening papers to read on the train. He always bought all three although each time he told himself that he did not know why he bothered.

The *News* had:

SUEZ SANCTIONS — EDEN AT CABINET

The little *Star* had

SUEZ: WE WILL BE FIRM
Gaitskell says 'Block Sterling'[31]

The *Evening Standard* had a triple-decker:

THE CANAL GRAB
Britain starts talks with Empire, France and U.S.
EDEN: FIRMNESS AGAINST NASSER[32]

Inside, a leader said:

Colonel Nasser[33] is a desperate man. That is the meaning of his Suez Canal grab. This is his face-saving attempt to restore the tottering prestige of the Egyptian dictatorship. In recent weeks, Nasser's reputation has taken blow after blow … Britain must resist Nasser's high-handed action. There can be no repetition of the foolish and weak policy which the Socialist Government pursued at the time of the Abadan oil crisis with the connivance of many Tories … The Egyptians are as incapable of operating the canal as on their own as the Persians were of running the oil wells … It is Britain's clear duty to do everything in its power to reverse Nasser's illegal act.

The Imperial Father was not surprised; it was the sort of jingoistic drivel people had come to expect of the *Standard*. Alongside the leader, in the Londoner's Diary section, another item caught his eye. It was headed

AN ANGEL OF MERCY

That dazzling new entrant to Society, Jessica Ross, together with her father, the illustrious newspaper proprietor Otto Ross, were early visitors to the bedside of Monty Evans, the *Daily Tribune* photographer, the brutal attack on whom was reported by the Londoner yesterday.

Miss Ross told us: "We felt that while this poor man's life hangs so precariously in the balance this was the least we could do to comfort him.

"I do hope that the police will soon catch up with his assailant and give him everything he deserves."

It has been pointed out that an item in yesterday's column may have been open to misinterpretation. The Londoner, together with the editor and proprietor of the *Evening Standard*, wish to make it clear that they believe Mr Ross to be an honourable, trustworthy and mild-mannered gentleman, unsurpassed in his profession and that nothing in yesterday's column was intended to imply, or could be read as implying, anything other than that.

Miss Ross herself is known to be virtuous, abstemious and demure. She did not witness the unprovoked attack on Mr Evans and had she done so she wishes it to be known that she would have tried to help him, as her conduct this morning demonstrates.

We sincerely regret any distress our previous report caused to the Ross family. The *Evening Standard* has agreed to make a donation to the cause of Miss Ross's choice, the Fund for the Abolition of Boxing.

There was no further news of the hunt for George Crawford. Perhaps the police were waiting for Monty Evans to die so they could step up their investigation to a murder hunt. There had not been a good murder trial since the House of Lords had rejected the Abolition of the Death Penalty Bill[34] a fortnight past. A good hanging trial would be very well received in certain circles.

On Jim's arrival at Blackfriars, it was raining heavily. He turned up the collar of his coat, held up the three evening papers to protect his hair from the rain, and set off to the plant of the *Daily Tribune*, arriving, dripping wet, at the open despatch bay.

Unlike the rest of the production staff there was no requirement on the Imperial Father to go in at any particular entrance. There was also a time clock but no one from one of the craft unions was required to use it.

Jim's route in was the previous night's path in reverse. There was no one in the despatch bay but there were already men at work cleaning down and oiling the presses. Cylinders for some early pages were already being fitted. It was a colourless scene. Little natural light filtered down into the press hall, even less than normal on a day such as this.

The exposed metalwork of the presses was either oiled metal with a dull sheen, self-coloured cast steel or painted a dark olive green, except for the numerous brass plates with engraved instructions. The only touch of colour was the red capitals on white-enamelled plaques warning people clear of the presses while they were in operation. The white lines on the floor delineating the safe pathway were stained with black ink, as were the men's coats and overalls, which had originally been brown or dark blue but were on principle never washed.

The Imperial Father greeted a few of the men and asked where Fred Dawlish could be found.

He located him by his feet, which were sticking out from inside Number One press, into which he had crawled to tighten the retaining nuts on a cylinder. The Imperial Father tapped on the sole of Dawlish's left boot and called: "Fred, how are you doing?"

"All right till you came along," was the indistinct reply as the Father of the National Society of Operative Printers and Assistants chapel[35] edged his way backwards out of the press.

"Bloody awful weather," said the Imperial Father.

"Yes," said the FoC. "Chimney stack of my house blew down last night. It's going to cost a fortune to put right. Almost killed my nipper."

"You property owners. You'll never learn," said the Imperial Father. He changed his tone to one as if reading from a script, and asked: "Does this weather have any effect on the print run? As you know, it's a big period for news and management's always trying to put on extra copies."

He received an equally formally toned reply: "It's funny you should say that. Damp in the atmosphere is never very good for the presses. It affects the tensions, you see."

"I do see," said the Imperial Father.

Dawlish said: "Added to which, water can seep into the reel store and collect on the floor, which sometimes means one side of the reel is damp while the other isn't. Bound to lead to web breaks with newsprint like that."

"Especially when management wants to put on extra copies," said the Imperial Father. "Is there anything that might cure the problem? I was thinking of an Extra Responsibility (Damp Weather) Allowance."

"Might do the trick."

"I'll see what can be done," said the Imperial Father. "Sorry about your chimney stack."

He continued on his round, stopping to have a cup of tea and a chat with the Linotype operators, most of whom had a small kettle kept hot by placing it on top of the pot of molten printing metal integral to their machines.

Jim collected half a dozen of the men to go with him to the canteen for their mid-day meal. This was something he tried to do most days; it kept him in touch with what was going on and it also gave him an audience for his political agitation.

"What do you think of this, then?" said the Imperial Father, stabbing at the damp page of the *Evening Standard* with its **ANGEL OF MERCY** item. "Rich bitch. I can't see why folk bow and scrape to people like her who wouldn't know what a day's work was like if her butler brought it on a tray."

In between mouthfuls of liver and bacon and mashed potato, the Imperial Father's dinner companions[36] mumbled general agreement, anxious not to provoke him into an analysis of the class structure of newspaper ownership, let alone a consideration of foreign policy implications of the American elections or the Suez canal affair.

"The Australians have accused us of nobbling the wicket to favour our spin-bowlers," noted Bill Enright, the deputy London Typographical Society FoC. "If we have been, we could even win the Ashes[37], helped by the rain and a few draws. What do you think, Jim?"

"Don't include me in your 'we', Bill," said Jim. "I'm not English — and my game's golf. You'd never believe who I met on the course this morning: Gudger. He looked most taken aback to see me. He had a loudmouthed Bromley alderman with him. Kept losing his ball in the bushes — must be some sort of Masonic ritual."

Enright gave him a strange look and said: "Never joke about the Masons, Jim." He went on: "I always feel a bit sorry for Gudger. He wasn't a bad Imperial Father. We're all supposed to hate him because he turned his back on the union to join management, but they made him an offer he couldn't refuse. We don't trust him, but I'd like to bet management don't either."

"I can't help that," said Jim. "I bear him no ill will, but he's decided which side he's on. He knows that if you try to stand in the middle of the road you get run over by a tram."

After dinner, Jim went to his gloomy corridor office to get down to some of the paperwork that piled up since the night before: stacks of leave forms to initial, the unofficial ghosting rota to work out (after all, there had to be someone to do the work, couldn't have everyone going sick or driving taxis on the same day), the names of that night's casual workers to pass on to the relevant FoC, the list of various departments' vacancies to be filled. He noted that there was a post in the library going and he wondered if he should ask the clerical FoC if he could offer it to Sheilagh; with a taste of working at the *Tribune* she might realise why it was that he was never home before midnight. There was a carbon copy[38] of the minutes of the previous day's production meeting and the agenda for that day's one. The usual: Apologies for absence, minutes, matters arising, production requirements, future issues, grievances, any other business.

The chairmanship and the secretaryship alternated daily between the union and management, the chairman and the secretary never being from the same side. Jim had been chairman the previous day and today was to be secretary. The agenda had been drawn up by yesterday's secretary, hence the wording "production requirements": the Imperial Father always wrote "production request". It was all part of the ritual battle for control.

Jim went to collect his deputy, Francis Josling, who was also FoC for the Association of Correctors of the Press. They went to the meeting in the oak-panelled, polished-floored, daylight-lit part of the building. Jim found that, in private, he worked well with Francis Josling, in spite of the public rows between them. In a difficult meeting it sometimes helped to have your strongest critic alongside, so he could not attack the negotiators afterwards if something went wrong.

As a member of the proof-reading department, Josling had the learning of a bygone time. You never could tell when you might need someone who had a command of Ancient Greek, Hebrew and Aramaic or who could tell you the names of Derby winners for a century and more.

Jim decided to make an impression on management as he entered the committee room. "A lot of tension in the air today, Francis," he said, loudly, as they went in. "As a result of what happens at this meeting, everybody might be going home early tonight. Didn't the Greeks have a special tense for describing times like that?"

"No," said Josling, deflating him. "You mean the paulo-post-future[39], but you'd be misusing it. You know as little about Ancient Greek as you do about politics."

Jim was glad to discover that his failed Classical reference had fallen on deaf ears, along with the implied threat of a stoppage. Gudger was the only other participant yet to have arrived. He was fiddling with his earpiece and adjusting a control knob on the hearing aid placed on the committee-room table in front of him.

The Imperial Father and the proffreaders' FoC sat down opposite him and waited for something to happen. The Imperial Father broke the silence by saying loudly to Gudger: "You want to watch out for the alderman, he's nobody's fool. Still, four and six is a lot of money to lose. It's more than an hour's earnings for very many people."

"Not at the *Tribune*, it isn't," said Gudger. "You're all overpaid."

"It's a good thing the meeting hasn't started yet," replied Jim. "If a remark like that was on the record and I believed it genuinely reflected management's attitude, it might bring about a very nasty state of affairs. Besides, why aren't you in the chair?"

"Just you wait and see," said Gudger, as the door opened.

In came Colonel Cumberledge, general manager of the *Daily Tribune*, every highly polished shoe of him, every silver hair and folded handkerchief in the top pocket of his well-cut suit. With him came the Printer, O'Brien, another silver-haired gentleman in an expensive suit, but slightly older, nearfng retirement age, and with a pipe in his hand. Gudger stood up till the two senior gentlemen were themselves seated but the Imperial Father and the proofeaders' FoC stayed where they were. The colonel took the chairman's seat and the Printer sat between him and Gudger, directly opposite the Imperial Father.

The Colonel looked at Jim and started: "I have been asked by the proprietor himself, who puts the utmost of importance on the production of tonight's newspaper, to take charge of these negotiations in person to make sure there is unimpeded production and no disruption to tonight's edition. Quite frankly, he is getting sick and tired of the continual failure to achieve full production."

Jim returned the Colonel's gaze and shook his head slowly from side to side. At the first opportunity, he said: "Colonel, with respect, and I realise you are new to this business, this is not the way things are done here. In the first place, this is not a negotiating meeting but a problem-solving one. If it was a negotiation we would demand parity of numbers. Secondly, you have to take matters in the order in which they are set out on the agenda and, thirdly, there has never, while I have been Imperial Father of the Federated Chapel," and here he glanced away at Gudger, "been any workforce disruption to production. Any shortfall in output has been entirely due to continual and chronic underinvestment by management. How we get any production at all is a miracle."

Jim believed what he said was more or less true. You couldn't be so obvious as to hold a pistol to the proprietor's head and say: pay us pots of money or we'll sabotage your paper. Far too uncivilised. You had to get to the same destination by using sophisticated and plausible arguments.

The same should be true for the other side — management could not hope to get anywhere by using pre-war tactics of overt confrontation — but this new man evidently had no idea of how to play the game. He had given away his intentions in the first seconds: he had virtually said that production of that night's issue was so important — why? Another Shock Issue? — that he would pay whatever was necessary. Jim set out with gathering enjoyment to separate the fool from his proprietor's money.

First he got rid of O'Brien. Since the Colonel wanted a negotiating session there had to be equal numbers. If the Imperial Father had to fetch another of his colleagues from the Federated Chapel Committee it would delay proceedings. It was also the turn of the Linotype operators to be represented and, understanding the Colonel's justified concern that they manage a full night's production, the Imperial Father was reluctant to see that vital department one man short just when a fast turn-round in typesetting was so critical. O'Brien said he was needed to sort out a problem in the reel-store and he was sure that Gudger understood enough about technical matters to stand in for him. The Colonel thought that was a reasonable compromise. Anything to get the show on the road.

"It's quite true what you say about how things have been done in the past," said the Colonel. "But do not take that as any guide to the future. I have received clear instructions from the proprietor that things have to change. In future there will be no interruptions to production. When management decides on a production target for the night, that target will have to be met, come what may.

"Anyone who does not pull his weight, or lets the team down, will be dropped from the side. No one's job is safe — and that includes management." Here it was the Colonel's turn to look at Gudger.

For Jim, it looked as if today was going to be fun. The Colonel was going to have to learn the hard way and Jim was going to enjoy teaching him. For Gudger, though, the public removal of his authority and the humiliating rejection of the style of management he had followed over the years was a noticeable shock. The Colonel, presumably used to shouting orders on the battlefield, or at the very least on the parade ground, would find that you couldn't treat printing workers like that. You couldn't dismiss them, or even threaten to. But Gudger's own post was different. He had no union to stand up for him anymore. So he just swallowed, said nothing, and looked at his hearing aid.

"Since we appear to be ignoring the order of the agenda today," said Jim, "I would like to raise the matter of the weather, which threatens to disrupt tonight's production. Now, of course, you can't sack the weather, any more than you can sack any of my members, so you will have to find another solution."

He talked at length and in great technical detail about the damage caused to the huge reels of newsprint by seepage into the store and the consequent difficulty of running the presses at full speed when they had to cope with different tensions at various part of the width. (It was to look into this problem that O'Brien had given for his excuse to leave.) The presses might have to run at half-speed if they were to avoid a series of web breaks.

The Colonel tried to follow the argument, which Jim made as complicated and technical as he could, explaining the presses in detail from end to end, starting with the newly fitted automatic-pasting device which meant that they could run continuously without stopping for reel changes. He described the device's 85-inch long, curved guillotine blades for automatically cutting off the flapping reel-ends, fully hydraulic and made in Dayton, Ohio, by the Harris Seybold Company, sharp enough and powerful enough to slice a man in two. He explained the safety devices of bells, hooters, flashing lights and automatic fast-acting brakes designed to stop that happening. He described in exhaustive detail all the features of the press from end to end. In all, it showed that printing a 1½d copy of the *Tribune*, at 40,000 an hour, was so complicated that only a man who had been born into a long line of printers and had undergone a long apprenticeship and detailed study could possibly be its master.

"Are you claiming that you can't print the *Tribune* even though that is the job you are paid for?" the Colonel asked.

"I'm afraid so," said the Imperial Father. "It's the fault of years of chronic underinvestment. Whoever heard of an unheated reel-store where you have to use duck-boards to avoid getting your feet wet? You can come along and have a look, Colonel. It will remind you of the Somme[40]."

The Colonel, who needed no reminding of the Somme and who looked as if he was not sure he could trust this plausible-sounding young Scot, had nevertheless no way of telling if he was being spun a line. "Is what he says true, Gudger?" he asked.

Sounding happy for the first time, Gudger said: "Unfortunately, yes, Colonel."

"So what can we do about it? The proprietor will be furious."

This was the turning point in the first battle. The Colonel had been forced to abandon giving orders and to throw himself on the workers' mercy: he had shown this by using the word "We". Now was not the time to throw out subtlety by demanding the Extra Responsibility (Damp Weather) Allowance. That could wait. Instead, the Imperial Father murmured: "Perhaps . . . no. It's too risky."

The Colonel grasped at the lifeline, not realising that there was a barbed hook embedded in it. "What's that? Is there a way out?" he said.

"Well — it's risky," said Jim. "We *could* try it, though. We could perhaps run at almost full speed, despite the variable tension of the newsprint stock, if we brought in an extra assistant for each press and made him monitor tension at all times, with his finger on the emergency stop, ready to push it the moment something started to go wrong."

Gudger spoke: "That's balderdash. Total rubbish. He's pulling the wool over your eyes."

The Colonel misunderstood and abruptly interrupted him. "Don't be such a spoilsport, such a stick-in-the-mud. Anything's worth a try. Don't you *want* the paper to get out?"

Gudger, who might otherwise have explained that there always was someone monitoring tension, that what was wanted was not just "almost" full speed, that it didn't take all that long to re-web after a break, that there was no budget for two extra casuals and that the Imperial Father would never have tried such an obvious hoodwink if the Colonel had been less of a dupe, but, in the face of the rude rejection of his views, decided to stay quiet and wait for the Colonel to come a cropper.

So it was agreed that two extra casuals be hired each night until the weather improved and that the reel-store be waterproofed and heated. Of course, with two extra people to supervise, the senior press operators would have to receive an Increased Responsibility Allowance.

They agreed the print run for the night and Jim said that, in a spirit of unity and in order not to delay matters further, he would hold over the grievance items till a future meeting.

"Capital fellow," said the Colonel.

That night there was indeed another of the *Tribune*'s Shock Issues. Not the Death of the National Health Service again, though. This time it was **Bloodlust: the Ring of Death**. Pages on how boxers beat each other to a punchdrunk pulp in the ring and how some of those tough enough to escape more serious injury nevertheless had their brains so damaged that, driven mad with a craving for blood, they stalked the streets looking for innocent bystanders to batter or kill. The news of the call for Egyptian assets in Britain to be blocked and all the other news, whether of the Suez crisis or not, did not start till page 4. The dragnet for fugitive fighter George Crawford took precedence.

Jim spent most of the afternoon at his paperwork, including the task of writing up the minutes of the production meeting. Just in case something went wrong, he made sure that the Colonel was correctly minuted as ordering the extra payments to be made and instructing the presses to be run at 95 per cent capacity, despite his own warning. He took the foolscap[41] sheet to be typed up and spent the rest of the afternoon moving around the various departments, checking on developments.

At evening opening time, fancying a pie and having had enough of the company canteen for one day, he went out to the printers' local pub, using the public bar so as not to have to rub shoulders with any journalists, who favoured the saloon or the lounge bars. There was an extraordinary incident, about which he was made to promise to say nothing to anyone. He left the pub, still worrying about the incident, and visited the *Tribune* press hall, where the final plates for the first edition were being bolted on. The front page was boxing, as news, and the back page was cricket and boxing as sport, the Moore-Parker fight[42]. No one saw fit to remark on the apparent contradiction.

O'Brien was in the press hall, as was Gudger. Jim saw the Colonel coming down the gangway and went up to greet him. "It's not really the done thing for the general manager to be here," he told the Colonel. "There's a lot of tension in the air tonight — but if you're with me, you'll be all right."

"Capital fellow," said the Colonel.

Jim took him to see Fred Dawlish, who explained in intricate and obscure detail everything that could go wrong with a printing press.

Both presses having been plated up and the final checks having been made, the electric bells and hooters sounded and the lights flashed for a full minute in their warning for all present to stand well clear. The start buttons were pressed. First one and then the other giant R. Hoe & Crabtree presses[43] started its slow run-up to producing the first smudged and off-register copies of that night's Shock Issue.

O'Brien took off an early, folded copy and called for adjustments. Over the next 15 minutes the presses built up to speed. There were satisfied nods all round, as the tone developed from a dull clanking to a seamless and noisy whirr. The Colonel in particular appeared to be enjoying himself. Jim cupped his hands around his mouth and shouted in the Colonel's ear: "It looks fine for now. No point waiting around: wherever you are in the building you'll know if anything goes wrong."

Nothing did go wrong for quite a time. The presses were halted, re-plated for the second edition and started again. So it was with the third, at about 10 o'clock that night. Jim was starting to be a bit concerned. He took Fred Dawlish to a spot far enough from the machines where they could hear each other without shouting, and said: "Everything appears to be going well tonight, Fred. Funny that; I had expected at least one web break. I thought it would be like your chimney stack — couldn't take the strain of the bad weather."

"I know what you mean," said Dawlish.

Within a minute there was a sharp crack from Number One Press, and a flying sheet of paper shot into the air.

Uncannily, there was soon a similar occurrence on Number Two Press. On each press the cylinders thundered uselessly around, printing their Shock Issue over and over again on to the same emptily revolving roller rather than on to a continuously moving web of newsprint. Alerted by the break in supply, the honed guillotine for the automatic paster slashed up and down, slicing thin air, rather than the loose reel-end it was expecting, and the conveyor churned uselessly on delivering no output to the waiting packers.

In spite of what the Imperial Father had promised the Colonel, there was no night casual atop each press, poised with his finger on a stop button. It was not really a lie — everyone in the print knew that it merely meant a book-keeping entry to add to the wages of those printers who were really there. Dawlish walked over to the wall and pulled the emergency power switch controlling both presses. A messenger had to be found and sent out to the pub where the operators tended to go between edition times to fetch the full press crew back. There was a delay of several minutes when the messenger could not attract attention at the door of the pub, which had been locked, with the drinkers still inside, at closing time.

Dawlish surveyed the mess. "It's going to take a long time to get this lot stripped down," he said to Jim. "Someone must have over-ridden the automatic emergency brake. There's also something jamming up the works. This mechanical newsprint isn't of the quality it was before the war."

He and his colleagues started stripping down Number One press. Attracted by the silence of the presses and the absence of the rumbling shake that could normally be felt throughout the whole building, even in the editorial fastness and the grand proprietorial floor, O'Brien, Gudger and the Colonel made their separate arrivals. O'Brien leant on a guard rail and watched, impassively. Gudger walked up and down the clear passageway between the two presses, while the Colonel went up to Jim and demanded to know what was up.

"I warned you it was risky," he was told. "We should never have tried it at that speed. Seems there may be a foreign body in the works; could be a rat, could be anything."

"Not with both presses at once, surely," was the Colonel's reasonable objection.

After blinding him with science, Jim wondered how he would react to superstition, and said: "There's a funny way with presses. Some of the older printers will tell you they're almost human, as if there was some mystical rapport between Number One and Number Two. I don't accept that, of course. I've been taught that there's a scientific explanation for everything."

"Or sabotage," said the Colonel.

"That's a serious accusation," said Jim. "It's a good thing no one overheard you. Some of these union people can be terribly belligerent."

The work on Number One Press continued at a measured pace. The tangled mess of newsprint was gradually cleared away and then large sections of the press were dismantled and laid out in an ordered sequence on the ground. The Colonel called Gudger over and in his presence expressed his worries to Jim: "What are they doing? Why's everything so slow? Why do they have to take it all to bits? Why can't they work on both presses at the same time?"

"Safety," he was told. "Besides, you don't have enough men to work on them both. It will save time to get Number One in production first; at least you'll get *some* production while they clear Number Two."

Gudger said nothing but disappeared behind Number Two press to investigate. He might not have wanted to be seen approaching the press from the main gangway — if anything would exacerbate a delicate situation that would. He must have been looking to see what it was they had thrown in to clog up the works. Might it have been the traditional rat again? Or could it have been chewing gum[44]? Perhaps he wanted to get evidence to expose Anstruther in front of the Colonel. He might have reasoned that that would show the interloper that he didn't understand industry practice and should leave tricky negotiations to Gudger. Then there would be no more unpleasant talk about people not pulling their weight, letting the team down and being dropped from the side.

Afterwards, it was clear what had happened: Gudger could see little from the sidelines, so he took off his coat, unstrapped his hearing aid, laid them on the ground beside the machine and crawled inside the press to investigate, exploring deeper and deeper in his search for the elusive cause of the stoppage. He crawled through the machinery, examining each part of the paper path for obstructions. In the darkness, he could see nothing out of the ordinary and might have begun to suspect that the machine had not been sabotaged at all, that the web-break had indeed taken place spontaneously. If that was so, there would be no excuse for stripping the press, he could tell the Colonel. That would save time. It might even restore the man's confidence in him. Perhaps, just before he crawled out of the machine he decided that he had better just make a final check on the automatic paster.

Eventually, Number One press was reassembled, the bodily remains of a dead rat removed, ready for the process of rethreading the newsprint, for which the electricity supply had to be restored. The operators set the Number One press controls to their base positions, started the warning bells, the electric hooter and the flashing light to caution everyone to stand clear of the presses and summoned a duty electrician to restore the 6,000-volt current.

Without his hearing aid, Gudger could not hear the bell or the hooter. Little light, flashing or not, penetrated the depths of the press.

With the power restored, the huge rollers of Number One press were able to be edged around to accept the complicated zigzag threading of a fresh reel of newsprint. No one had touched the controls of Number Two press since Dawlish had thrown the master power lever, so it burst into action where it had left off. With no newsprint running through its hungry maze, the machine started faster than it would have otherwise; with no newsprint running past, the automatic reel-pasting device sensed it was time to do its duty, the honed guillotine blade rising and then falling, swiftly, powerfully, cleanly.

Gudger would not have heard its approaching swish as it swiftly, powerfully, cleanly, cut off his head.

No one saw the accident take place. Dawlish was the first to the press to turn off its empty thundering. He then walked around the back, in preparation for clearing it down. He came across Gudger's coat, folded on the ground, with the hearing aid placed on top. In the pit under the press he saw a dark red pool of blood mingling with the printing ink.

"I think someone had better call an ambulance," he called out, before vomiting up the night's beer.

Shortly afterwards, Jim found himself in a reprise of that afternoon's meeting. The Colonel was again in the chair, O'Brien by his side. The seat previously occupied by Gudger was vacant.

Jim was saying: "I appreciate your desire to please the proprietor, Colonel Cumberledge, but I don't think you recognise the great esteem and affection for the late Mr Gudger. He was a greatly respected man; he must have been, otherwise he could never have occupied the position of Imperial Father of the Federated Chapel here before me. It is as a mark of common respect that the men have blacked any production on either press until the funeral.

"Shock Issue or not, the men have decided that the presses must stay silent until then. I take your point that a funeral could well be indefinitely delayed because of the need for an inquest. Perhaps we could be flexible on that point. It could be that we might persuade the men" — he looked at the Proofreaders' FoC for affirmation — "to allow Number One press to be used if Mr Gudger's remains are not released for burial within a month."

Gudger would have known what to do in the face of such a stance, but the Colonel was not in a position to call on him for help. O'Brien did not offer any assistance but just sat there, noisily smoking his pipe. The talking went on for a long time, the Colonel speaking of the importance to the nation of the continued publication of such a great newspaper, the proprietor's deep personal concern for his employees as shown by his care for a humble photographer, the precarious economic times, the cut-throat competition (a phrase he must have regretted), and the fitting tribute to a good friend that a prompt return to work would be. He even hinted that there might be money available in recognition of the unpleasant task of cleaning up the mess.

Jim spoke about the callous attitude shown by anyone who believed that the men's legitimate grief would be compensated for by a few pounds (the Colonel had in mind a few shillings), the necessity of leaving the evidence *in situ* for the murder inquiry that would surely follow, his own warning earlier that day of the riskiness of the undertaking — as demonstrated in the minutes — and the remarkable absence of grief displayed by the man who had sent his colleague to his death and who might be facing trial for murder.

The talking went on and on, which well suited the union representatives. At one moment, Francis Josling leant over to Jim and said: "I was supposed to be off two hours ago. Just think of the overtime I'm clocking up."

The clock passed the time when any further production would have been of use, even if the press crew had not in fact gone home hours earlier. It was no longer relevant to talk about that day but of when and at what cost there would next be any work done on the *Daily Tribune*.

The canteen had long closed and even the night steward with the keys to the executive drinks cabinet had gone home. From experience, Jim knew that hunger made some negotiators more anxious to settle, while others were made obdurate and argumentative. He feared that the Colonel might be a quitter, one of these people prepared to compromise, to back down, which would mean losing the opportunity to have a strike on such a perfect matter of principle. When the Colonel called a short break so he could visit the lavatory, Jim nevertheless followed him, to find out what was really on offer[45].

Alone in the polished-brass and white-tiled splendour, with three vacant Edwardian urinals separating general manager and Imperial Father, the Colonel said: "A great pity about Gudger, of course, but perhaps it was better that way. The proprietor wasn't too happy with him."

The Imperial Father waited to hear what was next. The Colonel said: "You seem a decent-enough chap — and a damned good negotiator, as I have just discovered. You can't remain a Red all your life: I think you'd make a great night manager. Of course, we wouldn't appoint you right away, have to advertise first, but, if you want it, the job's yours."

This was the mark of desperation, obviously the Colonel's last available card. The Imperial Father knew that if he acted firmly he could have a good quick strike over a matter of principle. He said: "I'm not interested in becoming night manager. The workers are going to take over the whole newspaper some time; it's a case of historical inevitability[46]. In the meantime, I don't need bribes, I need popularity. That's why you're going to get a strike — and it will be all your fault."

"It's not just workers who have 'solidarity'," said the Colonel. "I hope you realise that if we fail to come out tomorrow the Newspaper Proprietors' Association[47] will stop every paper in Fleet Street. They'll all be out on the street and they won't thank you for it."

"We'll see about that," said the Imperial Father.

On return to the negotiating table, he said, not altogether truthfully: "During our short break the management has made an offer which I believe the chapel will be willing to accept. It is for production to start at the normal time tomorrow night — using Number One press alone, Number Two press to be cleaned down by ambulance staff granted temporary membership of the union, and to come into full production within two days, the power supplies to each press to be separated permanently, for safety reasons, and management to undertake to institute any other safety measures the union is able to identify as being able to prevent a repetition of the accident, a £5 Special Production Allowance to every printing union member in the building, a day off for Mr Gudger's funeral, and a 10 shilling Special Responsibility (Grief) Allowance for all press crew members every night until the inquest, neither management nor union members to make any accusation of negligence against the other, and a two-inch obituary for Stan Gudger to appear in the first available edition."

This was too much for the Colonel. He said: "I came here in good faith. I've put up with accusations of murder, lies, doctored minutes, total fabrications and lies. I'm tired and I'm hungry and I'm angry and I'm going home to bed. You can have your strike."

Jim minuted the words, collected his coat and walked out into the dawning light.

By the time he arrived home the sun was almost up. Sheilagh stirred and turned over as he got in beside her, but she did not wake.

4

Early afternoon Thursday 26th July to 27th July 1956

As soon as the proprietor had extracted a promise that Monty Evans would be moved forthwith to a private hospital, under the supervision of the Charing Cross consultant, he returned to his waiting Humber[1]. Fibbins broke off his argument with a policeman about parking in a no-waiting area and opened a door for the proprietor, who got in. Jessica made as if to follow him but the proprietor said: "Where do you think *you're* going? I'm going back to the *Tribune* — and the car stays there. You're a big girl now; you'll have to make your own way home. I'll see you at 6.30 for supper."

Jessica thereupon decided not to stand up Lear and his invitation to the cinema.

She crossed the road, bought another copy of the *Evening Standard*, so she could re-read the Londoner's Diary item on her journey home. She walked through Charing Cross railway station and down the street to the Underground, where she waited for a Bakerloo Line train to St John's Wood. There was a long delay and when the train eventually arrived at the platform it was crowded. A middle-aged gentleman nevertheless gave up his seat for her, so Jessica was able to sit and read.

The front page of the *Standard* was about the car strike, which did not interest her overmuch. She read again the salacious item about the previous night. Even though the piece was lies almost from beginning to end, it helped her remember George. His sheer power and presence. The way he walked up and down with exuberant energy, waiting to pounce. His dark, tough, heroic good looks. His strength. And his obvious interest in her. That exhilarating crunch when he felled the photographer. The same powerful arms that held her, carried her, to a taxi. Her loneliness when he left her at the cab without even the kiss she wanted.

Until she could see him, there was merely the Hon Lear Farnsworth for company. Doubtless full of the Test Match, and horses.

As it was, the man who had protected her was now hunted by the police, probably at the instigation of the proprietor, who wanted him charged with attempted murder. If the nasty little photographer died, George might even be put on trial for his life. If they caught him before teatime tomorrow she might never even see him again.

When she arrived home, not having eaten for almost a day, Jessica got Mrs Burgess to bring her a pile of sandwiches, which she ate while watching television on the set in the library. There was little but cricket and horseracing on the BBC, but the new ITV had children's programmes until the mid-evening break. In the darkness behind the drawn curtains she thought of the fugitive George Crawford. She saw him as Robert Donat playing Richard Hannay in the old film, fleeing from the police who would not understand, cloaked by the girders of the Forth Bridge, herself manacled to him in his escape over the moors, in pursuit of the conspiracy of *The 39 Steps*[2]. She saw him as an RAF officer in *Reach for the Sky*[3], but that did not have a part for her in it, so she saw George Crawford as the mediæval Gerard in *The Cloister and the Hearth*[4], pining for his Margaret while on the run from his false accusers, their love growing only the more strong as the years and the leagues separated them. Thoroughly gloomy, but awfully heroic.

Lear, wearing a grey suit, turned up on the doorstep at 6.30 as he had threatened, before the return from Fleet Street of the proprietor. He was let in by Mrs Burgess, who told him not to drip on the hall carpet while he waited for Miss Ross. Jessica kept him waiting for only a minute or two, as she wanted to avoid meeting the proprietor, who was due back shortly.

She had changed from her daytime cotton frock to a burgundy-coloured woollen dress with a narrow white belt, drawn tight. It was raining again — this year must be breaking all records for rain, Lear remarked to her — so she put on her gabardine mac and tied a silk headscarf over her hair and under her chin. Doubtless Lear would supply an umbrella if they had to queue in the rain.

Lear's new motor car was a Paramount four-seater convertible[5]. "How on earth did you get it? The waiting list must be years long," asked Jessica, for something to say.

"Not at all," he said. "They're almost giving them away. I think the factory must be going bust. It's not as grand as it looks. It's only got a Ford Consul engine, that's why they call it a Jew's Bentley[6,7]."

Jessica gave him a fearsome glare, to which Lear reacted: "I didn't mean anything — it's only an expression, you know."

Jessica still glared, as Lear rambled on, saying: "I'm thinking of changing the car, anyway," as if it was the vehicle that was at fault. "It's a marvellous car but I've hardly had the chance to drive with the hood down all summer."

Water dripped through the join between the hood and the windscreen as they drove south to the Curzon cinema[8], in Mayfair. The noise of the rain on the roof and the slush-whirr-clunk of the windscreen wipers made further conversation unnecessary, so the pair said little until Lear had parked in a bomb-site car park.

"Half a crown[9] for parking! It's daylight robbery," he said.

Just as he was about to get out of the car, he said: "That reminds me. Here's your watch. I hope you like it." He handed Jessica a slim, leather box, while looking at her eyes for a sign of appreciation. Jessica opened the box to reveal the shiny Rolex. The gift was a bit of a blow. She had hoped he might have come up with a cheque instead, which she might somehow find a way of holding on to. Nevertheless, some display of gratitude was evidently called for, so she leant forward and kissed him quickly on the cheek and said: "Oh Lear — you are a brick."

Lear tried to encircle her with his arms but she sprang back too quickly for him. Lear looked as if this reward was rather less than he might have expected from a woman of the world who had just received a £1,000 gift and who had been publicly linked to him as a prospective bride, but he said: "That's all right. Think nothing of it. Any day."

Jessica was grateful for the rain. It did mean that she had to walk close to Lear's right side to share his umbrella but since his right hand had to hold the umbrella above them he was unable to make any advances. Lining up in the rain outside the cinema, Lear told her: "The last remnant of my regiment left the Suez Canal Zone in the middle of last month. Now, what with the antics of this new chappie Nasser, it looks like they may have to go back again soon, to restore order[10]. I'm still in Zed Reserve and that means I might well be called up. It's a dreadful bind, but if it happens I may have to miss the Olympics[11]. If I don't get called away though, mother and the BF would like you to come with us to Melbourne to see the Games. What about it? We have a paper there, you know."

Jessica did not know but was not surprised. The whole induction into the Farnsworth family was happening much too fast, she felt, but could think of no plausible excuse for saying "No".

So she said: "Yes, that sounds all right." Then, in resigned politeness: "Thank you, Lear."

The film was indeed foreign, as Lear had promised, but it was hardly the feast for the intellect he had implied. The heavily cut but still X-rated *Lady Chatterley's Lover*[12], while admittedly in French, with English subtitles, was pretty strange. An Italian, Erno Crisa, wore what appeared to be a postman's uniform to play a French-speaking English gamekeeper, Danielle Darrieux played Lady Chatterley and Leo Genn, Sir Clifford.

The plot was most difficult to understand after the censor's efforts. Jessica did not believe it really portrayed life in England. Nevertheless, she felt the choice of film demonstrated that Lear saw her as a sophisticated, daring woman of the world, gratifying in contrast to the attitude of the proprietor, who showed that he thought of her as child. What did George think of her as?

The film was not so bad that Jessica could not sit through it fantasising of herself as a dramatic Danielle Darrieux, George Crawford as Erno Crisa and Lear as the wheelchair-bound Leo Genn. Free from the umbrella now, Lear's hand started to wander from time to time. "Don't do that," said Jessica. "You'll make my dress grubby."

Apart from the main feature, there was a *Look at Life*[13] travelogue on Sarawak, the British colony in north-west Borneo, the Pearl & Dean advertisements, an intermission when Kia-Ora would be on sale in the foyer, and the newsreel. It showed the week's events in Suez, the wreck of the Andrea Doria[14], the car workers' violent strike, Southend's Miss Lovely competition, a strange new gambling machine called ERNIE which would pick the winners of the new Premium Bonds[15], Princess Margaret taking the salute at Sandhurst[16], the Bank of England bringing in coloured fivers[17], Marilyn Monroe leaving London after her honeymoon with Arthur Miller, and it showed the boxing. There were two parts. First there was Canada's great white hope, Parker, hitting the canvas in the ninth round, followed by the words ". . . and in London, another boxer is facing an unhappy time, as Scotland's George Crawford evades police anxious to question him in connection with a brutal assault on a newspaper photographer". There was a clip of Crawford in the ring, a fine figure of a man, though strangely unrecognisable as the figure of the previous night. It was terribly unfair but the newsreel compilers had chosen the fight where he had been defeated.

Lear leant over and whispered in Jessica's ear: "Seemed a nice enough chap last night; I had no idea he was like that. Makes me feel a bit guilty about leaving you alone with him. I hope everything was all right. He didn't molest you?"

"No." Jessica shook her head, feeling regretful.

After the film, when the National Anthem[18] was over, Lear tried to persuade Jessica to go to a coffee bar but she told him: "Lear, I'd love to, but the proprietor will be livid. I was supposed to have supper with him but I went out with you instead, without telling him. If I don't get back soon, there'll be hell to pay."

"Funny, that," said Lear. "I didn't know he treated you like a schoolgirl. I thought of you as the sophisticated type."

"No such luck," said Jessica. She did not make it clear whether she meant Lear was out of luck or she herself was.

"No," said Lear. The kiss on the cheek looked like being all he would ever get out of her.

The proprietor was not at home when Jessica was delivered back. Mrs Burgess said that he had gone back to the *Tribune*. "You treat him dreadfully. Don't you know he just adores you?" she said.

"Ah well," replied Jessica, "it's a good thing he has you to console him then." She went up to her bedroom.

Not to sleep, or not for several hours, at least. She thought of George, out huddled on the Embankment or wherever it was that fugitives huddled. Why had she named Swann & Edgar's as the meeting point, the most obvious rendezvous anywhere, teeming with people and doubtless under the constant eye of the police? She had not known at the time that the proprietor was so set on getting George captured and prosecuted, but that was no excuse.

She wondered why the proprietor was hounding the man; he surely couldn't know about Jessica's infatuation with him. The proprietor did have spies everywhere, though. But there could be nothing for the spies to report, just an innocent meeting at last night's ball, when George had very kindly got her a cab home. That was all. George, though, would be able to explain the reason for everything that was going on. If she ever saw him again. If he had not been captured and was not already languishing in a dark dungeon.

After a night of fitful sleep, Jessica rose, put on a nightdress so that Mrs Burgess would not realise that she slept naked, donned her dressing gown and went downstairs to tune the library radio in to the news to find out the latest on George.

When the valves warmed up, Jessica found that there was nothing but a crackle. The dial was still where she had left it, tuned to Radio Luxembourg[19]. She retuned rapidly, finding the BBC Home Service a few seconds after the news had started. There was nothing about George, so either he was still free, or else his capture had been covered so early in the bulletin that she had missed it.

The proprietor, attracted by the sound of the wireless[20], came into the library. He was already dressed in his office-going suit and had evidently been up for some time. Anxious as she was, Jessica dared not ask him whether there was any news of the fugitive boxer.

The proprietor complained to her: "I don't mind your going out with friends, especially not with young Farnsworth, of whom I have high hopes, but I do object to deceit. When I left you yesterday we made an arrangement to have tea together but when I arrived back you had gone out. It's not good enough."

"Sorry," said Jessica.

"I'm glad to see you taking such an interest in the news, though," said the proprietor. "I'll have to find you something to do at the *Tribune* soon. I understand you have told Mrs Burgess that you'll be going into town this afternoon. Join me at 6 at the office and we'll have a talk about your future in the car back home."

When he had gone, Jessica looked at the various editions of the *Tribune* and other newspapers that the proprietor had left behind. They did not make for cheery reading, particularly the *Tribune* Shock Issue on the National Health Service with the front page item Boxing Hero Crawford in 'Attempt on the Life of Our Monty'. Jessica wondered whether there was any precedent for a family member suing her own family's newspaper for writing lies.

At least, George seemed to have evaded capture so far, and she would be able to see him soon. For all her sleepless night she had thought little of what she was going to say to him. It was clear that she could do little for him — she had no hiding place to offer and not yet any noticeable influence over what the *Tribune* wrote.

Towards lunchtime and after begging another plateful of sandwiches from Mrs Burgess (who told her: "You haven't eaten properly for days"), Jessica set off to go up to town again. She wore a loose, sleeveless dress of artificial silk in the colour of pale olives. It fastened down the front with pearl buttons. She had new nylon stockings and high-heeled sandals in the same tan colour so that it looked, even if it did not feel, as if she was walking on air. She had spent a lot of time on her hair, brushing a sheen into it and pinning it up, to show off her long neck. In her white-gloved hands she carried a crocodile-skin handbag and when just out of home she stopped and took a deep-red lipstick from it and applied it carefully, using a mirror. She wanted to make a good impression and so, despite the changeable weather, risked going out without a raincoat, relying only on the Pac-a-mac and her polythene rainhood in her handbag. Would George have preferred her in her more normal jersey and slacks? Probably not. He was a working-class man and they were reputed to like their women to look the part.

She caught the Underground to Oxford Circus, changing trains for Bond Street. It wasn't raining yet although the skies looked likely to burst at any moment. The shops were toward the end of their July sales, the time of "further massive reductions in all departments". Jessica bought some Bri-Nylon undergarments in Fenwick's[21] before walking down to Simpson's in Piccadilly[22]. She liked going there, not for the store's old-fashioned 1930s decor or for its helpful but unpretentious shop assistants but because the proprietor maintained an account there and she could pledge his credit.

There was nothing she particularly liked but she managed to find a black dress with full, swirling skirt which she thought would do. She took the goods there and then, rather than having them sent — she wanted to arrive for her 3 o'clock meeting with George laden with parcels, hoping to give the impression that she was just passing through rather than having thought of little else for a day and a half. She was longing for the meeting but nonetheless forced herself to arrive exactly five minutes late by her new Rolex (which she noted kept exactly the same time as the huge neon clock at Piccadilly Circus). She walked slowly along

Piccadilly from Simpson's, paused for a silent prayer to Eros[23], and went down the steps to the Underground station.

There, pacing up and down in his animal way, in front of the concave curve of the Swann & Edgar window, was George Crawford. He had dark glasses and a large snap-brimmed hat tilted forward, but, to Jessica, there was no mistaking him. He had a dark suit and a dark tie with a white shirt and was carrying an umbrella. He was looking at his wristwatch in a way that demonstrated a certain agitation.

"George!" yelled Jessica, rushing up to him. She made such a spectacle that half a dozen passers-by stopped passing by to stare.

George looked startled. "Pardon me," he said. "My name's not George. You must be mistaking me for someone else."

"Oh my God," said Jessica, realising what she had just done.

George turned on his heels, muttered "follow me" and set off along the subterranean corridor and up the steps to the street, at the same time as a furious thunderstorm broke out. He was walking fast, the open umbrella held before him, and every few yards Jessica had to break into a teetering run not to lose sight of him. The rain coursed off her rainhood and down the back of her neck. Crawford walked into the rain back up Piccadilly, retracing in part the route Jessica had earlier used, past the Royal Academy, past Bond Street and up the left side of Albemarle Street, where he slowed down long enough for Jessica to catch up. He held out his left arm in a crook. Jessica rearranged the parcels into her left hand and clutched on to him under his umbrella as they walked up to Brown's Hotel[24]. "Good afternoon Mr Thomson. Madam," said the doorman, from under a huge umbrella.

"Good afternoon," said George, standing, dripping wet in front of the door. "I hope it's not too early for tea."

Sitting down shortly after, minus his hat and dark glasses, in a large airy room with the tables easily far enough apart for George and Jessica not to be overheard, he said: "That was pretty stupid, calling out my name like that. I've got into this mess entirely because of you. First, I protect you from those vultures and then you almost give me away. What are you trying to do to me?"

"I just didn't think," said Jessica.

"You 'just didn't think'! I've done practically nothing else but think for the past day and a half." He produced that day's *Evening Standard*, folded open at the **ANGEL OF MERCY** item. "What's your explanation for this?" he asked.

Jessica read, her skin feeling colder and colder as she went on. Her stomach turned over and she wondered whether she was going to be sick. She had appeared to betray her hero, and she could well understand why. George regarded her expressionlessly, through narrowed eyes, until Jessica said: "Believe me — this is the first I've known of this. I certainly never said those words or anything like them. It's total lies from beginning to end."

Intending to give extra force to what she was saying, Jessica added: "Far from supporting the Fund for the Abolition of Boxing, I've never even heard of it."

George said: "I suppose I'll have to believe you. You got me into this hole so I suppose I'll have to rely on you to get me out of it. I can't stay here for ever as I haven't any money to pay the bill."

"You mean you're staying at this hotel? Not dossing down on Trafalgar Square?"

"Of course," said George. "By the time I got back to my digs the night before last the police were already there. People from my background try to avoid any dealings with the police, so I just kept on walking. I never went back. I shouldn't have done it, I now realise, because the whole thing has grown into something far more than it really was in the beginning.

"Anyway, having walked past, I just kept on walking till the morning. I came here and booked in. I told them I'd just come off the night sleeper from Scotland and my luggage would be arriving later. I was still in a dinner jacket. As you heard, I said my name was Thomson — it's a name that used to strike fear into my father[25].

"This is a good hotel; it's full of Americans who are unlikely to recognise me. There are doors on to Dover Street as well as the street we came in at, so if I need to make a getaway it will be easier. I can eat in the restaurant and get the porter to supply such things as shirts and ties. I got this suit on approval, just round the corner in Savile Row[26]. It's amazing what you can get without any money, but they're already a bit suspicious and I'm sure they're going to present me with a bill soon. I can hardly go to the bank. So, how much money do you have with you?"

Jessica had only a 10-shilling note and not even enough coppers[27] for an Underground fare. She passed the brown note under the table to George. "That's all I have," she said.

"That's hardly enough to keep the sheriff's officer[28] from the door," said George.

"I told you, that's all I have," said Jessica. "How is it that no one spots you? You're not exactly unknown."

"That's the English class system for you," said George. "One of the few times I've had cause to be grateful for it. They'd never think of looking for a criminal in a posh hotel. In any case, I don't know very many people in London. The pictures of me in the papers have all been of me as boxer, not dressed in a suit, and in the films there's so much blood over the place I'm almost unrecognisable."

As he talked, his attitude was changing: the talking about himself was doing the trick. He was far less hostile to Jessica than he had been earlier, but he was still not proving to be the heroic figure she remembered. Hoping for a continuing improvement in his attitude and to get his mind off her treachery, she persuaded him to tell his life story. She expected tales of derring-do, but his history did not turn out to be particularly romantic, nor even very sordid. Just the tale of an ordinary Scots lad who was not very good at school except at sports and who turned out to be particularly good at boxing in the army. While he had made quite a bit of money in his brief career in the ring as a professional boxing champion, the trouble was that there was no training for what to do when your boxing career was over, as it effectively was for George from the time of his latest defeat, even if it had not been for his brush with the law.

The tea had been drunk, the scones and sandwiches finished and two cream cakes and two bowls of cherries from the trolley eaten. The waiter presented the bill, which George signed without inspection. He was not in a position to add a tip in cash, so the waiter went away, leaving the couple to get up from the table without assistance.

"I hope you'll be able to come to my room," said George.

Had the invitation come at any time in the previous 40 hours or so, Jessica would have been thrilled by such words — but by this time she was not so excited. The previously heroic figure seemed more mundane as he skulked in an unpaid-for suit in a West End hotel, avoiding the waiter's eye. So Jessica told him: "George, I'd love to, but the proprietor will be livid. I'm supposed to meet him at the *Tribune* and I'll have to walk there as I've given all my money to you."

He could perhaps have persuaded her but he did not attempt to. Neither did he offer to pay her trolley-bus[29] fare, but said: "Oh dear. I wanted to ask you something. We'll walk together then."

"Are you sure it's safe?" Jessica wanted to know. "Won't you be caught?"

"I don't think so," said George. "Not on foot. They don't really look at your face if you're moving."

So a wary Jessica and her runaway boxer set off eastwards. It had stopped raining, at least for the moment. The doorman said: "Good afternoon, Mr Thomson. Madam. Taxi?"

"No thank you. We're not going far, so we'll walk."

It was a very long distance indeed. They walked along Piccadilly, Haymarket, past the National Gallery and St Martin's in the Fields, past Charing Cross Hospital where Monty Evans had been carried by his fellow photographers, past the entrance to the Savoy Hotel where the drama had started, past the Law Courts and into Fleet Street. The narrow straps of Jessica's high-heeled sandals were cutting into her nylon stockings and through them into her feet. The strings on the parcels of shopping were cutting into her hands despite the white gloves. Why couldn't George give part of the 10 shillings back so she could get a taxi? Or even a bus.

As they walked, George talked, pausing only when other pedestrians came into earshot.

He said he realised that the whole clamour against him had been got up by the *Tribune*, probably on the direct instructions of the proprietor, whom, to Jessica's annoyance, he referred to as her father. The police probably wouldn't even have bothered if they had not been put up to it, he kept saying. Why, he had hit men before, other than in the ring, and nothing had been done about it. Jessica could clear him. She had only to speak to her father and get him to call off the campaign. In the meantime, until the clamour had died down she could send him enough money to enable him to pay his hotel bill. After all, he said, it was all her fault in the first place.

By this time, half-past five, the footsore Jessica and her complaining companion were nearing the *Tribune* building. It was threatening to rain again. Jessica stopped, turned round to George, transferred her parcels to her left hand, extended her right hand and said in cool formality: "Well Mr Thomson, thank you for accompanying me all this way. I am meeting the proprietor in half an hour and will certainly consider everything you have said in relation to him."

George ignored her outstretched hand, instead putting his right hand on her waist and saying: "We can't leave it just like that." There was a crack of thunder. George looked up, frowned and drew Jessica in at the just-opened door of the White Hart.[30] "At least let me buy you a drink."

He went up to the bar and, without taking off his hat or dark glasses, ordered two half-pints of mild, the cheapest drinks on offer. He got out Jessica's 10-shilling note. "It's better in the public bar," he said to her. "Cheaper, and there's not much chance of meeting a journalist."

There was in fact only one other person in the pub, a dark-haired, fair-skinned man of about 30 or so, standing at the bar with a beer and eating a pie with a fork.

"I know that voice," the man said, going over and looking closely at George. Then, in an urgent whisper: "Crawford, I haven't seen you since school. What on earth are you doing here? Don't you know they're after you?" He intercepted the barman on his way to George and gave him a florin[31] and two pennies. "Let *me* pay," he said to George. "Anyone who the *Tribune* has got its knife out for is a friend of mine."

He then looked at Jessica, who was taking her first sip of mild beer and finding it similar in flavour to tepid, soapy water. Her cool, clean clothing, bright shiny hair, and vivid lips were a startlingly unusual sight for the public bar. The man asked George: "Aren't you going to introduce me to your lady friend?"

George, received Jessica's 10s note back from the barman, put it in his pocket, and responded to all the questions together. "Of course I know what I'm doing, Anstruther. This is Miss

Ross, daughter of the *Tribune* proprietor. She's going to use her influence to get the hounds called off. For God's sake don't you interfere — and don't clype[32] on me, either."

Her introduction thus, and the air of proprietorship over her that George was assuming, were too much for Jessica. "I wouldn't assume too much, either of you," she said.

The Imperial Father of the Federated Chapel of the *Tribune* newspaper quickly downed his beer and said: "Now look, Crawford. Your secret's safe with me. I won't tell about meeting you but I advise you to make yourself scarce and I warn you against putting your trust in the class enemy — however glamorous she might be."

He nodded to them both. As he left the bar, Jessica turned to George and said: "Wow! Who was that? What does *he* do?"

"He's Jim Anstruther. He was a couple of classes above me at school in Dundee but I don't know what he does now.

"What do you mean I'm assuming too much? You can't mean you won't help me. I'm desperate. I could end up in gaol if you don't help."

"I'll think about what to do," Jessica said, noncommittally. She stood up and leant forward to give George a farewell peck on the cheek.

"I think I'd just as soon you didn't kiss me," said George, going on to mumble as if reading from a Bible: "One of you which eateth with me shall betray me ... Immediately, while he yet spoke cometh Judas, one of the twelve, and with him a great multitude with swords and staves, from the chief priests, and the scribes, and the elders."[33]

Jessica departed from the pub in the rain without taking any further sips of the tepid soapy water. As she turned her back on her fallen hero, she saw a wimp, a pathetic failure, and a gibbering religious maniac. She decided not to answer the telephone for the next day or two, just in case. As she walked around the front of the

Tribune building, there was Fibbins with the Humber, holding a door open for the proprietor. "Not a moment too soon," said the proprietor to her. "If you'd have turned up any later we'd have left without you."

As she clambered into the car, moving her wet dress past the proprietor's extended feet as she took her seat in the opposite corner, he said: "You're wearing lipstick. Doesn't suit you."

Jessica made no direct reply but, in a gesture of submission, flattened her lips for a moment so that less of the vivid lipstick would show. She said: "Why did you put that piece in the *Evening Standard* without asking me? I never said those words."

The proprietor looked at her, across the width of the back seat, paused for a moment, and then asked: "And how was the fugitive pugilist this afternoon? Have the consequences of his thuggish manners sunk home?"

Oh no! The man's spies were everywhere. How could he know? "What do you mean?" asked Jessica.

"Come on, now. You're not saying he stood you up at Swann & Edgar's? He's no gentleman, but I don't think even someone like him would do such a thing to my beautiful daughter."

"How can I deny it, if you've had your spies following me all afternoon?"

"Not spies. No one followed you. Mrs Burgess was listening on the extension."

"The bitch!"

"Don't use words like that, Jessica, especially not of Mrs Burgess. You treat her dreadfully. Don't you know she just adores you?"

"Ah well," replied Jessica, "it's a good thing she has you to console her then."

"The last time you made a remark like that, I almost hit you," said the proprietor. "Mrs Burgess stopped me. So I won't punish you this time either. You've obviously had a straining day."

Jessica suddenly sat up, and said: "Do you know? I was with George Crawford for three hours and he never once asked about the photographer. All he talked about was himself."

"I'm not surprised," said the proprietor. "Men like him — they're all the same.

"We could have stopped you, you know. Could have prevented your going. Could have had police waiting for him. But I'm beginning to think that you will only learn if you find things out for yourself."

Jessica moved away from her distant seat, edged across the car and settled herself down beside the proprietor, leant over and rested her head on his chest and said: "If you asked me now about that piece in the *Evening Standard*, I'd say 'go ahead'."

The proprietor stroked Jessica's pinned-up hair and said: "Good. You'll have a lot of work to do, administering the £5,000 for the Fund for the Abolition of Boxing."

Five thousand pounds was a vast sum but useless in someone else's hands, so Jessica did not leap at the prospect. She said: "Can't the people in charge of the fund do that, whoever they might be?"

"There is no fund," said the proprietor. "You're going to have to set it up. It will give you something useful to do.

"I've been thinking about what you should be doing. One day you'll have the *Tribune* to look after, but I don't intend to slough off this mortal coil just yet and I don't want you interfering with it while I'm still around. But, remember: I could die at any moment; everyone knows I'm not a well man. I can't have you spending your time swanning around town like a lady of leisure, gossiping and attending At Homes: that would be a futile existence in 1956. But I can't have you going out to work for someone else, so you'll have to run your own organisation. I thought a charity would be of interest to you: it will teach you about money and propaganda, which is pretty much all you need to know to be a newspaper proprietor."

He waited for Jessica to respond. When she didn't, he just said: "In fact, I sometimes think the *Tribune* must be a charity of sorts to carry on paying some of the layabouts on our payroll. In the meantime, it amused me to get Beaverbrook to stump up the money to get your charity going."

It sounded to Jessica like a thoroughly good idea. The £5,000 especially. "You *are* wonderful," said Jessica, by now snuggling against the proprietor's arm. "Does this mean I can forget about Lear Farnsworth?"

"Of course not," said the proprietor. "He's still part of the strategy. I understand he's invited you to Australia with him."

How on earth could the proprietor know that, wondered Jessica. "What are you going to do about Crawford?" she asked. "He thinks all the hue and cry has been got up by you. Are you going to let him get away with it?"

"I'm not quite sure," said the proprietor. "He's provided some very good copy for the *Tribune* — there's an excellent Shock Issue on him and his sort, out tomorrow. To tell the truth, I'm a bit bored with the whole thing now. I expect the whole business will die a death . . ." He smiled at Jessica and went on: ". . . unless the Fund for the Abolition of Boxing manages to maintain public interest in the affair."

5

Saturday 28th July 1956

After what felt like a very short sleep indeed, the absence of Sheilagh from the bed made Jim wake. Bleary-eyed, he went downstairs to see her. She was just finishing breakfast.

"So much for your coming home early," she said, without turning to look at him. Then, with ostentatious lack of interest: "What's the excuse this time?"

"I think it's the big one," said Jim. "We've got a strike on a point of principle. Management will have to stop the whole of Fleet Street on this one. It could go on for days."

"That's all very well, and I'm very pleased, but what about *us*?" said Sheilagh, giving up her pretence of unconcern. "Can't we even have the weekend? It's always that bloody newspaper with you; you never have any time for Party work these days, let alone for me. I might as well pack up and go now if we're never to have time together."

"Don't worry," said Jim. "You've got a half day today. We can have a cuddle at dinner time before I go off to see the union about the strike."

"I don't want one of your 'cuddles' — I want to talk about *us*," said Sheilagh as she buttoned up her pastel-green Orlon twinset and put on her mac. "Besides, I've arranged to go shopping in

London after work. Some of the shops have started opening on Saturday afternoons now."

Jim said: "Look; if you want to see more of me, why don't you get the staff to take action over working on Saturday mornings? It's an outdated practice. Even the Civil Service is stopping the five-and-a-half-day week. A union should be leading the way, not lagging behind."

Sheilagh, unlike the men at work, was always impressed by the language of Communism, so Jim quoted from *Capital*: "Remember, 'the shortening of the working day is the basic prerequisite for freedom'."[1]

By now Sheilagh was on the doorstep, delaying her departure only to reply: "You know that's not possible. They're suspicious of me already. If they find out I'm a Communist, I'm out — and you know that."

"Yes. Sorry, Sheilagh." Jim made to kiss her as she left, but she turned away on crossing the threshold and he kissed only the back of her departing head. He was once more left standing on the doorstep, shaking his head, in his dressing gown. This time there were a few of the neighbours already up and going about their Saturday morning business. Jim went back to bed and slept, something he had not managed to find time to do for days, he felt.

He would have slept far too long if he had not been woken by the doorbell. It was the baker's roundsman[2] wanting him to pay the week's bill. Jim paid and went back upstairs to put on his suit. He used the new sliced loaf the baker had left, with some Spam[3] he found in the fridge, to make himself a sandwich. He washed up Sheilagh's breakfast dishes and wrote a note to her.

> *Sorry to have missed you. I've gone to see the Industrial Organiser — as you say, the work of the Party must come above personal considerations. Afterwards, I'll have to call in at union headquarters to report about*

the Tribune *dispute and organise solidarity. I'll get back*
as soon as I can. Then at last we'll have that time together
that you've been missing. I promise I'll make it up to you
as soon as this current crisis is over.

love, Jim.

He suspected there was something wrong with the note but did not know what. The final sentence was a bit of a hostage to fortune and Sheilagh might keep the note to cast back at him in weeks to come. But he decided not to change the wording.

He rode his combination into Bromley as usual, although the Saturday traffic was pretty bad. He did not bother to rig up the parking light this time. Lighting-up time was still late and he expected to return well before evening. A night off would help the battery.

Being a Saturday, the two evening papers that had published were little but sports previews, but there was a short item about the *Tribune* troubles in the *Star*.

FLEET STREET STRIKE THREAT

Discussions are being held with printing unions tomorrow under the auspices of the Newspaper Proprietors' Association to avert a threatened strike prompted by industrial action at the *Daily Tribune*.

Trouble started when union members refused to work one of the newspaper's two presses. Under the NPA regulations, to ensure fair play, no rival paper may print while one of the association's members is strikebound. Evening papers and tomorrow's Sundays are not affected by the dispute.

It might not contain actual lies, but it wasn't the truth, either. Jim made a note to raise the problem of union members printing inaccurate reports about their own affairs. Might be able to get something done.

At Blackfriars station he changed to the Underground, and bought a District Line ticket to Charing Cross, where he walked up Villiers Street, crossed the Strand and passed the edge of silent fruit and vegetable market at Covent Garden, to King Street. The Regional Industrial Organiser had his office in Party headquarters, at number 16.

Jim was five minutes late for his meeting with the Regional Industrial Organiser but, as usual, the organiser, Sørensen, was late too. As Jim waited there was time for a minute of two's chat with some of the half-dozen other comrades who were waiting around for meetings.

Sørensen arrived outside his office smoking a pipe and looking very serious, as though responsibility for the whole world revolution was resting on his shoulders. Jim was never sure of where he stood with Sørensen, a man who took both himself and the Cause even more seriously than most other dedicated comrades.

Sørensen beckoned to Jim, sat down in his bentwood chair behind a piled desk and looked at Jim in silence. Jim found another chair and sat down facing him. Sørensen said nothing but looked expectant so Jim launched into a long report on his Party work in Fleet Street in general and at the *Tribune* in particular. He felt he knew what was required of him and the special language that was expected. He was facing a tough battle to get anyone at all interested in the Party or even in socialism, and the consequence was that he was not trying so hard as he once had. He did not tell Sørensen this, and glossed over the current political difficulties in favour of the great prospects revealed by the Gudger dispute.

Sørensen cut him off. "I know all that," he said. "You can save that sort of speech for the District Committee or the Central, if we ever decide to put you on. Just tell me how quickly you can get the men back to work."

This perplexed Jim. "I thought we were in favour of strikes," he said.

"Not when they threaten the existence of the *Daily Worker* we're not," said Sørensen. "The printing workers there are a seething hotbed of militant anti-Party agitators. They're the most disloyal people you could ever have working for you. They're going on strike in solidarity with the union at the *Tribune* and they say they won't go back till you do."

The Regional Industrial Organiser complained that the men at the *Worker* were putting their union principles before the Party — which could very well destroy the precarious finances of the paper, forcing it to close. He said that, as Comrade Anstruther knew, every time there was a strike on a Fleet Street paper, the proprietors of all the other papers declared their class solidarity by locking out all their workers too, suspending publication while one of their number was threatened. This was the logical thing for the ruling class to do. But some people in the printing unions deliberately ignored the class politics of the matter and insisted that the action must be spread to *all* national papers, including the newspaper of the working class. Comrade Anstruther's task was to stop them.

"I don't quite see how I can," said Jim.

Sørensen said he still had a suspicion about the Imperial Father's true loyalties. The Regional Industrial Organiser said he had a test for such people. He asked himself whether the comrade in question, if he had been involved in the Spanish Civil War[4], would have willingly given his life for the Cause.

Comrade Anstruther would have to be put to a peacetime-equivalent test. Sørensen said, in the way a judge might when reading out a sentence: "You'll have to use your position in your union to get the *Daily Worker* exempted from all industrial action. If that fails, or does not have the desired effect, you must attend a meeting of the chapels, or their officials, at the *Worker* and explain to them the errors in their analysis, tell them that the whole future of the paper is under threat if it closes for so much as a day and get them to carry on working through the strike."

Jim objected: "I can't try to get the policy changed by the union executive and then if I fail go behind their backs to ask the men to defy their own union. The union's got its own version of democratic centralism, too."

"The industrial struggle is only a mean to an end," said Sørensen. "The survival of the *Worker* is far more important. If you can't get them to work on, you'll have to stop the strike."

"That's ludicrous," Jim protested. "It's treachery to the union. The men are counting on me to win. I can't let them down."

"You'll have to decide where your loyalty lies — with your comrades in the Party or elsewhere," said Sørensen, between puffs on his pipe. "Whatever you decide, you'll still be alive. The comrades in Spain had no such choice."

He took another puff and said: "You won't be alone. Other comrades will have softened them up before we turn you loose on them. Remember, any loss of sales revenue could cripple the *Daily Worker*. Its circulation is not exactly healthy anymore."

Comrade Anstruther swallowed and accepted his Party duty. He stood up, pushed in his chair at the table and said: "I'd better go off to the union, then."

It was only a couple of steps to the door. As Jim was leaving, Sørensen took his pipe out of his mouth and stabbed its stem in his direction, saying: "Remember, the Party is counting on you."

Comrade Anstruther left the Party building, passed through the queue of gentlemen going in to Moss Bros[5], opposite, to collect formal penguin-suit wear for that evening's capitalist functions, and set out past the northern side of Covent Garden market and the back of the Opera House to the Underground station, where he bought a Piccadilly Line ticket to King's Cross. It was costing a lot in Tube fares.

At the London regional office of the union, there was a small gathering, largely of full-time officials of the various other print unions involved in the Printing and Kindred Trades Federation[6]. They were discussing tactics for the meeting the next day with the Newspaper Proprietors' Association.

"Glad you could find time to come, Anstruther," said the union organiser, Baverstock, as Jim arrived. "What was wrong? Couldn't you face working on a Saturday?"

"No," said Jim. "It wasn't that. Trouble at home." He could hardly admit to having been at a Communist Party meeting getting his instructions. Besides, there *was* trouble at home, even if it had not caused his lateness.

Jim outlined the compromise settlement which had already been offered, but predicted further trouble with the cleaners' union if their members were not involved in the removal of the carcass.

"I'll sort something out with them before we meet the bosses," promised Baverstock. "How long do you think we can run this action for? I only give it a day or two, myself."

Jim, pointing out that feelings were bound to run high when a point of principle was involved, said it was likely to last much longer. Especially since every day the body was not moved the stench would get worse and the men would be even less anxious to go into the building, let alone move Gudger's earthly remains. If management brought in undertakers or ambulancemen to do the job, without the relevant union tickets, it could result in the press being permanently blacked.

Jim did not wish to raise the matter of the *Daily Worker* directly, so that he could not be later accused of undermining union policy which he had been a party to setting. He whispered to Phil Jones, from the Farnsworths' *Forward!*, who was sympathetic although not actually a Party member, to ask about the other papers.

"Everything going to plan, except at the *Daily Worker*," said Baverstock. "The Reds are egging the men on to blackleg on the strike. Pleading poverty or somesuch. Such arguments from employers leave me cold." He made the remarks with especial directness, always having suspected many of his members, particularly that man from the *Tribune*, of being Communists.

"Thank you all for coming," he said, dismissing the meeting. "I'll not be needing the lay members at the NPA. They always insist on top-level negotiations being carried out by full-time officials only[7]. I'll let you know afterwards how it went."

Jim had a feeling that there was no such rule but, since he would be fully occupied trying to break the strike at the *Worker* and could not simultaneously be present at the meeting to further the strike, he did not protest. He went home, to his first evening with Sheilagh for weeks. By the time he arrived, she had already started cooking tea. "I don't know why I risked it, bearing in mind your recent attendance record," she said, while opening a tin of peas and ostentatiously failing to look at him. "What did you mean by that insulting note — the evening together *I've* been missing! I don't suppose it matters to you at all. And another thing: I resent being lectured by *you* in a note left on the kitchen table about my duty to the Party."

Jim found himself saying, in his first words at the start of their first evening together for weeks: "Look, Sheilagh, if you were looking for someone who expresses himself in perfectly rounded phrases every time and can write the perfect letter, perhaps you should have found a journalist to move in with, not a printing worker from Scotland."

Sheilagh stopped ignoring him, to glare in a hostile fashion.

"I think it would be better if I went out and came in again," said Jim, proceeding to do just that. On the second entrance the couple were more civil to each other, although in being polite their conversation lacked the intimacy of the earlier attacks. Hostilities further declined as the pair co-operated to find a way of getting the hot Fray Bentos steak and kidney pie[8] out of its tenacious container and on to plates.

Over the kitchen table, Sheilagh asked: "What are you looking to get out of our being together?"

Jim was rather shocked at this way of looking at things. Analysis might be a tool to be used on political matters but it had never occurred to him to use it in personal life. He had never really thought about Sheilagh as a problem to be analysed. He did not know what to think, let alone say. He tried: "I don't have any aims, except political ones, I suppose. All I want to do is get through tomorrow. The Party has set me a test of loyalty."

"Loyalty!" Sheilagh seized on the word to switch the subject back. "Things aren't like that anymore. I'm not your chattel. I don't have to be loyal to you. I'm not beholden to you for anything. I'm free to live where or with whom I please, and damn convention. We've chosen to live together in the form of a family, but I don't have to. There's nothing to bind me to you, no laws, no property relations, so I do so of my own free will, because I want to. Can you imagine why?"

Jim was undergoing a political crisis and all he was getting from Sheilagh was Marxist jargon about the origin of the family. "No," he said. "I just know that you do and I'm grateful that, of your own free will, you decide to live with me." As an afterthought, he said: "I do do the dishes, you know."

"It's not gratitude I'm looking for — or even the dishwashing — it's understanding. And love."

"That's my incapacity with words again." Why was he always apologising when he was with Sheilagh? "I thought the love went without saying. As for understanding, I'll bet I can outdo you in the theory of Scientific Socialism any day. What about Fourier's belief that monogamy was part of the war of the rich against the poor?"

Jim didn't know why he had said that. He didn't even know that he knew it, or what it meant, or why Fourier[9] believed it. The truth was that Jim was suffering from sexual yearnings which were increasingly unfulfilled. Since Sheilagh had moved in he had become far happier with himself but the spirit of daring adventure that had attended their previous illicit guest-house couplings had gone. Before Sheilagh could rebuke him, he stood up and reached across the Formica-top, his tie dipping in the remains of the steak and kidney pie, embraced Sheilagh and said: "I don't know why I said that about monogamy. I must have been thinking about how it used to be."

Sheilagh gave an amused half laugh, took Jim by the hand and, saying "I think you may have reminded me of one of the reasons", led him upstairs. They stayed in bed together all evening, touching, licking, consciously trying to recreate something that had earlier happened spontaneously. They kissed, stroked, received, were penetrated and did the penetrating, without talking much. The talking was where the difficulty arose.

Afterwards, Sheilagh leant over to Jim's ear and said: "What do you mean the Party's set you a test of loyalty?"

He told her of the task that had been laid out to him, and said: "I'll do it, of course, but I'm worried the Party may be calling on me for more than I can give. I've been in the Party and the YCL[10] before it since 1941 and everything I've ever done is just used so they can ask for more.

"They're burning me out. Using me up. It's not as if all the work is doing the Party any good. We've fewer members now than at any time since before I joined. The more reactionary this government gets, the more people, even ordinary, decent working-class people, vote for it."

"Don't worry about it all, Jim. You claimed to be able to outdo me in the theory of Scientific Socialism, but you can't. You've just got no staying power, except, possibly, in bed."

"What do you mean by 'possibly'?" asked Jim, before falling asleep.

Sunday morning was more like the early days of Sheilagh and Jim's dalliance, as they went off on the motor cycle for a spin in the country. Jim wore his windcheater and Sheilagh put on trousers as well as a mac and her headscarf. She eschewed the use of the sidecar, leaving it to carry the packed picnic, and rode on the pillion, holding loosely on to Jim's waist. There was too much wind and noise to talk, and Jim spent the time running over his options for that afternoon's *Daily Worker* speech.

The idea was to find a secluded spot for an early lunch (and possibly a reprise of their earlier habit of open-air coitus) but the gathering storm clouds and the threat of what later turned out to be a hailstorm of appalling severity drove them, chaste and picnic-less, home.

Jim took out his winter motor-cycle gear out of the cupboard for the trip to the station. On arrival, he was so wet and dispirited he kept the protective clothing on for the train journey. At Blackfriars he set off on foot to Farringdon Road to the *Daily*

Worker plant at William Rust House, named after the Communist pioneer.

He went in at the main door, showed both his Party card and his union card to the attendant in his fortified locker and walked upstairs to the composing room to find his opposite number, the Imperial Father of the Federated Chapels of the *Daily Worker*. There was no one around, so he went into the case room in search.

In spite of the recent construction of the building, the equipment inside was far more antiquated even than that at the *Tribune*. Most of the pots for the molten printing metal used in each line-casting machine were still heated by naked gas flame, rather than the electrical operation in use at the *Tribune*. No two of the machines were identical, each having been bought, frequently second-hand, as and when Party appeals had come up with the money. Many of the machines had small, brass plaques attached to them, naming the comrade fallen in the Spanish Civil War in whose memory they had been bought. Jim looked at the plaques and recalled Sørensen's test of Party loyalty.

Manning on the *Daily Worker* was always as low as the unions would permit, but there appeared to be very few people about indeed. Possibly not even enough to get a paper out even if Jim was successful in appealing to them to work. He put the absence down to it being a Sunday as well as the spreading of the rumour of the strike, coupled with the hailstorm and gales.

Even the *Worker*'s Imperial Father had not turned up, but eventually a group of various FoCs and chapel officials did assemble. One of them, Alf Riley, introduced himself as the senior FoC. He said: "We don't have to listen to you, you know. It's against the rules of most of our unions for us to be addressed by people from another branch without the sanction of the national executive, but we've decided to hear you out anyway."

Before Jim could thank him, Alf Riley said: "If the unions want to know why — we're hearing you as a spokesman for the *Daily Worker* management. Before you say anything, I think you should know that most of us aren't Communists. In fact, we hate the Communist Party. They're right bastards to work for."

Duly put in his place, Jim started out by saying: "I certainly haven't come to lecture you, and, whatever you may think, I'm not a representative of management. And I never will be, either." He was trying to put out of his mind the strangely tempting offer of joining the *Tribune* management made to him two nights before. He had not told anyone about it, especially not Sheilagh. One of the troubles about being offered a bribe, apart from temptation if the bribe was high enough, was that it showed that at least one person believed you to be corrupt. And he was worried about the possibility that he might indeed be so.

The audience was a difficult one. At about 10 or a dozen it was too large and too small at the same time. Too small for oratory, too large for a chat. "I've come here as a representative of the *Tribune* workers, to tell you about our dispute and to ask for your solidarity," he started.

"We thought you'd come to tell us *not* to strike," said Alf Riley.

"So I have," said the Imperial Father, glad to be getting any response at all, even if hostile. "That will be your way of showing solidarity. Look at it this way: the unions are in control of production. We can stop it whenever we want to, although there would come a point when a weak newspaper would have to close rather than pay us. In fact, the proprietors like the high costs our insistence on quality creates, as they stop new rivals setting up — the *Daily Worker* knows just how difficult that is. That is why employers don't mind paying decent wages, as long as they are more or less equal across all titles."

A cry, from where Jim could not identify, of: "We don't need a lesson in economics."

"All right, I'll move on. When one newspaper is strikebound, all the others in the proprietors' association suspend publication too, so that they do not gain circulation at their rival's expense. Thus, there is less pressure on the first employer to settle the dispute quickly. He's only losing a day's profit, not his position in the marketplace. As far as he's concerned, the strike can go on and on, and the unions have lost their bargaining strength. Eventually, carried to its conclusion, the men could be starved back to work."

The same voice as before: "I've had enough. Did you say you were concluding?"

"Almost," said Jim. "That is why your fellow workers at the *Tribune* want your help. The *Worker* is not part of the NPA, not having a proprietor in the normal sense of the word. You aren't party to this anti-union plan to starve us back to work. If you carried on producing a paper, as well as getting a pay packet at the end of the week, it might help force the NPA to back down, especially if circulation shot up as a result."

"Now we know he's a management nark." The same voice again.

"Not at all, it's the workers from the *Tribune* who are asking this. I might add that this isn't a dispute about money: there's a matter of principle involved. Management is trying to get us to operate a press with a dead body still inside it."

He had quite a lot more to add, but Alf Riley interrupted: "All right, you've had your say. Now I'll set a few facts straight. You never get a straight line from the Commies. I've been working here since the Thirties: first they call for a Popular Front against Fascism, then they invade Poland along with the Nazis and denounce what they call the 'Imperialist War'. Later they cosy up to the employers and denounce wartime strikers as saboteurs and call for them to be shot. I don't want anything more to do with them than I have to."

Jim made to protest, but he was told: "You've had your chance, now listen to me for a change. The matter before us is quite simple. First, the unions are founded on the one-out, all-out principle. We won't blackleg on our colleagues. Secondly, the aims of the NPA and of the unions are the same on this one. It's a jointly-arrived-at policy. Nobody wants newspapers to have to fold because of an industrial dispute; this way we can have a dispute even at a weak newspaper without it going to the wall. If there wasn't some such agreement, wage rates would collapse. Far from one dead body causing Fleet Street to stop work, the place could be stacked up with them like a morgue and nothing could be done about it. Thirdly . .."

Here the union organiser, Baverstock, who had just made an entry, whispered in Alf Riley's ear. "Thirdly," continued Riley, "it's a union instruction. I'm surprised to hear someone from the *Tribune* asking us to blackleg on his own strike. He needs as much support as he can get, especially now that it's being said by the employers that it was he who pushed the unfortunate man into the press in the first place."

Jim butted in: "That's a rotten lie. I'll tell you what happened..."

Baverstock grabbed hold of him and said: "Oh no you won't. Not here. You can say what you want on the pavement outside in the rain."

In a quieter, even more menacing tone, he said: "I'm going to have words with you later. What you have just done is totally inexcusable. It's an expulsion offence — and you know what that means: you're out of a job and no one will have you, even if you re-train as a street sweeper."

Baverstock turned to the wider audience and said: "I've just come from the NPA meeting to inform you that negotiations have broken down. The strike's official. There will be no production tonight, or any night until it's settled."

Everyone, including Baverstock, dispersed, the men going to collect their hats and coats against the vicious weather outside. Only Jim was left. He moved over to an Intertype[11] machine, sat down on the operator's seat and stared at the brass plaque before him. Presently Sørensen came in, stood behind him and said: "Nice try. They were never going to give you a fair hearing, but you did your best."

"Yes, I did," said Jim, swivelling the seat round, "but how did you know?"

Sørensen looked at him pointedly, and slowly turned his head so that his left ear was inclined toward the seated man. He tapped the ear twice with his left index finger and said: "Only the best Soviet equipment."

6

Monday 30th July 1956

For Talbot Posner, the day should have started with his 9am news meeting but, instead, he found himself in a meeting with the controller of programmes in another part of the building, the part with carpets in the corridors. He was receiving the television equivalent of a dressing-down.

"I want you to be absolutely clear," said the controller, "I think, and everyone on the board thinks, your programme is the best since the invention of television. It's far and away the most lively, the most incisive, the most telling, the truest slice of life, the most honest current affairs show anywhere in the world."

"You didn't take me away from today's news planning session to read me an Oscar citation — so what's up? Was it the vampire story?" said Posner. He did like praise, and agreed with everything Howard Hay had said, but wanted to get the forthcoming reprimand out of the way quickly.

"Absolutely nothing wrong at all, Talbot! I just thought that as there is less than two months to go before our first birthday it would help you if you were aware of how everyone saw *As It Happens*. It occurs to me that some old squares, particularly the stick-in-the-muds at the Independent Television Authority[1], might not see it our way. In fact, I had an informal chat with one of the stick-in-the-muds over dinner last night, and he didn't go for the show at all. Or at least he said it wasn't bad, but unless we hardened it up he wouldn't allow us to count it against our current-affairs quota. He wanted to reclassify it as light entertainment."

"I hope you told him to go boil his head."

"Of course I did, Talbot! That only angered him and he reminded me that the law requires us to broadcast 'nothing which offends against good taste or is likely to be offensive to public feeling'."

"Since when have I broadcast in bad taste?"

"As far as I'm concerned, Talbot — never. But the ITA man claimed that the competition to find the potato that looked most like Pandit Nehru's[2] head was not a particularly inspired contribution to the debate on the Commonwealth. Neither did he like the piece on 'Is Your Neighbour A Werewolf?'. He had many other complaints but one I can remember is that he believes you have an obsession with film-stars' busts."

"Of course I do," said Posner. "Doesn't everyone? Why else do you think these girls get to be film-stars if they don't have big ones? Even the Queen is obsessed — why else do you think she has Marilyn Monroe, Anita Ekberg and Brigitte Bardot to the royal film performance and then insists they come in wearing twin-sets buttoned up to the neck[3]? It's a legitimate current-affairs question. I really resent these complaints."

"Look Talbot, no one's complaining. I think you've misunderstood the purpose of this meeting. Perhaps I shouldn't have even mentioned the chap from the ITA. I called you here to say how happy everyone was."

Posner found himself trapped in the quicksand of bonhomie. The more he struggled to speak straightforwardly the more he faced this underhand barrage of love.

The controller continued: "I want you to know that everyone here is one hundred per cent behind you. We all think the programme is absolutely marvellous and couldn't possibly be done better by anyone. There is no complaint from anyone within the station. We're not asking you to give up on the juicy bits, or the funny bits, or for the studio to be filled up with talking heads, or at least not for ever. Just for the next few weeks, while the ITA prepares its periodic review. Oh yes, and this doesn't bother me at all but it upsets the accountants and we've got to keep them happy: you're wildly over budget."

"What exactly are you asking me to do? You know the law prevents us from having anything that is scheduled to be discussed in Parliament in the next 14 days[4]. So the only politics you can discuss is the boring bits that even the MPs don't bother with. So that rules out politics from the current affairs show. What else do you want — needlework classes? Do you want the ratings to slump, or what?"

"Nothing like that, Talbot, old chap," said the controller, getting up from his chair and walking round his desk. "Glad we've had this chat," he said, extending his left arm in Posner's direction as he walked toward the door leading from his office to the anteroom containing his secretarial staff. Only really senior people got to use the door that led directly on to the corridor. Posner followed the controller to the internal door. He could not reply to Howard Hay's ultimatum in front of the witnesses, he felt. The two, controller and programme editor, walked through the complicated maze of passages, past the part where the carpets gave way to linoleum[5], the controller's left arm around Posner's upper back. They walked, the controller smiling left and right to studio employees as they progressed.

"I just loved Friday's show," said the controller as they reached the *As It Happens* office and Posner opened the door. "How about some more humdingers like that?" he said as he gave Posner a playful parting punch in the kidneys.

The open door released a cloud of tobacco smoke and a hubbub of chatter. The two dozen occupants of the editor's office looked out at the editor and controller and came to varying conclusions about what had been going on. The controller checked himself in mid-turn and, instead of returning along the corridor, said to Posner: "Hey Talbot! Why don't I sit in and see how you manage to put such a marvellous programme together? Perhaps I'll learn something."

He stepped in to the crowded office, saying: "Is that all right with you? Just say if it isn't."

Trapped, Posner forced himself to smile broadly and say: "I'm sure we'd all just love you to." To the assembled staff, as he followed the controller in, he said: "OK, OK, settle down. There's work to be done."

His own leather-covered seat was vacant but the half-dozen other, smaller chairs were occupied by the programme staff, mostly the middle-ranked members. The most senior and the most junior were variously seated on the floor, perched on filing cabinets or leaning on the bookcases. Everyone was either drinking tea out of paper cups from the canteen, or smoking. The controller took a few steps inside the doorway and swept his arm through in a follow-on motion for Posner to move to his seat. Once they were both in the room, the controller took a couple of steps back and sat on the floor beside a pile of old newspapers, his back resting against the closed door. Posner moved through the office delicately, tiptoeing between the used film-cans that served as ashtrays. He stepped in a zig-zag way, in the type of route a draughts piece[6] might use on a crowded board. He hopped between the long, parted legs of one of the new, blonde, production assistants, who was wearing tight, black pedal-pushers and a well-filled jersey. He decided that if he survived in his job for more than a few days he would have to take the new girl on a lengthy shoot, under his personal supervision and to some exotic and distant location, to teach her about the exciting business of television.

In order to survive that long, though, he would have to reconcile his conflicting instructions for making the show more boring, saving money and keeping the ratings up. He did not wish to be seen to back down, either.

"Right," he said, on reaching his desk, "I've just been in a meeting with Howard Hay, here. He says he just loves the show and so does the board."

The controller beamed, nodded his agreement, and said: "Just carry on as if I wasn't here. I won't contribute anything to the meeting. I'm just here to learn."

"So," said Posner, "let's give him some more of what he likes. It's going to be easier for you today, because there are no newspapers to cloud your thinking. No more pinching ideas from the *Daily Sketch*[7], you'll have to come up with your own stories. And I don't mean the sort of crap the BBC will have on *Highlight*[8]: they'll think the 14-day rule prevents them having anything at all about Suez so they'll witter on about the car strike, I shouldn't wonder. That Cliff Michelmore[9] should never have been allowed on television."

He rubbed his hands and said: "This meeting is half an hour late starting, so you've all had plenty of time to think. What ideas have you got for me?"

After a few minutes of the meeting, which looked like taking far longer than usual as every member of the team felt it necessary to perform before the controller, Posner had jotted down the first few items in a provisional running order. As luck would have it, there was so much hard news around that it looked as if he would be forced to drop a few of the fun items. This would be a blow to his self-esteem, as Howard Hay might think the new seriousness was the result of his words. Nevertheless, the spaghetti-eating competition and the backwards-walking race would have to be put off for a further day or two.

First on the list was last night's weather, with lots of pictures of people rowing down the flooded high-streets of towns within easy driving distance of London. If the floods had all gone by the time the cameras arrived, he wanted pictures of a 100ft factory chimney, made unstable in the gales, being pushed down. Should be easy enough to arrange.

Come out of that to petrol panic at the pumps — all this Suez crisis was bound to have its domestic effects and, if there was no panic already, there would be once the show had gone out.

Then another Suez scare, perhaps "Will I be Called Up to Fight?" Not likely to be affected by the 14-day rule; if the Government wanted a call-up it would just do it, never mind Parliament. It was a good excuse for some more vox-pops[10] on the streets, even if on a more serious subject than normal.

Then they'd have to do something about the newspaper strike, he supposed. Get the editor of the *Daily Whatsit* in to say what he would have printed, perhaps.

One of the reporters, making a suggestion while presenting his best profile to the controller, wanted to do a filmed piece on the Communist agitators doubtless responsible for the strike — but there were no more crews available. It was a good story idea so Posner enjoyed ruling: "Any more items, however visual, will have to be done in the studio. Even if a plane crashes on Kingsway[11]. Just find the man behind it all, bring him in and we'll nail him in the studio. Don't blame me, blame the accountants."

The reporter complained: "We can't leave an important interview like this to Huw in the studio. He's not up to nailing a kipper to the fish counter."

Posner stopped him: "Justin, I know you think you would be a better presenter than Huw Proudfoot, and doubtless a better prime minister than Mr Eden, and I'm sure your chance will come. Your job today is just to catch the kipper[12]. We'll do the cooking."

The meeting wore on, the programme suggestions more and more fanciful, but everyone wanted his — and her — turn to shine before the controller. He, however, seemed to have lost interest in the proceedings and was thumbing through the pile of old newspapers by his side, apparently ignoring his employees' attempts at promoting themselves.

Ordinarily, individual staff members, having been assigned to a story, would have left the meeting to get to work on it, but this time they were anxious to stay to see if anything happened. Besides, they could not have left the room as the controller was blocking the door with his back. At length, Posner decided to close the meeting but, as he about to do so, the controller held up a recent edition of the *Tribune* and asked: "Does anyone know whether they've caught this runaway boxer?"

There was a general mumble, until one of the researchers, Giles Hope-Jones, said: "I don't think so, but then they probably weren't looking very hard. The whole business is a put-up job if you ask me. That Hungarian chappie, Ross, is up to something very funny. I was at a charity ball last week when Crawford — he's the boxer — was pawing Ross's daughter."

"Pawing?" said the controller.

"Yes. You know. Touching her up. Getting amorous. Mind you, she seemed to be enjoying it. Funny thing is she's now turned up as the boss of something called the Fund for the Abolition of Boxing."

"Weird," said the controller. "Why don't you do a filmed report on the whole business?"

"He can't do that," said Posner to the controller. "He's only a researcher, not a reporter; second, he's assigned to the weather story and, anyway, there are no spare crews. We're over budget as it is." What did the controller mean by trying to run the show himself? Posner decided to read his contract very closely and to get legal advice on dismissal procedure. He was sure he was on his way out.

"Yes. I see," said Howard Hay. "Why don't you get the girl into the studio? It'll make a welcome relief for the viewers from a fire-eating Communist."

"I'll see what we can do," said Posner, trying to keep his options open.

At around mid-day, Jim was still at home, writing a report on the background to the *Tribune* dispute for his union executive committee, when the telegraph boy rode up on his red Post Office BSA Bantam motor cycle[13] and rang the doorbell. In exchange for a sixpenny tip he handed over the telegram, which read:

```
      CONTACT US IMMEDIATEMOST TO LEARN
   SOMETHING TO YOUR ADVANTAGE + JUSTIN
               SILCOCK +
         ASSOCIATED-REDIFFUSION
         TELEVISION + FLE 6000
```

These television salesmen were getting aggressive. Jim put the telegram in a pocket and went back to his writing. An hour or so later he had finished. Again regretting that he could not use a typewriter, he folded up the handwritten sheets and collected his overcoat and gauntlets for the ride to the station.

Just then, Justin Silcock himself, blond-haired, earnest and enthusiastic, arrived on the doorstep and rang the bell.

"You'd better be quick," Jim told him. "I'm going out. And I'm not buying anything."

"Are you Mr Anstruther?"

"Who wants to know?"

"I'm Justin Silcock, of Associated-Rediffusion Television. You didn't reply to my telegram." The lad looked most taken aback, as if upset at not being recognised.

Jim said: "I told you I'm not buying anything — and I'm not hiring anything, either."

"Are you the Mr James Anstruther who is the Imperial Father of the Federated Chapels at the *Daily Tribune*?"

"Why should my post be of interest to you? If you don't mind, I'll have to go now or I'll be late for my next appointment," said Jim, leaving the house, pushing past Silcock, pulling the door behind him and making for his motor cycle combination.

"Don't worry about that, I'll drive you wherever you want to go. I'm not a salesman, I'm here to get you to appear on television." Sensing confusion in Jim's reaction, Silcock went on: "We want to give you the opportunity to tell your side of the story, to set the record straight, to give you a chance to answer all the accusations."

Jim, wrongfooted by having started the conversation at cross-purposes, still didn't quite understand what was going on. What accusations? His side of what story? Setting which record straight? He said: "If I take you up on your offer of a lift, how will I get back afterwards?"

"Don't worry about that, Mr Anstruther," said the reporter, hustling him into the front passenger seat of his black Ford Consul parked by the kerb. "We'll get you home in one piece, I guarantee you that."

As they drove, they agreed the details of Jim's television début. For some reason he found himself more concerned with trivial details than with the forthcoming interview. How could he let Sheilagh know that he was going to be on television? Silcock would send another telegram. But how would she be able to find a neighbour with a set that could receive ITV? Silcock was sure that that would be no problem. There were lots of television sets around, these days. In the London region and the Midlands, the two areas where there were ITV stations, there were now more television licences than there were for sound radio[14]. Where both channels were available, ITV was watched for 79 per cent of the time, the BBC just 21 per cent.

As Silcock bumbled on, the Imperial Father remembered about his report. "Make a detour," he said. "I've got to get my report to the union."

Silcock slapped him on the shoulder. "Don't you worry about that, old man. We'll arrange a messenger to deliver it for you."

"But I've got to get it typed-up first."

"Don't worry. I'll get someone to type it up for you."

They appeared to have got everything covered. Jim gave himself up to the care of Associated-Rediffusion. He did regret though that the decision had been so rushed that he had not been able to get advice from the Party. Was it politically acceptable to appear on commercial television?

On arrival at the company's building in Kingsway, close to the end of Fleet Street, Silcock escorted Jim to the canteen. He took Jim's handwritten report on the dispute, promising to get it typed up and sent by courier to union headquarters. Silcock told Anstruther to order anything he wanted from the canteen, and left, promising to return soon. He was gone for a considerable time.

For Jessica, the call, which did not come until well into the afternoon, took a different form.

She was in the library at Avenue Road drafting an appeal for sponsors to be sent to members of the House of Lords identified by the proprietor as likely touches and an appeal for money to be sent to everyone listed in the *Medical Register*, when Mrs Burgess put through a telephone call from the proprietor.

"You know how I said yesterday that I'd help you all I could with your Fund?" he said. "Well, I have. You're to appear on television tonight, on a programme called *As It Happens*, on ITV, to speak about it."

"I can't go on television, I don't know what to say," said Jessica.

"Don't worry about that. You'll think of something. Take the Shock Issue if you want to mug up on the facts, but I'm sure they'll have a chap there to prompt you with questions."

Jessica was truly terror-stricken but didn't know how to justify the fear. "I haven't got anything to wear," she tried.

"You'll only be seen from the shoulders up," said the proprietor. "I'm sending the car to take you to the studios. It'll be with you in about three quarters of an hour. I'm sending our editor, Artemus Jones[15], with you to hold your hand. You'll like him, although he's a bit of a quiet chap sometimes. A churchwarden, I believe. I've got the television people to do an interview with him as well, about something totally different, to do with the newspaper strike. They wanted me to do it, not Jones, but I said people wouldn't understand about a proprietor rather than the editor being responsible for the spirit of the newspaper, so they'd far better have the editor.

"Remember, this is all part of your training. They're bound to respect you after this."

And that was that. Jessica abandoned her appeal letters and went upstairs to change out of her pants and chunky sweater. Into what? She decided on the brilliant-white dress she had worn to the hospital. Since that visit, she had associated it with carrying out worrying and unpleasant tasks at the proprietor's instruction. *Vogue*[16] had said about it: "It is pretty enough for informal dining and dancing anywhere, cool enough to win envious looks. Wear your stiffest petticoat — and you're ready for a gay evening." Jessica wasn't so sure what sort of an evening it would be. She added a couple of dabs of Hartnell[17] scent behind her ears, even though the viewers would not be able to see it, and took her handbag.

When the car arrived, Fibbins came to the front door of the house to collect her. When he opened the car door for her to get in, Jessica found the man she assumed to be Artemus Jones already occupying the seat normally used by the proprietor. She had to step over his feet to get in, and, as she did so, she felt Jones's hands grasp her waist. It was the type of ostensibly helpful but unwelcome gesture that you could not quite complain about for fear of being accused of over-reacting. As she moved across the car, Jones's hands slewed around and up, the fleshy insides of the man's wrists pressing against her brassiere. Jessica was disgusted with herself for not complaining. She also feared that the man's grip meant that later she would find greasy hand-stains on the sides of her radiant-white dress-top.

As Jones slowly withdrew his hands, Jessica looked down at them: pale and rather pudgy, with brown blotches on them and tufts of red hair on the backs of the fingers, all except one, where the hair was partly flattened, sprouting sideways from under a broad, gold ring. Jones used the ring to tap twice on the glass partition before calling: "Drive on, Fibbins."

Jessica saw Fibbins wince. It was not the way he was used to being spoken to, even by the proprietor.

Jones, his hands at last in his lap, smiled at Jessica, revealing yellowing teeth, and said: "You must be Jessica. I must say, you smell as good as you look. I'm very glad to meet you after all this time."

Jessica looked at his rounded, grinning features, his otherwise-red hair with the patch in front that was yellow with tobacco smoke, his brown suit and his squint bow tie. He had already forced her to occupy a subservient position in the car, reinforced his mastery by groping and pawing, and was now using her first name without even being introduced. How might Lady Farnsworth deal with such a situation? Jessica did her best to look haughty, even imperious, but felt she was failing when she said: "And who might you be? Are you from the television company?"

It didn't manage to put off Jones, who said: "You know who I am, my dear. Your father asked me to come along and hold your hand."

He leaned over again, grasped her right hand out of her lap and drew it to his lips. "A very lovely hand, too, I might say."

Things were getting out of hand indeed. As his lips descended on her fingers Jessica regretted that she had not put on gloves. Lady Farnsworth might well have stabbed Jones with a hatpin, decided Jessica. She knew she ought to slap him in the face or, at least, get into the front of the car alongside Fibbins, but somehow was not able to do either. Instead, she jerked her hand free from Jones's grasp, crossed her arms across her body and held her hands under her armpits. She squeezed herself firmly into the corner of the car as far from Jones as she could manage. She decided to look straight ahead and say nothing until the car arrived at the studios. Her concentration on that task helped take her mind off the forthcoming ordeal by television.

Jones did not appear to mind, or even to be much put off by her aggressive silence. He kept up a constant self-promoting chatter for much of the way, unfazed by the ostentatious lack of audience response.

"This your first time on television?" No response.

"Thought it might be. I've done lots, of course. It's as easy as pie. Want a drink to steady your nerves? No? Well, I hope you don't mind if I do," Jones said, reaching down to a briefcase on the car floor and taking out a silver flask. He unscrewed the cap and waved the flask toward Jessica. Receiving no response, he put the flask to his own lips and tilted his head back.

"Just what you need in the middle of the afternoon, to help see you through the day," he said after a few swallows. He again offered the flask to Jessica. Receiving no response, he wiped the open top with his handkerchief and offered again, before giving up and putting the flask away in the briefcase once more.

"Funny thing, this television," he said. "It'll never take over from newspapers. Can't take a television set to the toilet with you when you're taking a break from the production line. Can't hang it up in strips in the toilet, either. Can't take one on the train to work. Can't prop one up on the toast-rack to avoid speaking to the wife in the morning. Can't even use one to wrap up the fish and chips or line the budgie's cage. Oh yes; there'll always be newspapers."

Between puffs of a series of Senior Service[18], he said: "These television johnnies just don't have the news sense, you see. When there aren't any papers they just don't know what to do. That's why they want me there. I'm to tell the viewers what would be in the *Tribune* today — if there was a *Tribune*, instead of Fleet Street being closed down by a bunch of malcontents.

"After my piece, they tell me they've got the bolshie swine who's responsible for all the trouble. One of ours, I'm told. A chap called Anstruther. One of Khrushchev's mob[19] by all accounts — thinks he can put the world to rights. I know about Communists, bunch of workshy layabouts. Bloody great chip on their shoulder, every one of them. Just because we can't all have something, they want none of us to have anything.

"Asked for me specifically, they did. Recognise quality, you see. I heard your old man on the phone to them. He said it was a job for him, the proprietor himself, appearing on television. They said the public would get the wrong idea about who was responsible for what goes in the paper and it had to be the editor or nothing. That's it. Nobody else would do for them. It had to be me: yours truly, Artemus Jones. I'm a bloody good editor, that's why."

When the car pulled up in Kingsway, Jessica got out, inhaled the cigarette-free air, and encountered the television people as rescuers, with relief rather than dread. In the foyer, she met Giles Hope-Jones, who said to her: "Hello, Jessica. You're looking smashing."

"I didn't know you worked for television. I thought you were just a friend of Lear's."

Giles looked at her radiant white dress, saying nothing about its unsuitability for the screen[20]. "The two don't rule each other out, television and being a friend of Lear's," he said. "I'm supposed to be responsible for looking after sports here, but this editor doesn't use a lot of sport so I'm really just a bit of a dogsbody." He took Jessica by the arm in a businesslike manner quite different from Artemus Jones's earlier fumbling.

"I'll take you up to the Green Room. Jones is going off to make-up and then we'll take him straight to the studio. There's a fire-breathing Communist in hospitality and we don't want Jones and him to come to blows until they meet in the studio. I've got to rush off — there's lots of things I have to do — but just ask for me if you need anything."

"Giles, nobody's told me anything," said Jessica, beginning to show her panic now she no longer had to keep up appearances in front of somebody who might have jumped on her at any sign of weakness. "What's going to happen? What do I have to say? Who's going to interview me? Do I have to put on make-up, too?"

Giles looked a bit perplexed. "Sorry. Hasn't anyone told you? No need to worry: you'll be interviewed by Huw Proudfoot. I'll get someone along to tell you what the questions will be but you don't need to be worried about Huw: he's a big softie. Couldn't knock the skin off a rice pudding. All you really need to do is look sweet and smile. I'm sure you can do that."

He took her into a windowless room with walls that were not green but cream. There was a mushroom-coloured carpet with cigarette burns; there was a fug of cigarette smoke in the air and half a dozen or so men standing around with drinks in their hands, not talking to each other but trying to appear as if they were not scared.

Giles told Jessica, quietly, about the other people in the room: the man from the Meteorological Office, who seemed somehow familiar until Jessica realised that she had seen him on television, an elderly man whom Giles said was a retired general, and the joint parliamentary secretary at the Ministry of Transport and Civil Aviation, called John Profumo[21], there to talk about the Suez canal.

Giles told her about the 14-day rule but said politicians hated it as much as the television people and they connived to get round it. He whispered that the Ministry had only a tenuous connection with the whole thing, but the editor had taken it into his head that he had to have a Government Minister and this was the only one who could be found at short notice, so he would have to do. The man was a friend of the ITV system as well as being an up-and-coming Minister and the management wanted him on as often as possible. There was a Labour MP expected later.

Then Giles, no longer whispering, said: "Miss Ross, I don't know how much you involve yourself with the *Tribune*, but you might like to meet Mr Anstruther, who works there."

Jessica grabbed Giles as he was about to go, and said: "You still haven't told me what's happening."

"Nothing to worry about. It's a piece of cake," said Giles, releasing her anxious grasp and leaving the room.

Jim looked at her and said: "I thought I might be getting the proprietor himself, but evidently not."

Jessica stared at him, standing, glass in hand, in a not very good suit and tie. Tallish, with dark hair and craggy features, but his face covered in extraordinarily thick and overstated make-up. As he bent his head toward her to catch her reply, he appeared like Bela Lugosi playing the blood-sucking Count Dracula[22]. He was so much the crazed bomb-throwing agent of the Cominform[23] that Jessica was not even certain that he was the same man she had met just three days before.

"Are you the man who called me a 'class enemy'?" she said.

"And 'glamorous'," said Jim. "What are you going to ask me? Are you going to stick to this particular dispute or do you intend to go wider? Is there going to be anyone else in there or is it just us two?"

"You're not saying I have to appear with you?" asked Jessica, her earlier terror quickly returning. It wasn't just that he looked like Dracula, he was obviously there to talk about a newspaper strike about which she knew nothing. "I thought they wanted me to talk about the Fund for the Abolition of Boxing."

"If it's not you who's going to attack me, who is it?" Jim wanted to know.

"I did come in the car with a thoroughly nasty man called Artemus Jones," said Jessica. "But he said he was coming to talk about what would have been in the papers if there had been any.

Nobody has told me anything about what to expect. I've never done anything like this before. Even if the interview is about boxing — I don't know anything about that, either."

"I don't think they tell anyone anything," said Anstruther. "Certainly not me. I just made the assumption that they wouldn't allow a left-wing trade unionist on television on his own without someone to attack him. What's nasty about Jones? I've never met him but I'm told he's harmless. A churchwarden apparently, but they do say he has been seen in Dieppe with a lady who was not his wife."

"He's got greasy hands and he puts them everywhere," said Jessica. "You might call him harmless. He said you were a bolshie swine and a workshy layabout with a chip on your shoulder. Is it true you're a Communist?"

"Yes, since you ask," said Jim, taking the question as the cue for the routine he had practised many times before. "Lots of people are Communists. We want to end exploitation. We're part of a democratic organisation trying to achieve a socialist country where people will contribute according to their ability and receive according to the work they do, with full democratic rights, a steadily rising standard of living and an equal opportunity to enjoy a full and happy life."

"Seems reasonable enough to me," said Jessica, rather surprised that he had not mentioned Russia, revolution or bombs. "Look, it's an awful cheek but, since no one's telling me anything about my interview, will you test me by asking a few questions?"

"As long as, afterwards, you'll interview me about my plan to destroy Britain's freedom-loving society, starting with the *Daily Tribune.*"

So they did. Sitting on a sofa, Jim got Jessica to explain her new-found horror of boxing and prompted her to call for a Private Member's Parliamentary Bill[24] for its abolition. He said he didn't approve of boxing as it involved two members of the working class trying to hurt each other to amuse the rich. They started into the rehearsal of his own interview, with the Imperial Father of the Federated Unions Chapels of the *Tribune* newspaper, who was by now known to Jessica as Jim, asking Jessica, as she had become, to accuse him of murdering Gudger so he could practise his reply. Then Jessica was called away to make-up. The make-up lady, who said she was called Doris, spoke Cockney[25] and had a face as elaborately made-up as a Marshall & Snelgrove beautician. She was not able to tell Jessica anything about her part, either. As Doris worked away on her face, adding layers of pan-stick, Jessica realised that there was no mirror and that she was unable to check on what was being done to her. She feared that she might be made to look like Countess Dracula, if there was such a thing. Vampires kept themselves away from mirrors. She questioned Doris.

"Don't worry about that, dear," she was told. Did everyone in television say Don't Worry all the time? "He's *supposed* to look like a Communist. *You're* supposed to look glamorous. Mind you, haven't the wardrobe people said anything about that dress?"

"What wardrobe people?" Jessica wanted to know. "What *about* my dress?"

"Don't worry, I'm sure it'll be all right," was the unsettling answer.

When she had finished, Doris took Jessica back to the Green Room, which was now empty, except for the motherly lady tending the drinks cabinet. There was still a fug in the air and a litter of cigarette ends overflowing the ashtrays. No General, no weather man, no Government Minister, and no Jim. Just a large television set in the corner, with a picture unblemished by interference, showing the opening moments of *As It Happens*.

"I'm sure they'll come for you when they need you, dear," said the drinks lady.

On the screen, Huw Proudfoot was saying: "On the day of the big clean-up after vicious storms and gales swept the country, on the day Britain said 'No more guns for Nasser', we bring you, as ever, the news and the people making it, As It Happens. We've got a very full programme for you tonight, when we ask: could *your* hubby be called up to fight, and could the petrol for *your* car dry up? We'll also be meeting the glamorous young lady who wants to KO the noble art of boxing." As he said the words, a photograph of Jessica, taken the previous year, briefly filled the screen. She was dismayed and reassured at the same time. Huw Proudfoot continued: "But first, today's big mopping-up operation, as the nation counts the cost of last night's calamitous storms. Here, for those of you still with television aerials, is how it looked across the country. First, a reassurance for the hundreds of worried people who have phoned us: there is no risk of your aerial attracting lightning to your house."

There followed a film of a reporter in wellington boots splashing about in a few inches of water in a nearly deserted shopping street. The film lasted quite a while. The reporter interviewed a succession of shopkeepers, who each agreed that the weather had been truly atrocious, absolutely diabolical, quite terrible and really horrible. Each of them had some personal tale, of the floating away of a baker's entire stock of meringues, the blowing away of a week's worth of washing hung out to dry, and the escape of a pondful of goldfish.

Then, in the studio, the man from the Meteorological Office was interviewed by Huw Proudfoot about the year of appalling weather. He said that it wasn't true that it had never been so wet within living memory, it just felt like it. He said neither the opening of the first atomic power station nor the testing of atomic bombs had anything to do with the weather.

Upstairs, in the gallery overlooking the studio floor, Talbot Posner shouted to the director, sitting two feet away from him: "If he won't say what's he supposed to — get him off."

The director shook his head. By the time he got a message to the floor manager to make a signal to the presenter, the item would be over anyway. Posner turned to the group of researchers sitting behind him and yelled at them, generally: "Why didn't you tell me he was going to say this? I should never have listened to you. Next time, it's back to the man with the seaweed. At least he'll say what you want him to."

Posner was angry with himself really. He did not like having to make boring television programmes under instruction. This rubbish he was forcing himself to put out was indistinguishable from the BBC. If stories kept crashing around him he might even have to let Howard Hay get his own guest on the show. He had hoped to get away with introducing the anti-boxing item at the start of the programme and then failing to reach it.

He would then have said that Hay's guest would have been impossible to use since it would have meant three people representing the one newspaper in successive items. That, in fact, was why he had chosen Artemus Jones rather than any other Fleet Street type. Might as well give up making television if you allowed the administrators to dictate who and what had to go into your programme.

On to the next item, Will You Be Called Up to Fight Nasser? It was street interviews largely, with a succession of real people uttering entirely predictable lines. Over to the General in the studio. We don't want to fight; but, by Jingo, if we do, we've got the ships, we've got the men, we've got the money too[26]. North African desert a fine place for a tank battle, Rommel[27] could tell you that. Wasn't too sure about the need for a call-up, though.

What the tanks couldn't handle, a couple of brigades of Gurkhas[28] could mop up, pdq[29].

Oh dear, thought Posner. At least with spaghetti-eating contests it didn't matter if people said the wrong thing.

The next piece was a film opening with two men rather stagily pushing a Standard Vanguard[30] along the road to a garage. As the car arrived there was a shot of a blackboard reading: "Sorry. No Petrol. Blame Nasser." More of the same, with several minutes of contrived queues, vox pops and an ending with a man who had resurrected his wartime Jowett van that ran from coal gas out of a large balloon on the roof[31].

Back to the studio again, where Profumo had meanwhile taken the place of the General. The Labour MP who was supposed to turn up to counter the Minister had never arrived. The statutory balance of "due impartiality" was provided by an empty chair. It was either that or drop the complete item, which would mean using Hay's anti-boxing heiress. Posner was not going to give in that easily.

Profumo, invited as friend of ITV, was introduced by Proudfoot: "Welcome to *As It Happens* Minister. I'm sure the viewers would like you to put their minds at rest by telling them how many weeks' stock of fuel there is to keep the wheels of Britain's transport turning."

The Minister said: "There is no panic about petrol supplies. That item suggesting that there is was the most irresponsible piece I have ever seen on television. How can you possibly justify it? As for asking me a strategically important question like how long our fuel supplies will last, I'm shocked. Information like that is of vital importance to the enemy."

In the gallery, Posner yelled: "Get to the commercial break as soon as you possibly can."

Huw Proudfoot would have only a minute to splutter on. He doggedly continued with his prepared questions as the floor manager signalled him that there was a minute to go. "We can only report what we see, Minister. The camera doesn't lie. Perhaps you could set people's minds at rest by saying whether we have enough aeroplanes to transport troops to Suez in a hurry, if needed."

"I really think that a lot of people in this country are panicking quite unnecessarily. There will be no petrol shortage, because Britain knows how to stand up to tyranny. It is absolutely defeatist to suggest otherwise. If we had been firm with Hitler from the beginning we would not have needed the last war. We will have to get together with other responsible nations to show this jumped-up popinjay who's boss, to tell him he can't get away with twisting the tail of the British lion."

He looked set for a good rant and Posner regretted having brought the commercial break forward, but Huw Proudfoot was already winding up the interview: "Thank you very much, Minister. I'm sure those strong words will have given Colonel Nasser something to think about. After the break we'll be finding out about life without Fleet Street and what great headlines the world has been missing. We'll also be meeting the man who managed what Hitler couldn't and closed down the British press. See you soon."

The advertisements played: Tipped Weights[32] Have the Player's Taste, followed by Persil Washes Whiter, You Can't Tell Stork from Butter, Esso Motoring Means Happy Motoring (a bit unfortunate after the Petrol Panic item), Gibbs SR Toothpaste[33] and Laboratory-tested Anadin[34]. Three of them featured men in white coats.

During the break, the Minister was removed from his seat alongside Huw Proudfoot, amid much protest. "You told me I'd get five minutes and I got less than one," he said. "Cliff Michelmore always lets me talk as much as I want to. I've been a supporter of ITV all along and this is the treatment you give me."

In his place was seated Artemus Jones, with Jim Anstruther in the Labour MP's empty place. Jones did not look in a good way. Maybe his lunch was disagreeing with him, maybe it was the whisky in the car or the bright lights in the studio, but he was sweating profusely. The perspiration started out as beads on his face but turned to streams, causing his make-up to course down in rivulets and stain his collar. The make-up lady moved forward with a towel, patted him dry and dusted more powder on his face. Within seconds it joined the rivulets.

Huw Proudfoot looked at Jones with concern. Jones was dripping wet — and the wetter he was the more likely was his speech to dry up. In the minute Proudfoot had left to him between getting rid of the Minister and the programme starting again, he attempted to make Jones more at ease.

"These lights are a bit hot, aren't they?" he said. "Perhaps we should all wear those green eyeshades you editors use."

No response. So, while picking up his script to memorise his opening line for the second half of the programme, Proudfoot said to Jones: "The sound engineers need to have a sample of your voice for what they call 'level'. So, please tell us what you had for breakfast."

"Same as I always have," said Jones. "Bowl of Cornflakes and a small Irish whiskey." The studio crew members laughed, whether or not they were supposed to, even though it was not clear from Jones's voice or expression that he was indeed telling a joke.

"And you, Mr Anstruther," said Proudfoot, "welcome to the programme. Just want to check. Have I pronounced your name correctly?"

"That's how most people pronounce it," said Jim. "Some snobbish people pronounce it Ainster, but I don't mind either."

"I was told you were a Red, but now I find out that you're a Liberal, really," said Proudfoot. He then spoke to both the men in front of him: "I'll start with you Mr Jones. We'll talk about editing the *Tribune* on a day when it isn't printed and then we'll widen the issue to include you, Mr Anstruther. Don't be tempted to come in before I introduce you. Is that all right?"

Before either of them had a chance to reply, there was a shout of "Silence" in the background and Proudfoot turned to a camera, smiled and said: "Welcome back to *As It Happens*, the programme that lets you meet the people behind the news.

"Well, there's certainly been plenty happening yesterday and today, and you've seen some of it right here. But one place you haven't been able to see it happen is in the newspapers, because there haven't been any. So, in the studio with me we have Artemus Jones, distinguished editor of the *Daily Tribune*, to tell us what we've been missing." There was a change of picture to include Jones, who was staring vigorously down at the table in front of him. "Mr Jones: I imagine you would have done the same as us and led with the effects of the terrible weather?"

Jones looked at the presenter in terror. "Weather. Ah, yes, the weather. Yes, I suppose we would."

Proudfoot waited a second to see whether his guest was going to add anything and, when it became obvious that he was not, said: "But there's lots of other things in the news. The Suez crisis for one, as we've seen tonight. What would you have said about that?" Nasty question that. It wasn't just a prompt but genuinely required a thought-out answer — and one couched in terms avoiding the 14-day rule.

More sweat broke out on Jones's face, and his soggy bow tie began to droop. "Suez. Ah. Yes. Suez," he said. "Terrible business Suez. They just don't know what to do about it, do they?"

Proudfoot sat back in his chair, evidently hoping to force Jones to go on. The silence was broken by Jim, who butted in with: "I don't see what's terrible about it. The canal runs through Egypt, it was dug by Egyptian working men almost 90 years ago. Thousands of them died in the process. It's perfectly natural for the Egyptians to want to control the canal. People in this country would feel it pretty strange if a foreign company owned the Thames, say."

While he was speaking, the shot changed to include the three protagonists and again, to show Jim, in his Dracula make-up, alone. Proudfoot kept trying to interrupt and eventually succeeded, saying: "James Anstruther, the printing union leader at the *Tribune*, did you close down the presses just because you are against Britain in the Suez crisis?"

Upstairs, Posner saw his television programme being shanghaied by a rule-breaking revolutionary, and felt his job slipping away from him. He was no longer shouting. He just said quietly to the director: "We'll have to use the boxing girl after all. Just get rid of this fiasco as soon as you can."

"It's not as easy as that," said the director. "We can't clear the seats without a film or a commercial break to cover it. Even if we did manage to, because you took the break early we've got a long time to fill before the end of the show."

"Oh my God," said Posner, seeing before him the prospect of 25 years as press officer for the company's late-night religious programmes, which they were obliged by law to air, although the audience numbers were particularly small.

Behind him, Giles Hope-Jones said: "You can't have Jessica Ross yet, anyway. I left her to stew in the Green Room like you said; she's not on the studio floor. And if things are anything like they were last time I saw her, she'll be totally sozzled by now. Even if, by some miracle, she isn't, her dress is so bright, the cameras might go up in smoke."

Posner whimpered out loud. At last he said: "You'd better go and get her, anyway. Tell me whether you think she's up to it. If she is, and her dress is as bad as you say, they'll just have use her in tight close-up, to cut the dress out. And, since you're going to the Green Room, bring a very large whisky back for me."

Back on the studio floor, and in the homes of more than a million ITV viewers in London, Jim was realising that when everyone had told him "No need to worry", they had been quite right.

"I didn't stop Fleet Street," he said. "The unions didn't stop the presses. The owners of all the newspapers are refusing to run them in a sympathy strike on behalf of the proprietor of the *Tribune*. I didn't even stop the *Tribune* presses — they broke down because management wouldn't spend the money to protect them against bad weather. They don't bother about that sort of thing. A printer even gave his life trying to repair the presses and they won't even make arrangements to clear his body away. He died at his post, trying to make a profit for the owners, and they've left him there to rot. It's been three days now. I can tell you, Mr Proudfoot, when you get attitudes like that every day of your working life, you come to question what the ruling class have to say to you about other things, too."

Proudfoot turned to Jones: "Mr Jones, we've come to this rather earlier than intended. I had rather hoped to get an insight into a few of the gems from the pen that we might have been missing from the *Tribune*, but Mr Anstruther has made some pretty outrageous claims. I'm sure you'll want to put him straight."

Jones nodded. "Oh, yes. Very much so."

When he appeared disinclined to continue, Proudfoot asked him: "This trade union official claims that your presses broke down of their own accord, that someone has died trying to repair them, and the closure of Fleet Street during this time of crisis is due to some agreement between the newspaper owners themselves. Is any part of that true?"

"I'm only the editor," said Jones. "I'm not responsible for printing the thing." He paused, and then said: "Mind you, it sounds plausible, doesn't it? What do *you* think?"

If ever there was a natural end to an interview, that was it, but Proudfoot was getting no signal to move on, so he had to struggle through as best he could. "I suppose you've got some great scoop lined up for when the papers come back, though," he said.

Jones looked at him, paused, and said: "I might have, and I might not. If I had a scoop and I told you what it was, then it wouldn't be a scoop any more, would it?" He leant back in his chair with a squelch and tapped the side of his streaked nose with his index and middle fingers, saying: "Mum's the word, eh!"

Still no wind-up sign for Proudfoot, so he ploughed on: "Mr Anstruther. You're in charge of all the unions at the *Tribune* and, even if you didn't do so in this case, you have the power to close the paper down. Is this the sort of job that should be entrusted to someone who has been accused of being a Communist?"

"I don't know about being *accused* of being a Communist. I'm quite proud of being a socialist and equally proud of being a member of my union. I was elected to my post by my fellow union members, who all know my views. I don't think they put me in despite of my views but because of them. They know that I'm not corrupt and that I'll do the job I'm there for and stick up for their interests."

Out of camera shot, the floor manager held up a board with the words "Weather next". Sensing some activity behind him, Jim decided he might not have long to go to get his point across, so he rapidly changed the subject. "Now, take this Suez crisis; I believe it signals the end of Britain as an imperialist power."

That was as far as he was able to get before Proudfoot said: "That's as much as we have time for of this fascinating subject. Let's hope the newspapers are back on the streets soon. As we saw earlier, there was some real havoc caused by the elements last night. Now, to tell us whether we'll have to batten down the hatches again tonight, here's George Prosser from the Meteorological Office, again, with the latest forecast. Afterwards, I'll be back, As It Happens."

The picture changed again to show the weather man, with billiard cue and chart, in another part of the studio, as he gave an unscheduled forecast. It was extended and highly detailed.

As Jessica was moved into the wet seat vacated by Jones, Proudfoot was handed a note written by Talbot Posner.

George can keep
going for ever
on the weather,
but we'll stop
him after three
minutes. Do your
best with Jessica
Ross. Remember, she's
the heiress who has
set up a campaign
called The Fund
for The Abolition
of Boxing.
Ask her why.

So he did. After Prosser's words "and so the weather doesn't look very promising for our cricketers and other sportsmen this week," Proudfoot smiled at the camera and delivered his link.

"I have with me one person who would be perfectly happy if one particular sport was blown away for ever: Jessica Ross, the 22-year-old belle of the ball who has decided on a bare-knuckle fight to the finish against the noble art of boxing. So, Miss Ross, is this a contest that will go the distance?"

Jessica felt strangely detached from what was going on. As if she was not part of her own body, a spectator rather than a participant. She was conscious only of sitting on a wet seat and listening to someone asking a question she could not understand. Since she could not work out what the question meant, or even if was indeed a question, she decided to answer one that Jim had put to her earlier.

"I'm not going to wait for Parliament to clean up the law on boxing. I want the police to take action now," she said. There had been no chance to take a reading of her voice for level and Jessica's nervousness caused her speak loudly. The sound boomed out, which, coupled with the big close-up necessary to avoid her damagingly bright dress, had a particularly dramatic and forceful effect.

"The attempt by two men to knock each other senseless isn't legal in the streets, so it shouldn't be legal anywhere else. The people who promote it are guilty of conspiracy to cause an affray and people who watch it are accessories to a crime. I want the Attorney-General to prosecute any television company which broadcasts a boxing match. Without the publicity, and the money, they get from television, and with the police on their trail wherever they go, boxing promoters will soon have to give up the fight."

Watching in the gallery, Posner cheered up slightly. Get out of that one, Howard Hay. It's your guest who, in giant close-up and at top volume, has asked for television companies to be prosecuted.

Jessica reproached herself. Every time she was nervous, she reacted aggressively. She knew it didn't help her make friends but she was unable to stop herself. There was nothing she was able to do about it. She hoped that Giles had been right in saying Proudfoot couldn't knock the skin off a rice pudding.

"Oh dear," said the interviewer. "I don't like the sound of that. How can a young girl like you decide to take on something that has been causing pleasure to thousands and each year providing a ladder to success for dozens of young fighters?"

"I may be young, Mr Proudfoot, but I have seen what boxing really does to people. Even for those boxers it doesn't kill and for those whose brains it doesn't beat to a blancmange it does affect them — it makes some of them into selfish and violent thugs who believe a fist in the face is the answer to any argument. For them, it isn't a ladder to success, it is a slide down into the gutter. And it's not only the boxers themselves who suffer. A similar process happens in the hearts of the spectators, too. They are brutalised by blood-lust into a similar pattern of belief in the power of the fist. The whole business makes me, and many other people, utterly sick. That's why we're going to stop it."

Proudfoot decided on a hit below the belt: "Tell us about your friendship with the boxer George Crawford, who, I understand, is still wanted by the police."

"It's true I've met him, but he's hardly a friend. People like that don't have friends, they're out for anything they can get and they care for no one but themselves. Society needs to be protected from them, but they, too, need to be protected from their own violent instincts. It is to carry out work like that that we have started the Fund for the Abolition of Boxing. Until we get a permanent address, donations can be sent to me care of the *Daily Tribune*."

"You aren't allowed to make charitable appeals on ITV," protested Proudfoot.

"It's not a charity, it's a political campaign," said Jessica.

Which was worse, but there was no time for Proudfoot to say so. Just a quick: "Good night from me, Huw Proudfoot, until tomorrow night when we again look at the people who make the news As It Happens."

Huw Proudfoot and Jessica Ross disappeared from London's ITV screens, to be replaced by a fresh-faced lady with a beehive hair-do, who said: "Thank you Huw, wasn't that fun! Next there's *I've Got a Secret* with Maurice Winnick. Chairman Ben Lyon helps Catherine Boyle, Dick Bentley and Zoë Gail guess the exciting secrets sent in by viewers. But first, a short break."

The harsh television lights went off, section by section, and the background lighting reasserted its wan presence. Doris arrived with a shoebox from which she took a cream to remove the make-up from the presenter's face. As she worked, she handed another jar, a roll of cotton-wool and a hand mirror to Jessica. "You're a girl, so you'll know how to take off your own make-up," she said.

The presenter spoke to his former guest. "Boxers bedamned: I'd hate to confront you on a dark night."

"I'm sorry if I was too aggressive; I didn't know how else to react," said Jessica.

"Don't worry," said Proudfoot. That phrase again. "It was good television. I wish I could say the same about every item I was given tonight."

Jessica concentrated on dabbing at her face while the presenter talked on. She obviously had to take off the stagey make-up, which was too overdone even for a streetwalker, but she didn't want to be out in the evening without any make-up at all. She realised she had left her own lipstick in her handbag in the Green Room. In the meantime, she tried to compromise with the make-up removal, resulting in a strangely messy effect.

Proudfoot was still talking. No one except Jessica was paying any attention at all and even she was only half listening. "For months they make me interview Mynah birds with halitosis and pirates suffering from dry-rot in their wooden legs," he was saying. "Today, for the first time, they at last come up with some respectable hard news interviewing, which, believe me, should be far easier. Instead of that, they mess me around so much I'm made to look an idiot. They couldn't run a piss-up in a brewery, excuse my language. Can I take you for a drink in hospitality?"

"Oh yes, please," said Jessica, her attention again attracted. She was grateful for a guide through the maze of corridors so that she would be able to get back to her handbag. The Green Room was not the hushed reception area for the nervous she had found before. Instead, it was crowded with people talking at the tops of their voices. The General was just leaving but the rest of the guests were there, together with most of the programme-makers.

The Government Minister had encountered the new production assistant with the long legs and the well filled sweater. He was leaning toward her, his upper body supported by his extended left hand, which was flat on the wall above her right shoulder. He had a half-full whisky glass in his right hand, which from time to time he waved round in expansive gestures. The gestures came at moments when it appeared that the young lady might otherwise edge out of the confined space left to her.

Giles Hope-Jones, who had earlier that day been allocated as researcher for the weather story, was in conversation with George Prosser, from the Meteorological Office. He was trapped by politeness, but smiled and waved as Jessica passed.

An ebullient looking man was with Artemus Jones, and as Jessica passed, with Huw Proudfoot, on the way to the drinks cabinet, she heard a snatch of conversation. "Oh yes," Jones was being told, "you were quite excellent. Particularly for a first timer. I see you as a future television presenter. You have the right gravitas." Jessica seemed to recall Jones claiming to be far from a first-timer on television, but could not remember whether he had detailed any of his supposed earlier triumphs.

Huw Proudfoot told her, as they reached the drinks queue: "That was our programme editor. I think he'll be looking for another job tomorrow morning."

Someone interrupted. "Not because of anything *I* said, I hope." It was Jim, his face still streaked with the remains of the Dracula make-up. Jessica was immediately conscious of her own blotched mess of a face and of the damp patch at the back of her dress and the greasy-palm stain up one side of it. She had not yet managed to locate her handbag.

"Not you alone," said Huw Proudfoot. "Not the General, the Minister, the weather man, the editor, or even this young lady, alone, either. All of you together. At least I hope they blame the programme editor. Otherwise it will have to be me buttering up Artemus Jones for a job at the *Tribune*."

The heiress to the *Tribune* and its chief union official raised their eyebrows at this information. They exchanged surprised, silent glances. Proudfoot noticed, saying: "You two obviously know each other. Where did you meet?"

They both replied at the same time, using, inexplicably, the same words: "In the public bar at the White Hart." The glances between the two turned to perplexed stares. They laughed with nervous reserve. Jim spoke to Jessica: "I thought you were absolutely brilliant in there. You were in total command and absolutely convincing. It was a joy to see. You were so nervous beforehand — how did you manage it?"

Jessica blushed through her blotches. "I had such a good act to follow. I saw you wiping the floor with that creep and felt so pleased I didn't mind what happened next."

Huw Proudfoot, who had been standing on the sidelines as the two talked, blustered in: "Thanks a lot! So you give you the chance of your lifetime and I'm a creep."

Jim spoke for Jessica: "She didn't mean you — Miss Ross was talking about Jones."

"Oh," said the presenter, taking a moment or two before convincing himself that no one could possibly have thought he was creep. "He wasn't exactly Richard Dimbleby at the Coronation, was he?"[35]

Just then a fourth person, the reporter Justin Silcock, joined the group and said: "Huw, Howard Hay says he'd like a word when you've got a moment."

The presenter again looked taken aback. "I'd better go, then," he said. He handed Jim some handwritten sheets of folded, lined foolscap.

He said: "You'd better have your notes back. I'm afraid I didn't have time to read them." And left the room. Jim looked at the notes and then at Silcock. "Do you mean you never sent these off?" he asked, moving toward him, glowering.

"I think I must have forgotten," said Silcock, edging backward.

Jim spoke slowly, with a hard edge in his voice. "But you didn't forget to show my private papers to anyone who might use them against me."

"No harm done, was there," said Silcock, in a voice at once breezy and ingratiating.

"I'll give you 'no harm done'," said Jim, taking a step forward. "Do you realise the damage you have caused by the union not getting this report on time?"

Jessica, who found herself attracted to Jim in a way similar to her initial attraction to George Crawford, feared a repetition of the incident outside the Savoy Hotel. She laid a calming hand in the crook of Jim's right elbow. He did not shake the hand off, and stopped moving toward Silcock. He said to the reporter: "I'll have to take it myself and hope it still arrives in time to be of some use. Where's that car you promised me?"

"It won't take more than a few minutes to whistle one up," said Silcock.

"You mean you haven't even ordered it?" said Jim, beginning to raise his right arm toward Silcock. Jessica tightened her grasp for a moment, to attract Jim's attention, and said: "If it'll help you get where you want, why don't you come in *my* car?"

She didn't know at that stage that Jim lived in the opposite direction to her, and it wouldn't have stopped her anyway. She then gave the second of her two reasons for the invitation: "It'll help protect me from that lecher with the wandering hands."

Silcock took the opportunity to step out of fist range. Then he shook his head and said: "I'm afraid not, Miss Ross. Your car has already left with our editor and Artemus Jones. I'll go and see about getting another car. You evidently don't mind sharing."

As Silcock scuttled off, Jim said to Jessica: "Thank you. I'll try to keep my hands to myself." Jessica wondered whether he was saying he wouldn't punch Silcock or whether he was promising not to embrace her in the style of Jones. She did not know what to say to let Jim know that really didn't fear for herself at his hands. They never taught you useful things like that at school, even in Switzerland.

They waited until the Green Room was almost empty and the drinks cabinet had been closed, but Silcock never returned. There was no news of any other car. They looked out of the window and the rain appeared to have stopped, so Jim suggested he tried to get Jessica a taxi in the street.

They stood on the street corner together, periodically raising a hand toward passing taxis hurrying through the glistening streets. It was difficult to see whether the For Hire arm on the taximeters was up or down until the cab was very close. The only time they thought they might be lucky it turned out that the cab was stopping for someone else.

Jessica had neither coat nor umbrella. Jim, who had been on his way out of the house when collared to appear on television, had his motor-cycling coat. It was large enough to drape over both their shoulders. After a while, it started to pour with rain again and Jim ran with Jessica to a nearby café. They sat opposite each other, clothes dripping and knees occasionally touching, supposedly accidentally. For a while they just talked about their screen débuts and railed about the television company, Silcock, and Artemus Jones. Then Jessica asked what was in the report Jim was so anxious to deliver. He would not say, claiming to be more anxious to know about Jessica, in particular how she had come to be seen by him in the public bar of the White Hart with George Crawford.

For little reason, Jessica was inclined to trust the man. He had a straightforward air of honesty to him. He was leading a strike against the proprietor, her own adoptive father, but seemed to bear no personal grudge. He was also someone to talk to, and even more than normally, after the stress of the television studio, she wanted to talk about herself. Jim did say he wanted to hear.

So she talked. Not in strictly chronological order, she told of how she had been picked up by Crawford, although she had probably been asking for it, about her misery of a life, her loneliness, about the strange way the proprietor had of knowing what she really wanted when she didn't know it herself, about his spies all over the world who trailed her and reported back, and about her decision to accept the task of running the anti-boxing campaign to prove to everyone that she wasn't a nincompoop and that given the chance she would make it a hit. The campaign had got off to a fine start and she was quite pleased, really, with the television thing, but did Jim have any ideas?

While she spoke, Jessica fixed her eyes on some part of the table or on Jim's clothing and used her hands to touch herself in a fidgety way. As she talked, Jim looked at her too, rarely directly into her eyes but at various points about her face. He nodded from time to time, said "mm", or "uh-huh" at various points and occasionally gave short prompts, such as "yes?" or "then what?" or "what do you feel about that?" He didn't reply directly with any ideas for the activities of the Fund for the Abolition of Boxing. Instead, he asked: "Why do you call him 'the proprietor'? I thought he was your father."

So Jessica told him about that, too. About being ashamed to herself about having no memory of her real father or mother or of anything before her adoption. About never having got over the death of her adoptive mother, either.

"What do you call the proprietor at home?" Jim wanted to know.

"Nothing, if I can avoid it," said Jessica. "I just can't bring myself to call him 'father' or 'daddy' or anything like that. I don't speak to him very much. Before they sent me away, there was always mummy there — that's my adoptive mother. If I need to say something to him nowadays I don't call out, I go to find him. That way I'm able to say 'you' rather than use a name. As you know, if I need to speak *about* him I call him 'the proprietor'."

Jim looked directly into her brown eyes for the first time, with a sad expression, and then looked away before saying: "I imagine it upsets the man terribly."

Jessica, deciding not to take up the implied reproach, said: "I imagine it does."

Neither of them had eaten for a long time, so they took a pile of buns and jam doughnuts between them, as well as the two foaming, milky coffees, which were served partly in glass cups and partly in the corresponding saucers. Sitting opposite Jim in the coffee bar with its hissing espresso machine and new wallpaper made in imitation of bare bricks, Jessica tried to work out how to say she wanted to see more of Jim without appearing to be forward.

Jim said: "It seems to me that you could solve two problems at the one time if you were to use some of the money to get some good offices. You need a base to run the organisation from and an address to give it respectability instead of it being seen to be something to do with the *Tribune*. If the offices were large enough, you could almost live there and free yourself from being beholden on your father — the proprietor, I mean."

It was good advice. Jim even promised to help her look for premises, as long as they weren't seen together too often.

"It wouldn't look good for either of us. It's not true that I, or anyone else, is fireproof at the *Tribune*. They can only not sack me on an issue where I would get the support of the workers. I don't think the union would back me if I was interfering with the boss's daughter."

Jessica tentatively touched his hand: "I don't think I'm being interfered with, Jim."

He leant over the table and grasped her hand, and half stood up to lean across the table and kiss her. Jessica did not turn her blotched cheek toward him but offered her mouth. That night before going to bed she discovered a trace of Jim's Dracula make-up on her upper lip.

The pair made arrangements to meet on the Wednesday at 10, when Jim said he would help in the hunt for an office for the Fund for the Abolition of Boxing. The Tuesday would be too soon to get lists of available property.

They were to bump into each other in the basement of Gamages[36], among the ironing boards and electric toasters. They swore themselves to punctuality as they had no way of getting in touch — Jim daren't telephone the proprietorial residence and Jessica could not possibly call him at the *Tribune*, where the switchboard operator would recognise both their voices. Jim was not on the phone at home. There was a three-year waiting list on the RAVensbourne exchange.

There was a lull in the rain as they got up to leave. They should abandon trying for a taxi and should run for the Underground, they reckoned. When it came to paying for the buns and coffee, Jessica realised she had lost her handbag. Jim said he didn't remember seeing her with it, and Jessica could not remember having it since before being rushed into the television studio. Jim paid the coffee-bar owner for them both and gave Jessica a shilling for her journey home. She had no pocket or bag to put it in, so kept it in her hand.

Jim said: "It's far too late to deliver the report. I've no idea what excuse I'll give for not handing it in, though. I can hardly tell them the real reasons — that first I was hoodwinked by a journalist and then I failed in my duty because I preferred to hold hands with a young lady."

They walked together to the Underground station, side by side. Within Holborn station they walked closely together until the passages to the westbound Central Line for Jessica and the eastbound for Jim diverged. They stopped and kissed goodbye.

"Do either of us really know the danger of what we are doing?" asked Jim.

"Probably not," said Jessica. "But you must promise to be there. I'll be devastated if you don't turn up."

"I'll be there," said Jim.

As she turned to go her separate way, Jessica realised that she knew next to nothing about the man.

She arrived home looking rather more dishevelled than when she had left. It was a cold and wet night and she had no coat, the rain had got through her white dress, petticoats and girdle and she was soaked to the skin. Her bare arms were goose-pimpled from the cold and her shoes were scuffed from the walk. She was remarkably cheerful.

Mrs Burgess let her in. The proprietor was in the library, sitting on a sofa, reading a typewritten report which ran to dozens of sheets of quarto paper[37], stapled together. Jessica went to him and said: "Hello Daddy! I've had a wonderful time."

"I know, I saw you on television," he said, putting down the document. "You were marvellous — which is more than I can say for my editor. Why the 'Daddy' business? Has appearing on television transformed you that much?"

"I won't call you 'Daddy' if you don't want me to," said Jessica. "It's just that I'm feeling so happy." She had difficulty in bringing herself to use the name, but she felt she should, to please Jim. The proprietor extended his arms and Jessica moved closer, sat down beside him in her dripping dress and was enveloped in his arms. "I'm happy too," he said. "My only daughter's come home to me, and it looks like I've still got a newspaper after all."

Jessica looked up to him from the crook of his arm and said: "What are you saying about the newspaper?" Then: "I'd have been home earlier but your editor took the car without waiting for me."

"Oh dear," said the proprietor. "I'll have to speak to him about his manners. In fact, I haven't been happy with him of late about a number of things, for example putting up such a pathetic performance tonight — I should have agreed to do the programme myself. Now the unions have given in and I've got my paper back again, I may just take the opportunity of getting myself a new editor. Pity I can't get a new union, too."

Then: "How did you manage to get home?"

"I had to go by Underground and then walk. I'd left my handbag behind and I had to borrow the money from someone for the fare," said Jessica, hoping he would not press further. She should try to get him to talk about something that interested him more. "Why did the unions give in?" she asked.

"Which someone?" the proprietor wanted to know.

So far Jessica had not told a lie, but felt she might have to, soon. She said: "I'm glad you saw the programme. What did you think of the General?"

"They were all useless, except you and, I'm afraid to say, that Bolshevik[38] agitator of mine. I do think the General might have brought you home instead of lending you your tube fare. It's not safe for young girls out alone at night. Did you meet this Anstruther chap?"

"Yes," Jessica felt she had to admit, knowing that the bald answer would not be enough.

"Well — what did you think of him? Remember, I haven't met him myself. It may well be a good thing he wasn't at the negotiations tonight. The full-time officials who were there appeared to have no idea what had been going on at the *Tribune*. You'd have thought they might have got some written report or something, but apparently not. We just told them it was all the fault of some Communist agitator, and they seemed to accept it."

Jessica, who had had little to eat except the buns in the café, started to feel sick, although defiant. It had probably been a mistake accepting such a man as her father. She thought she might give up calling him "Daddy". She risked hinting at what she felt, saying: "I found him quite charming and very clever."

"Oh dear. That's just what Colonel Cumberledge said. That type's the most difficult to deal with, but deal with him I shall. I can't just sack him, but I intend to find some way of getting him out of my hair. I can't guarantee on the union selling him out every time. I'll either have to promote him, or get someone else to take him on, or make things so bad for him he quits, get him arrested or arrange a nasty accident. Which do you think I should try?"

Jim arrived home after a long wait at the main-line station, a walk to the bus stop and another long delay in the driving rain before a 227 bus turned up. He was greeted by an angry Sheilagh as he let himself in.

"Where the hell have you been?" she said.

"Didn't you see me on television?"

"Don't make jokes with me," she said.

"They promised to send you a telegram saying I was to be on. Didn't you get it? What did you think of me? Do you think I wiped the floor with them?"

Sheilagh looked at him coldly and said: "You'll have to do better than that, Jim. There was no telegram. I've been watching television all night and you certainly haven't been on."

"It was ITV," said Jim.

Sheilagh narrowed her eyes and said: "I suppose appearing on television, if that's what you say you've been doing all day, would explain the make-up, but not the perfume. I've had just about enough of you, Jim Anstruther. If you've found another comrade to believe in you, good luck to her, that's all I can say."

7

Tuesday 31st July 1956

Jessica had a terrible night. When she slept, she had unpleasant dreams, which woke her. Awake, she worried, particularly about her role in bringing down the strike against the proprietor.

In the morning, she had a lengthy, deep and hot bath, in which she washed her hair and removed the final traces of the television make-up. After Mrs Burgess's breakfast, she spent the forenoon on the telephone to commercial estate agents, asking for written particulars of small office premises. It was almost a mechanical operation, which she carried out because she had planned to do it, rather than in any prospect of succeeding. She thought of the acquisition of the office as Jim's project and felt it unlikely that he would want anything more to do with her following the collapse of his strike. She had to take a large share of the blame for that.

If he didn't turn up on Wednesday she could not get in touch with him. She could not telephone him at work and did not know his home address. She might never be able even to tell him how much she regretted what she had done to him. She knew almost nothing about the man. He could be married, even. Perhaps, in years to come, she might see him in a corridor in the *Tribune*. He would pass by, muttering "class enemy" so softly only she could hear.

To have something to do, Jessica kept telephoning the estate agents with her requirements. A couple of rooms would do, but there had to be a telephone — nobody could be expected to face the wait of a year or more to get the GPO[1] to allocate a new line. The place had to be available to move into straight away, and it would help if it was fairly central and not too expensive. She had not realised quite how many estate agents there were, nor how unhelpful they would all be. On the telephone they tended to sound like spivs or else they affected exaggeratedly public-school accents. Either way, their reaction was the same when they heard Jessica's simple specification. They gasped in astonishment and said they didn't think she quite realised what a difficult request she was making.

After a lunch spent telling Mrs Burgess every detail about her television appearance, missing out only the most important parts, she continued with the telephone calls. After an hour or so, the exchange operator broke in just as she was dialling another agent, whose advertisement she had seen in the *Evening Standard*. "HAMpstead 3404? I've a caller here who's been trying to get through for almost an hour. He says it's awfully urgent," said the operator.

The urgent caller turned out to be only Lear, but he was in a bit of a lather. He said: "Jessica, I've some bad news to tell you. I've been called up."

"Oh," said Jessica. "What's bad about that?" She really had stop taunting the poor boy.

"It's a bit hush-hush, I think. It's not official yet, and the BF says it won't be in the papers for a day or two. He should know, after all. It seems they want the regiments with Suez experience to go up to maximum strength. That means they want me."

"Sorry to hear it, Lear," said Jessica, in apology for her earlier quip.

"I'm not sorry; a bit of action sounds like fun to me," said Lear. "I called it 'bad news' because if this shindig goes on for any time we might have to miss the Games. I felt you might be upset."

"Upset? I'm mortified."

Lear either did not appreciate or decided to ignore the ostentatious insincerity. He said: "I need to see you before I go. And I'm going soon."

That did not appear to be too much of a problem. "All right, fine. Any time except tomorrow morning."

Lear's voice almost exploded. "But Jessica! That's the only time I have. I have to join my regiment on its way to Cyprus tomorrow afternoon. Be reasonable! I don't ask much of you."

"Look Lear — tomorrow morning's absolutely impossible. Why don't you come round now?"

"But I've got to go to Gieves & Hawkes² to get fitted for my uniform. And there's a regimental dinner tonight. What can possibly be so important that I can't see you in the morning? If I died without your having said 'goodbye', then you'd reproach yourself."

"Don't be silly, Lear. You're beginning to sound like the proprietor. You're not going to die. This is peace-time. Send me a postcard — although I doubt if you'll be going anywhere more exciting than Catterick³."

It would be a pity not to have Lear to taunt any more. Jessica hoped he would not tell anyone about her unbreakable Wednesday morning appointment.

After she had run out of estate agents to call, Jessica had tea and spent much of the afternoon and evening watching television. At first there was nothing but cricket on the BBC. The rest of the programmes were similarly dull: At 5 o'clock Desmond Morris's *For Children* took another tour of London Zoo, after which there was Jimmy Hanley and *Jolly Good*, and then *Mick and*

Montmorency, in which Charlie Drake and Jack Edwards set off on their summer holidays. At 6, programmes closed down, for tea. Over on ITV, at 7, television started up again with the ITN news, read by Ludovic Kennedy, followed by the comedy *Topper*, then *Jack Hilton*, followed by *Bob Hope*. After her own appearance, she was a convert to the undemanding trash on ITV. She was able to watch it and worry about other things at the same time.

Tuesday was not a normal day for Jim. When he woke, Sheilagh was not in the bed, and the ordered state of the sheets made it appear that she had spent the night elsewhere. Going downstairs not yet fully awake, he glanced at the doormat for the *Daily Worker* before remembering the industrial dispute. In the kitchen there was a cereal bowl in the sink with traces of Rice Krispies. He found the package for his own breakfast but there was no milk in the refrigerator. He collected that day's bottle from the doorstep and, passing the sitting room, saw a blanket on the sofa, where Sheilagh had evidently spent the night.

Even if it had not been for the row of the night before, he would have felt disoriented. The morning ritual had been upset, and there was the worry about the undelivered report. He dressed and walked to the telephone box at the end of the road. In went 2d and he dialled the union regional office. When, after a minute or more, the union's switchboard answered, he pressed Button A[4] and asked to speak to Mr Baverstock. Better not mention the missing report, yet.

"Anstruther here. Can you tell me how the meeting with the NPA panned out?"

"Fine. You're back at work."

Surprising, and unsettling, news. "But what about the body?" Jim asked — he was, after all, as far as he knew still Imperial

Father of the Federated Chapels of the *Tribune* newspaper. "How did you get over that problem?"

"The body isn't there anymore. That's all we need to know. Whether it went by theft, natural decomposition, or got up and walked away by itself, it's not there. You can run the presses as normal," Baverstock told him.

"I don't think the lads will like that," said Jim. "What else have you got for them?"

"An excellent collection of benefits. There is to be no victimisation, full compensation for the two days' lost wages and a two-inch obituary for Stan Gudger in the first available edition of the *Tribune*. I think that's pretty good going. The national executive has approved the deal. You're to start work immediately."

"Isn't there a Special Responsibility (Grief) Allowance? An Extra Responsibility (Damp Weather) Allowance? Two extra casuals per night? Did Gudger die for nothing?" said Jim over the crackly line.

"This is the first I've heard of any allowance being asked for," said Baverstock. "You never told us. We've got nothing in writing from you. If I was your Combined Chapel Committee, I'd be pretty angry that my Imperial Father couldn't even put his demands on paper. You've got no complaint against me. You've got no right to be angry. If you try to spread lies about me, I'll tell your members the truth about you."

Jim saw how good the result was for the Party, which would now get its *Daily Worker* back on the streets. He wondered whether Baverstock was one of the secret Communists the Party was believed to have in place for emergencies. With a "good morning to you," the union organiser hung up. Outside the telephone box there was a queue of people waiting for Jim to finish using the phone.

Dejected, he went back home, locked up and got on his motor cycle. At the station, the evening papers were available as usual. Jim looked at the front pages. Not unnaturally, they were all about Suez. He felt that the *Star*, probably unintentionally, summed it all up with **SUEZ: GOVT FIX DEBATES.** He scanned the sports pages so that he would understand what was said to him in the canteen — there appeared to be another Test match going on. Then he just stared out of the soot-stained carriage window at the succession of junk-yards, coal depots, bomb-sites and people's overgrown back gardens.

Within the *Daily Tribune* there was a sullen mood. Most people had arrived back grumpily after the extended weekend. Some of them had been contacted at home by their relevant FoC by telephone. They in turn had passed on the news to fellow workers who lived nearby. Some, who, like Jim, had no telephone and did not live in East London or Essex, had not come in.

Jim was greeted in sullen fashion in the despatch department. In the print hall he ran the gauntlet of silently expressed hostility until Fred Dawlish stopped his path. "What the hell went wrong, Anstruther?" he asked. "We had an issue here which we should have milked for all it was worth. Yet you've let the union betray us. We've gone back to work for nothing. No advance at all. How am I going to pay for my chimney repair?"

"Yes, I know, Fred," said Jim. "It's appalling. The lesson we've got to learn is never again to let national officials meddle in our affairs." A small group of press hands gathered quietly around the pair.

Fred Dawlish said: "They've taken away the body. God knows who did it, because it wasn't any of us. But they've left behind an all-too-human stench. How are we expected to work like this?"

The air was indeed fœtid. The gales had subsided, after what the Meteorological Office had described as the worst July ever known (thereby contradicting their representative who had just denied that very claim on television the night before). The dampness in the atmosphere had built up over the weekend when there had been no heat from the working machinery to evaporate it. There was a cloyingly sweet smell overlying the dampness, which could well have been the lingering presence of Stan Gudger.

Jim sniffed, grimaced and said: "It doesn't smell too good."

To general assent from the small knot around him, Fred Dawlish said: "If you'd have actually fought in the war, instead of skulking on the Home Front, you'd know that smell for what it is: rotting human flesh."

"Come on, Fred. You can't attack me for that. You know I tried to join up but they wouldn't have me. They knew I was a Communist."

Dawlish made a logical point: "If you're a Communist, why aren't you calling for a strike?"

Jim told him: "You're quite justified in being angry, but we can't have another strike on the same issue so soon. We can't defy our own unions. They've done a deal and it would be anarchy for us not to accept that. That's part of what solidarity means. We'll just have to find another issue to get our own back. I'm sure something will turn up within the next day or two."

Over dinner in the canteen, Jim encountered more hostility.

"I see England has been accused of nobbling the wicket again," he said to Bill Enright.

Enright said: "Look Anstruther, we know you're not really interested in cricket, so why pretend? Just tell us why we aren't on strike?"

Francis Josling interrupted. "I'll tell you why. It's because he's a Communist. He takes his instructions from King Street, not from us. I don't know what it is, but they've obviously got their own devious reason for wanting our strike to fail."

"That's just not true, Francis," said Jim, his sausage and mash growing cold upon his plate. "I take my instructions from the union. That means the members, but it also means the elected national executive. What would be the point of management even bothering to talk with us if we couldn't guarantee to stick by our side of a bargain? Our only strength is sticking together. If it wasn't for the union, they'd be able to pick us off, one by one."

"That's not true," said Francis Josling. "It's in the nature of union officials to sell out their members."

As Josling developed his theme, the rest of the print workers hurriedly finished their food and left the table.

Jim was in a dejected mood all afternoon and decided to return home early, arriving back at about 7.30pm. Sheilagh had preceded him by a few minutes. She scrubbed and boiled some potatoes while Jim opened another tin of peas to eat with a tin of Waveney corned beef[5]. They did not speak about their row of the night before but nonetheless had an argument, this time about politics. Jim told her about the events of the day and particularly about the canteen discussion. The claim that Communists and union officials were doomed to sell out their members had upset him more than he admitted at the time, he told Sheilagh.

Sheilagh told him to ignore the insidious rantings of Trotskyites[6] and other traitors. All around the world such people were planting their deadly lies. They might use left-wing words but in reality their arguments led to reaction. Objectively, they were fascists. They should be exposed as such, and shot.

Jim maintained that the days of shooting people were over. Khrushchev's secret speech earlier in the year about the excesses of the Stalin period had been right. The Communists in Poland were showing the way to a world free from fear and exploitation, where you could go to bed at night without keeping a bag packed in case the secret police came for you.

Sheilagh called him a deluded fool. The Polish United Workers' Party[7] was being misled by bourgeois opportunists. Unless it came to its senses, the international proletariat, led by the Red Army, would have to show it who was boss. Once the working class had got control it should never again allow power to be wrested from its hands.

Jim said it was easy for someone from a middle-class background who had never soiled her hands and had never know poverty to romanticise the working class she knew nothing about. Sheilagh said that Jim made her sick. She didn't want him anywhere near her.

That night it was Jim who slept on the sitting-room sofa.

8

Wednesday 1st August 1956

Her actions demonstrated the muddle Jessica's mind was in. She believed Jim would not turn up for the meeting but nevertheless she still went herself. She also avoided the white dress and the olive-coloured one with the pearl buttons, as he had seen them both. She put on tan nylons, a pleated navy-blue skirt and a close-fitting jersey, to which she added a narrow navy belt and an amethyst brooch. She put on low-heeled shoes and, after looking at the gathering clouds, took out her black gabardine, belted waterproof coat and covered up her carefully chosen clothes.

A large number of letters arrived for her, most of the envelopes bearing the names of estate agents, and many of them managing to introduce spelling errors into her simple, four-letter surname. She packed the letters, unopened, into a dark brown leather music case of the proprietor's. She practised clutching the case under her left arm.

To make sure of being at the appointed spot at the right time, Jessica felt she had to leave the house at 9 — which turned out to be just the time Fibbins arrived with the car to take the proprietor in to the *Tribune*. The three met in the hall.

"I see you're going out," said the proprietor. "What are you doing?"

"Looking for premises for the Fund," said Jessica.

"There's no need for that," said the proprietor. He made a sign to Fibbins to go out to the car and wait. He said: "Now Jessica, you know you can have the use of whatever space you want at the *Tribune*. In fact, I won't hear of anything else. Come with me now and I'll make the arrangements."

There would have been plenty of ways of avoiding a confrontation. Jessica could have accepted the offer, or said she was just looking to see what sort of place was available, or given some other soft answer to turn away wrath. Instead, she used grievous words to stir up anger. "The only reason I'm doing anything with this Fund is to get out of your clutches," she said.

The proprietor did not check himself either, before saying: "I'd remind you who originated the Fund. I can get Beaverbrook to stop a cheque as well as write one."

The two stood, facing each other in the hallway, exchanging looks of outraged propriety and defiant challenge. After a while, the proprietor extended his arm softly and said: "Come with me."

Jessica replied: "I'm going in totally the opposite direction to you." She turned her back and retreated up the stairs to wait for the proprietor to depart. She wondered what she would do if he saw her going into Gamages, which was in fact very close to the *Tribune* building.

The Underground to Chancery Lane was crowded with men in dripping hats, wet umbrellas and steaming overcoats. It was so crowded that there were many women standing. Jessica had little space to open her letters with their purple, Banda-duplicated contents. She arrived far too early at Gamages. In the basement, in a space behind a stack of pots and pans, she stood slitting open her letters with the handle of her comb.

The outwardly meaningless language of buyers' premiums, reversionary tenures, flying freeholds and full repairing leases helped steady her nerves. She tried to look as though she was just passing the time while waiting for someone, which was indeed the case, but various shop assistants and, on one occasion, the floor-walker, kept asking if they could be of assistance to madam.

To escape their attentions, she found a place behind a huge, cream-coloured Kelvinator, with unique recessed insulated compartment in the door with integral heater for housewives to make sure the butter was always ready for the table. She hid behind the concealing refrigerator and kept reading while waiting for the time of the appointment, when she planned to move to somewhere more prominent. Her new Rolex told her it was five minutes to 10.

Just as she was settling in, a voice close behind her asked: "Can I be of assistance to madam?"

She turned round sharply, then saw who it was. Jessica had expected to have had time to prepare herself for the meeting, if Jim was indeed to turn up. Instead, she had been taken by surprise, almost like a schoolgirl caught smoking an illicit cigarette in the coal cellar. She said: "You gave me a fright. I didn't think you'd turn up, you know."

"Perhaps I shouldn't have, Jessica," said Jim, whose naturally dark hair and craggy features looked better without the fearsome make-up. "I'm not so sure what we're doing is very sensible for either of us, but here I am." Then he said: "I see you've got some estate agents' lists."

Still feeling rather flustered, Jessica stepped out of the confined space before she answered.

"It's good to see you, Jim. I'm glad you decided to come." She asked: "Don't you blame me for losing your strike?"

"I don't see why I should blame you," he said. "Even if you were totally on management's side, which I suspect you're not, for some reason, the damage was done long before I met you the other day. I should never have gone to that television thing. I should have spent the time reporting to the union, instead.

"Still," and here he removed his gaze from a spot on the floor and looked straight at Jessica, who was gradually regaining composure, "it was great fun. I wouldn't have wanted to miss it. Or miss meeting you, come to that."

Jessica gazed at him and smiled.

Jim paused in embarrassment at what he had said, made a grab for some of the sheets of paper in Jessica's hand, and said: "Which of these offices do you think we should look at?"

A shop assistant at that moment appeared, and said: "I see you're interested in the Kelvinator. It's the best on the market you know, but despite that there's not a very long waiting list. It's only 51 guineas, and that includes the purchase tax."

The assistant glanced at the estate agents' lists that both Jessica and Jim were holding and, looking first at Jessica and then at Jim, said: "Setting up house are we? If you put your name down for the Kelvinator, it will make any house a dream-home."

"It's not what you think," said Jim, hurriedly, as the two escaped toward the stairs up to the street exit. They giggled as they found themselves walking along High Holborn. To get out of the rain, they jumped on to a trolley bus which turned out to be heading for the West End.

They managed to get a pair of seats together, inside the bus, with Jessica closest to the nearside window, and they sat looking through the sheaf of agents' particulars. From time to time, Jessica passed a bundle to Jim with a shake of her head, or picked a sheet out and gave it to him for his comments. Without photographs, and with descriptions generally limited to the number and size of rooms, measured in square feet, the offices were difficult to visualise. What was clear was that they were almost all either far from the centre of town, had no telephone, were restricted to a certain use or were unbelievably expensive. After a while, Jessica had excluded every offering except one from a house agent which had crept in by mistake. It was described as a "bijou pied à terre" in Shepherd Market and had two furnished rooms, with a kitchen and bathroom.

"You can't have that," Jim said in her right ear. "It's 15 guineas a week and it doesn't say anything about 'office use'."

"You're beginning to sound like the proprietor," said Jessica. "Telling me what I can't have. Come with me to look at it, at least."

They got off the bus near Piccadilly Circus and walked in the drizzle through the Mayfair streets until they found the agent. It was near both the cinema she had been to with Lear and the hotel she had been to with George. Jim said he would wait outside for Jessica, in spite of the weather. It was her own workplace she was looking for and her decision to look at that particular flat. He said he did not want a supercilious agent making the wrong assumptions about them. In fact, thought Jessica, he looked a bit embarrassed about the whole thing, less in command of himself in the West End than he had been in his own area near Fleet Street or even in the television studio. Perhaps he didn't want to be sneered at by a snooty man in a tailored suit.

Inside the agent's panelled office, it was Jessica on her own who was to be sneered at.

To begin with, when she entered, in her black gabardine mackintosh, there was a polite, even obsequious, welcome. A middle-aged man with tidy, short, white hair approached her and ushered her to an upholstered seat in front of a large, polished desk, saying: "Good morning, madam. My name is Freddy Fanshaw. How can I help you?"

Jessica put the music case on the desk, unbelted and unbuttoned her coat, took it off, handed it to Fanshaw, and sat down. She sifted through the pieces of paper in the case and by the time Fanshaw had returned from hanging up her coat she found the sheet about the bijou pied à terre. She handed it over to him and said: "I thought I might have a look at this."

Fanshaw's attitude immediately changed. From being polite he became familiar. He kept the same distance but his manner changed from professional aloofness to fastidious distaste. "Oh," he said. "I didn't realise you were a business girl."

"It's not exactly business," said Jessica, slightly foxed. "More a sort of charity."

"I'd never quite heard it put like that, before," said Fanshaw, coldly.

Jessica, whose only previous experience of estate agents had been talking to dozens of them by telephone the day before, did not know what to make of his odd manner. She was anxious to get out of his office as soon as she could, but had a couple of questions.

"I have to know: does this place have a telephone?"

"Oh yes. All the girls insist on telephones, nowadays. That's how most of you get your trade, after all."

Another strange answer.

"This piece of paper doesn't say anything about business use. Are there any restrictions?"

Fanshaw stood up, looking shocked. He glared, and said: "This firm has built up a reputation for confidentiality and discretion. There is no way we would countenance any illegality, so we have a policy of not requiring clients looking for a certain type of property to give too much information. You can get up to what you want, so long as you don't involve us in it."

He bent down, opened a desk drawer, took out a key with a label on, and dumped it on the desk between him and his client and said: "We want the keys back within an hour — otherwise you might start using the place rent-free for trade."

He turned his back, and said: "I'm sure you can find your own coat. Good morning to you."

Outside, Jessica met Jim, slipped her arm through his, and said: "If you'd have come in with me you might have got them to treat me a bit differently."

Jim said: "They'd have got quite the wrong idea if I'd have been there. A young lady going into an estate agent with a man — not everyone is modern-minded, you know."

"I suppose not," said Jessica.

When they reached Shepherd Market itself, they found a freshly painted quiet lane which could almost have been in a seaside resort. The houses lining each side were almost twee in their dolls-house quality. There were some Italian cafés, an ironmonger with a window display that, prices apart, could have been left over from before the war, and a few slightly tatty-looking antiques shops, specialising in small, portable items. In many of the doorways, even at 11.30am, stood girls and women of various ages huddling against the drizzle. They were all heavily made-up and wearing cheaply provocative clothes.

Jim started talking quickly to Jessica, perhaps in an effort to stop himself being accosted, or possibly trying to divert her attention from the scene around them.

"I really can't say what an astonishing person you are," he said. "You're totally unlike anyone would expect. It's unusual enough to find a member of the ruling-class with an enlightened attitude — but one quite as unconventional as you is almost unbelievable.

"I mean, you look normal . . ." He blushed. "I mean, a lot better than normal. So many rich liberals seem to think that, because they reject the politics of the Tories, they have to go round looking like bin-men. Real members of the working-class tend to find that a bit condescending, a bit off-putting."

His talking had not diverted Jessica at all from taking in the scene around her, even though she was particularly pleased at the first compliment Jim had ever paid her, even if it was only "a lot better than normal".

They reached the doorway of the bijou pied à terre. It was beside a clean Italian café. There was a blowzy-looking woman leaning on the doorpost, sheltering from the weather. She edged over to let Jessica put the key in the lock, and looked Jim up and down.

"You're new on the patch, aren't you, love?" she said to Jessica.

Jessica smiled at her in a way she hoped would be thought enigmatic. Walking up the lane it had come to her why Fanshaw had acted so strangely. She wasn't shocked, though: more amused. That this street-walker had made a similar mistake was funny, too. The idea of these people living on the edge of society, as they did, was quite attractive. It was tinged with danger, with public outrage, and for Jessica it was therefore tinged with glamour.

Jim answered instead of Jessica. "It's not what you think," he said, in an embarrassed way. Jessica was having difficulty with the stiff doorlock. He put his left hand on top of Jessica's right and helped her operate the key. It was the turn of the young woman in the doorway to provide the enigmatic style. She looked at Jim and said: "That's what they all say. Things never are what they seem."

She edged over, squeezing more tightly into the doorway, to allow Jessica and Jim to pass while still keeping herself dry.

Inside, there was a narrow passage, leading to a flight of stairs. The linoleum on the floor was littered with dead leaves. On and beside the doormat there were various uncollected letters in manilla envelopes and a bright coupon for 3d off a packet of Tide. The stairs were carpeted, but the leading edges of the carpet were worn and the stair rods had not been polished for some time. There was a damp smell of disuse.

Once Jim had entered after her, Jessica reached back past him and shut the door. She turned her head back toward the stairs and raised her chin in a suggestion to Jim that they should go upstairs.

"Do you really think you need to see any more?" he asked.

"Ooh yes," she said, taking a pace toward the stairs. Jim followed.

At the top of the stairs there was a narrow landing with a carpet-runner and a banister. Dim light from a square of diffused glass set in the high ceiling showed four brown-painted doors.

Jessica opened the one to her left, into a tiny room that had most recently been used as a kitchen. The once-patterned lino was worn in the centre, torn at the edges and dirty everywhere. There was a stained, chipped, low-level butler-sink of the type used in the scullery at home for cleaning the muck off muddy boots. Into it dripped one green-encrusted brass tap. There was a green-painted meat safe with a broken hinge, and a plain, solid, deal table with a cast-iron gas ring standing on an asbestos mat near the edge closest to the sink. The short rubber gas piping leading to it was attached to a nozzle behind the sink, preventing the ring from being sited anywhere else. As Jessica stood on the threshold, the sun briefly shone into the room, through a gap in the clouds and through the grime on the window, on to a glass in the sink with a dead, but preserved, daffodil. Jessica did not enter the room, and pulled the door to after a brief look. Over her shoulder, Jim made a loud sniff.

The door next to the kitchen entrance led into a room which had been part dressing-room, part sitting-room. It was equipped with a bedroom-style grate that could not have given out much heat, but the room looked more promising than the previous one. The Chinese-patterned carpet was serviceable, in spite of a few cigarette burns, and there was a deep, comfortable-looking, buttoned sofa. Dominating one wall was a magnificent, mirrored dressing table in kidney-shape style in white-stained wood with pinkish edges. Centrally, in front of the mirror, stood a cut-glass vase, with a few faded dried flowers. A plush music-stool stood, ready for use, in front of the dressing table, and there was a Bakelite telephone, silent, on the floor beside it.

Jessica stepped into the room and placed her case on the stool facing the dressing table. She took off her coat, folded it, and placed it on top of the case. She crossed to look out of the window, down at the street.

Jim came into the room too, but did not cross to the window. Jessica turned to him and asked, brightly: "Well, what do you think?"

"I'd always wondered what one looked like," said Jim.

"One what?"

"Tart's boudoir," said Jim. "I don't think this is a place for someone like you. Perhaps we'd better be going. There's still time to look at some other places."

"Don't be a spoilsport," said Jessica. "I haven't even looked at the place, yet. If you don't want to look, stay here."

She moved toward the door, which was behind Jim, whom she would have to pass. As she did so, she paused, with the intention of giving him a small kiss to show that she did not resent his words and that he should not resent hers.

She tilted back her head and, part closing her eyes, puckered her lips. Her lips were met with his. He moved closer and wrapped her in his arms, one high and the other on the small of her back. Jessica relaxed into his embrace for as long as she felt she should allow herself and then edged back from him. She felt herself grinning widely.

"Whatever made me call you a spoilsport!" she said.

"I don't think we should have done that," said Jim, looking abashed.

"Of course we should," said Jessica. "Now just let me look at the rest of the place. Stay there if you prefer."

On her own, she looked into the bathroom. It was opposite the kitchen and no larger, but at least it had a hot water supply, fed from a gas-operated geyser. One side of the bathroom was entirely taken up by the geyser and an enormous, Edwardian cast-iron bath with claw feet. There was a long dark-brown stain on the white enamel. A small handbasin and old WC pedestal stood, side by side, under a window opposite the door. A piece of raffia replaced the normal chain of the WC's overhead cistern.

The fourth door was to the bedroom. If Jim had called the sitting room a tart's boudoir, what would he say when he saw this! Apart from the fireplace, there were just two, enormous items of furniture. They dominated the room, leaving only enough exposed floor for a small fur rug. There was a vast old wardrobe, its front entirely covered in mirror glass, which reflected in its dusty surface the largest bed Jessica had ever seen. There did not appear to be any bedclothes on it except for a maroon counterpane of crushed velveteen over a lumpy bolster. There was another enormous mirror on the wall behind the bed-head and a third on the wall opposite the window.

Jim was right, of course. The flat was almost entirely unsuitable. Jessica had come out looking for an office. This was dirty and expensive and had dubious neighbours. It was, though, the dubious neighbours which gave the flat its perverse, louche charm. There was a certain magical sophistication about the place. Jessica felt that, if she moved in, it would be the end of her days as a schoolgirl. Even the proprietor would have to accept that she had grown up.

She did have to admit that it was not the perfect address for her office. The thousands of visitors the Fund would doubtless attract would be most nonplussed, but there might be nothing wrong with creating an air of mystery.

Although she had decided that she wanted to have the flat, she wanted to be *told* she could have it. It was her decision, but she wanted to feel that it had been someone else's, and that she had just acted on it. She looked around the preposterous bedroom once more and returned to the room next door, where Jim was sitting at one end of the couch, the end with the raised back. He had taken off his raincoat. Jessica's opened case was on the seat beside him and he was flipping through the estate agents' lists. He looked up and smiled as she came through the door.

"I want it, Jim," she said.

He looked a bit concerned and said: "I know it's none of my business, but you did ask me along for advice . . ."

Jessica felt that he was not going to provide the instant support that she wanted. He was set on being difficult, it would seem. He was going to tell her not be a silly, little girl, to grow up and be responsible. But what he said did not turn out to be as bad as she expected. It was quite wise, really.

". . . I think you should look around once more, and write down all the good things and the bad things about it. Then go home and do nothing about it till tomorrow, to give yourself time to think. Then, if you're still set on it, you can talk to the agent again."

It was quite good advice. If only the proprietor was as sane and calm in his judgment.

Jim stuffed the estate agents' lists back into the case and put the case on the floor by his feet. He put his right hand, palm downward, on the couch and said: "Why don't you sit down?"

Jessica moved over and sat down on the spot indicated, and then edged an inch or two closer. She looked, slightly upward, into Jim's eyes. He said: "I think you've got to decide why it is you want this place. It's obviously totally unsuitable for using as offices, but I think you know that."

Jessica nodded, as she was bidden. She feared what might be coming next.

"I suppose you want to prove your independence, to get somewhere where you can set up on your own, to prove that you can think, and act, and live for yourself. The whole idea is nothing to do with the Fund, is it?"

Jessica nodded in a contrite fashion. She saw herself back at one of her schools, having been found out in some misdemeanour. "You won't think the less of me because of this? I know I'm being silly," she said.

She reached out with her right hand, half turned toward Jim and, for a moment, gripped his hand firmly.

Jim beamed. "Far from it," he said. "I envy you. When I was your age I was still living with my father and mother. I didn't manage to get my own place till much later. Even then, I didn't have nearly enough points for the council to rehouse me, so it was a bit corrupt, really."

Jessica looked perplexed. She didn't understand about council houses.

Jim said: "After all, ordinary people couldn't possibly afford a rent like this. Even then, I think they'd prefer a bit more respectability for their money. After all, a council rent could be 13s 4d — it would always be less than £1. If you've decided to get a flat, why don't you look at some others?"

"But it's this one I want," said Jessica. "I didn't realise it until we came here, but now I know."

"Why? It's not the nicest of areas."

Jessica paused for a moment and then, recognising her own real motive, sighed. She said: "It's because it's so naughty, I suppose. The proprietor will be livid when he finds out I've got a flat. If he knew who my neighbours were, he'd go apoplectic! There's no telling what he'd do."

Jim said: "Are you sure that angering him is the best basis for making a decision?"

"You bet!" said Jessica.

Jim looked impressed. "I've rarely come across such strength of feeling, even in a Communist," he said.

"How do I become a Communist?" asked Jessica. She paused, looked at the expression in Jim's face, and said: "I'm not just being flippant. It's a serious and genuine request."

"They don't take just anyone, you know," said Jim, at first leaning back and then bending forward till his face was less than six inches from Jessica's. "They have to be convinced that the Party will gain from your joining."

But then he said: "I wouldn't mind trying to convince them, though."

He brought his right arm around Jessica's waist. She moved toward him so their bodies were touching, and tilted her head back to be kissed.

At the end of a long embrace, Jessica tried to think of something to say to defuse the tension. "Have I passed the exam?" she said.

Jim took his hands away from encircling her body to loosen his tie. He undid his front collar stud and the three top buttons of his shirt, took hold of Jessica's right wrist and guided her hand inside his shirt. His own hands returned to her upper body, holding her tightly to him once more. They kissed again.

Jessica was glad the deciding was being done for her. As she was being kissed, she readjusted the position of her trapped hand, and felt the warmth of Jim's chest at her fingertips. Through the shirt material and the wool of her jersey, the back of her fingers encountered the hard stitching of her own brassiere. So this was what being naughty felt like.

Jim disengaged his mouth from hers to murmur in her ear: "Don't stop; I like it."

Jessica didn't know what it was she hadn't to stop, but she was pleased Jim liked it, whatever it was. For herself, she wasn't so much enjoying what was going on as being interested in it. The whole thing was really very funny. Nothing like this had ever happened to her before. She wondered what was supposed to happen next in such circumstances.

Jim stopped stroking her through her skirt and sweater, undid her belt and put his hand, then half his arm, inside her jersey. He started feeling her again, his fingers beginning to explore under the edges of her brassiere. Jessica supposed that she ought to be doing something. In the books, the heroine would slap his face and yell something. But then he might stop and she wouldn't find out what happened next. Either that or he wouldn't stop, and then Jessica would have to admit that she had lost control. So she didn't slap and she didn't yell, which made her feel guilty. At the same time, she felt concerned because she was not enjoying herself, even though she had so longed to be taken in Jim's arms. Perhaps she should be trying harder. As she lay there, not knowing quite what to do, Jim undid his fly buttons, took Jessica's left hand and guided it inside his trousers to his humid and bulging underpants.

She didn't feel called upon to say anything, which was a relief. She might very well have said the wrong thing. Jim was not in a position to say very much, either. He was no longer kissing her lips but had taken her jersey off and unfastened her brassiere. He was massaging one breast and had the nipple of the other between his teeth. The humid mound in Jessica's hand grew in size and firmness.

It was as if Jim had been waiting for a cue. Disengaging from her breast, he whispered in her nearest ear. "That's it," he said. The rush of breath was exciting. "Now take my clothes off."

Jessica started to have second thoughts about her desire to be dominated. Jim started taking off his clothes unaided, fairly slowly because he kept pausing to kiss and touch Jessica in some new place and to strip her clothes off too. He had a certain amount of difficulty when it came to her girdle, but managed well enough. Jessica noted that he had evidently performed the manoeuvre before. He appeared to have finished when he himself was entirely naked. He'd even taken off his socks, she noted. Her own girdle had gone, but Jim apparently wanted her to keep one of her stockings on. At any rate, it hadn't joined the other clothes cast into a muddled heap on the floor at the end of the sofa.

Jessica found herself to all intents naked and squeezed into the back of the narrow piece of furniture. Jim was pressing his large, muscled, pale body against her. In her hand she still gripped his enormous, hard, ugly penis. At least Jessica assumed it was enormous; she had not seen others for comparison.

She did not let go, but said in what came out as a rather half-hearted squeak: "I think we'd better stop now, Jim."

He pushed his body firmly against hers, took her whole ear into his mouth and breathed: "Not now. We're just getting to the interesting part."

Might there be no let-up? Jim squeezed harder, and then he put the fingers of one hand into her mouth. Jessica supposed she was intended to suck them. What strange things people did to each other. She rejected the passing thought of biting them off, and sucked. The wet fingers next manifested themselves between her legs.

"No, you mustn't," she said, with alarm. "Stop! Stop!"

"Bourgeois conventions aren't for us," said Jim, his fingers stopping their rubbing, but not withdrawing. "We can fight the class war here as well as on the streets."

Jessica could not see any logic in the remark, but, perversely, felt unable to wrest herself free from Jim's firm embrace. She didn't want to upset him. He was forcing himself on her but Jessica felt embarrassed about resisting. Pathetic. She went limp, let go of the man's pulsating penis and decided to abandon herself to whatever might take place.

Jim stopped and, slipping his fingers out of her, murmured: "What's wrong, Jessica? Have I done something to upset you?"

"No Jim. It's just that I didn't expect my first time to be like this. I expected something different."

Jim looked surprised. He slowly twisted round to sit up, moving Jessica with him. As they sat up, beside each other, Jim naked and Jessica with nothing on but her Rolex and one tan stocking, he said: "You're a virgin?"

Jessica, taken aback at the use of such a word, looked apologetically down at the clothes, most of them in an untidy pile, the rest scattered around the dusty room.

She nodded and, tension released, burst into laughter. Jim laughed too, but rather more ruefully. "I'm sorry, Jessica," he said. "I didn't mean to take advantage of you. I didn't want to hurt you." She noticed that what she had thought to be a huge penis was by now just a small and shrivelled piece of flesh.

Jim moved around the room, retrieving items of clothing and either putting them on or passing them to Jessica.

"I hope, despite my filthy behaviour, you'll see me again — but I suppose your office-hunting may be over," he said, while sitting down, putting on his socks. He stood up and made to look around for his shoes, while saying, as if incidentally: "It's a terrible thing to admit, but I think I'm falling in love."

"What's so terrible about that," said Jessica, enormously relieved. "I've been in love with you ever since I first saw you."

"It was a sort of half-joke," said Jim, by now fully clothed except for his raincoat. "Certain misguided revolutionaries followed the 'glass of water' theory: that Communists should avoid emotional entanglements and should satisfy their sexual lusts as they would drink a glass of water, quickly and in order to survive, but without any personal love to distract them from the revolutionary cause. I don't agree with that myself."

At Jessica's request, which she made to sound casual but which was heartfelt, Jim agreed to return and teach her more about revolutionary theory. It seemed to be accepted that Jessica would be renting the place. Jim promised to help her move in, starting, estate agents willing, in two days. At the top of the stairs the two kissed once more. Just before they parted, as a silent declaration of intent Jessica put her hand on Jim's crotch and squeezed the concealed bulge.

Jim descended the stairs, went through the front door and pulled it shut behind him. The streetwalker was still in the doorway, sheltering from the continuing slight drizzle. She said: "It wasn't what I thought then love?"

Jim shook his head slowly and said: "Things never are," before walking down to Piccadilly to catch a bus to work.

As he went he thought about Jessica's statement "I've been in love with you since the moment I first saw you" and wondered why he had not replied in kind. Perhaps, he thought, he did not wish to admit certain things to himself by putting them into words. It was always easier to make jokes or to talk about politics.

There was nothing much doing at the *Tribune* and Jim left work far earlier than he had been managing of late. He got back to Bromley before Sheilagh had even started making tea. "You're early," she said, without the trace of hostility Jim had come to expect.

"There's something we've been missing from our lives," said Jim, as he drew her close and undid the top button of her blouse. He then took her by the hand and led her upstairs to bed, where they spent the whole evening.

At the beginning of their partnership their explorations of each other had been infrequent, clandestine but long-drawn-out and majestically exhilarating. When Jim had managed to get the house they found themselves in sexual coitus sometimes several times a day, in every room of the house and on, under and beside every item of furniture, particularly the kitchen table. But the passion had not lasted. As the couple learned quick ways to receive and provide pleasure their intercourse became less frequent, less protracted, and more mechanical.

This night, somehow, was a return to previous times. Jim wondered whether it was their last time. Into the night, as they lay together in a soggy heap of bedclothes, Sheilagh stroked Jim on the chest and said: "It's over now, isn't it, Jim?"

Jim thought of misconstruing the question, or statement, not wanting an argument at such a time, but in the end he said: "We've had a good time, Sheilagh."

"Yes," she said. "Is it anyone I know? Is she a Comrade as usual? That would make it worse."

"How on earth did you know?"

Jim looked glum, the euphoria of the evening's sexual excitement having rapidly disappeared. Sheilagh pulled the wet bedsheets up to her neck and said: "Well, is she a Comrade?"

"No, but I think she's going to become one," said Jim.

Sheilagh said she hoped Jim was not going to try to turf her out of the house, because she had nowhere else to go. This was something Jim had not thought about; he had not looked that far ahead. Sheilagh said a decision was urgent, since, although she had been sleeping with Sørensen, she was unable to move in with him since his wife suffered from small-minded petty-bourgeois attitudes and wouldn't have a rival in the house.

"This is outrageous," said Jim. "You mean to tell me you've been going to bed with the Regional Industrial Organiser of the Communist Party, who has been setting me loyalty tests, and you have the cheek to say it would 'make it worse' if I'd been seeing a woman Comrade!"

"You make me sick," said Sheilagh. "Sørensen warned me that you'd be like this. You've no concept at all of revolutionary morality!"

9

Thursday 2nd August to Wednesday 31st October 1956

After her unpleasant experience with the estate agent, Jessica conducted her negotiations about the flat over the telephone. She had held on to the key to avoid having to confront Fanshaw again. She even managed to get a reduction in the rent to 12½ guineas a week, after stressing stressed the long-term nature of her interest and the purpose of high moral value for which the flat would be used.

Jessica had by now opened an account at Drummond's[1] into which she paid the Beaverbrook cheque. She gave her new address to the bank for correspondence.

When she told the proprietor of the find she had made, he did not refer to his previous insistence on her using offices at the *Tribune*. She did not know how to explain his new attitude but assumed that he had failed to stop the cheque in time. The proprietor did not even object to the address, and went so far as to compliment Jessica on choosing Mayfair, a district with known social cachet. He offered to lend the services of Fibbins for a day or two to help her get the office furniture moved in but Jessica said that that was already taken care of. Mrs Burgess said that she would come and help supervise any cleaning that had had to be done, but Jessica said that that was in hand, too.

She had decided on the flat in order to shock the proprietor, but by now she was feeling rather too embarrassed about her decision to capitalise on it. She realised the decision might have been more to convince herself that she was capable of anything than actually to shock the proprietor. If she was really going to be independent, minor acts of rebellion would not be needed anymore.

Jessica was not intending actually to live at her flat. The sitting room would become an office and the bedroom would there as an added extra — the room for her and Jim, she hoped. She still knew next to nothing about him, not even whether he was married. She believed he might be, and tried to convince herself that this made him even more exciting and their forthcoming liaison even more desirable.

On the Friday morning, Jessica went by Underground to Sloane Square to buy bedsheets at Peter Jones[2]. The ones in Mrs Burgess's linen cupboard were not large enough for the oversize bed in Shepherd Market and, even if they had been suitable, their absence would have been noticed. When it came to paying for the sheets, Jessica had to put them on the family account as her chequebook had not been issued. The appearance of a set of sheets on the monthly bill would be just as difficult to explain as a pair missing from the linen room, but Jessica decided to ignore the problem. She added some cleaning materials and a pair of rubber gloves to the bill. She certainly wasn't going to wait to have the goods delivered, and took the large parcel with her on the Underground to Green Park and on foot through the streets from there. At least this day was the first for a long time when it wasn't raining. Jessica passed the ever-present group of streetwalkers who, she noted, never appeared to get any daytime trade, and let herself into her new flat.

It was dingier than she remembered. The dirt was unpleasant, rather than charming. Jessica went into the bedroom, looked in shame at the preposterous arrangement of mirrors, and then made up the bed with her expensive, fresh, new, white sheets.

She started some dusting in the room she thought of as the office. She abandoned the task half-done and turned to cleaning the windows from the inside. The job threatened her dress, which was a bright flowered print on a largely white background, so it was partly with a sense of relief that she saw Jim walking up the street. He was carrying his raincoat folded over his left arm, partly obscuring the small, brown-paper bag he was also carrying. He was on time, but for Jessica that was far too early for her to have sorted herself out. Could he not come back next month, next year? The closer he came, the more fearful Jessica became. Perhaps she wasn't grown-up enough for what she was doing. She was in love, a state which was ideal when she was thinking about Jim in his absence and yearning for him. His actual presence, the fulfilment of the dream, was an intrusion.

Jim himself may have been feeling something similar — he disappeared from view when opposite the street door and there was a disturbingly long delay before he rattled on the letterbox. Jessica peeled off her rubber gloves and went downstairs, stepping on the edges of the stair treads to avoid making any creaks. She stood just inside the door, her hand on the latch. Please make him go away.

Jim waited for possibly half a minute before knocking on the door. Jessica opened it, and said, breathlessly, as if she had just run down the stairs: "I've missed you, Jim."

Jim came in and pushed the door closed behind him. The two of them stood in the dingy corridor and kissed. Jessica held him in both hands, while Jim clasped her round the waist with his right arm. His left was still holding his coat and the paper bag.

Jessica did not want the embrace to end, because she did not know how to tell Jim what she wanted him to do next. She wanted him to take her into the bedroom and get the whole business over with. Instead, when he stopped kissing her, Jim took the paper bag and offered it to her, saying: "I'd like you to have this. I've had it specially made for you."

Jessica withdrew a slim volume, bound in red cloth boards. There was no title on the cover. When she opened it, she saw on the flyleaf the handwritten words *To Jessica Ross on 3rd August 1956. From Jim Anstruther. We have a world to win.*[3]

As she took the book, Jim said: "You don't know much about me, and I felt this might explain."

Jessica could still see no title page. She said: "Thank you, but what is it?"

He told her: "It's the *Communist Manifesto*, by Marx and Engels, 1848. This edition comes from the Soviet Union, but I've had some of the lads at the *Tribune* bind it specially. It's more useful work for them than printing the paper."

Jessica said she was sure it was, and took Jim upstairs by the hand, to the door of the bedroom. "I don't think you've been in this room yet, Jim," she said, opening the door and leading him in.

Jim looked at the multiple reflection of the vast bed in the arrangement of mirrors, appeared a bit shocked, and said: "I thought you said you were a virgin."

Jessica shut the door, summoned up her courage, and blurted out: "I don't think I will be by the end of the day."

What followed was unlike what she had expected, imagined, hoped for or feared.

She had not so much wanted to have the encounter as wanted to be able to look back on it. She wanted to lose her virginity not for any possible pleasure in the act itself but so that she could believe herself grown-up. Naked in bed, their clothes again strewn around the room, she looked at Jim's body. The rugged face and the hairy chest were not followed up with a corresponding physique.

He had muscles, but not like those of the men with shirts off who dig up the roads. He was neither skinny or overweight and his skin was pale. Jessica would have welcomed a few tattoos; real ones, like a serpent wrapped round a dripping dagger. Perhaps she might get tattooed herself, so she could look at it in the mirror.

The whole business of losing one's honour appeared to take a particularly long time. Jim was being most considerate, which denied Jessica the thrill of abandoning herself to fate. He was evidently nervous about hurting her, which meant that, instead of being swept along on a tide of helplessness, Jessica felt that she would have to make the moves herself. In doing so, she felt for the first time dirty. "Take me, Jim, take me," she shouted.

"I'd better put this on first," said Jim, picking a foil packet out of a pocket of his discarded trousers. So he'd known what they would do that morning.

It was not as painful as she expected, but it carried with it very little other emotion, either. She did not at first realise that it was over but when Jim ceased his rhythmic thrusts with a sigh, and Jessica realised that the act was probably completed. She wondered whether she would ever learn to enjoy it, and what there was about it that could ever be enjoyable. With Jim a spent force alongside, his dwindling penis still inside her, and a small patch of blood on the new sheets, Jessica wondered what to say. Sorry, perhaps. Or, I'll try harder next time.

Jim, though, didn't seem to expect anything to be said. He lay there, smiling to himself, stroking her naked body with far more genuine affection and less mechanical purpose than he had shown before. "That was perfect," he said. "I'd always wondered what it was like with a virgin."

It struck Jessica as an unpleasant remark, startlingly impersonal after what they had just done. Jim sensed her reaction and said: "No one in my whole life has given me anything as beautiful as you just have. I don't deserve to have someone as good as you as my lover."

The words — particularly "my lover" — thrilled Jessica. Jim rolled over, releasing a small further flow of fluids on to the sheets, took off the French letter and hung it over the bedhead. He sat on the edge of the bed and started putting on his clothes.

It appeared not to be the done thing to talk about what they had just done. "They've started calling up the Reserves today," Jim said. "They've got no idea what century it is. Such behaviour was out of date even in 1856."

Jessica dressed too, putting on her discarded, bright summer dress. She felt strangely empty and lonely for a minute, and then followed Jim into the next room. She asked him how he'd known about the call-up; Lear had said it was to be a secret. It was in the first edition of the evening papers, apparently. She told Jim that she was worried about Lear, even though she did not even particularly like him. She still knew nothing about Jim, and the *Communist Manifesto* wasn't likely to answer the sort of questions she wanted answers to. Despite their recent intimacy she felt inhibited about asking.

Picking up from the remarks about Lear, Jim did tell her, though. He had been living with "a certain person," he said — not letting Sheilagh's name past his lips. Apart from that he was fairly honest, particularly about how he had been much to blame for their drifting apart, and his shock at the revelation that she had been living with him while sleeping with Sørensen, whom he described as "a senior Party official". He did not mention quite how recently this had taken place and was vague about their current sleeping arrangements (as he had to be since he didn't know himself whether either or neither of them would sleep on the sofa until Sheilagh moved out).

The words "a senior Party official" allowed Jim a natural way back into talking about politics, a subject he was more at ease with. Apparently, he was not going to allow this act of treachery affect his devotion to the Communist Party, although he might find it more difficult if this particular official set another test of discipline for him like the last one, when he had to try to talk a group of angry strikers into blacklegging on their own dispute.

That day was to prove the precursor of many similar ones. As the weeks went by, what was almost a routine developed. Jessica would have breakfast, frequently with the proprietor and Mrs Burgess. At the same time as the proprietor set out by car to the *Tribune*, Jessica would go by Underground and on foot to Mayfair. Jim would arrive shortly afterwards and they would talk, usually politics, and then go to bed. Normally that way round. Frequently they did not use the bedroom with its huge, groaning bed and opulent arrangement of mirrors but chose instead other areas. Jim seemed particularly fond of the new office desk. She didn't see why they had to use the desk or the kitchen table when they had such a good bedroom, but Jim insisted that it was a perfectly working-class thing to do. After a while, Jessica began to enjoy the sexual act for its own sake rather than just as a way of proving to herself that she was grown-up and naughty. Still, however inventive and enthusiastic she became she never quite felt herself totally a participant and always something of a spectator. Sometimes she marvelled at what it was she was up to.

In the early afternoon, Jim would go off to the *Tribune* by bus and Jessica would turn her attention to a few hours of work for the Fund. She had a brass plaque made for the front door. Sometimes visitors would call, afternoons only, by appointment. She got a typewriter and managed to produce her own letters. She put the telephone in a drawer so that its bell was muffled and she did not feel required to answer it when she didn't want to, as was the case principally in the mornings.

She worked hard on the Fund, the first real job of her life. She tried a bit of fundraising by sending letters out to likely prospects but always received far more messages and resolutions in support than she did cheques. Still, apart from the rent and a few postage stamps, her costs were not high and the Beaverbrook money would last a long time. She started building up a file of press cuttings from such magazines as *Boxing News*[4] and each time a boxer was injured in the ring she used to send off letters to the editors of the various newspapers. Sometimes they were printed — the *Tribune* in particular had a good record on this.

Because of her late start she generally found it necessary to work late into the evening, which was good because it meant avoiding having arguments at home. She started to make a bit of a name for herself and was a great help to Lords and MPs, generally Liberal or Labour, who agreed with her campaign. By and by, people began to call on her at the office to look at her files. The Labour MP the Right Hon Dr Edith Summerskill[5], who had just published a book on *The Ignoble Art*, was one of her more frequent visitors. Occasionally a punch-drunk boxer would call by, hoping for a handout, but Jessica explained that she had no funds for individual cases. She dreaded the possibility of George Crawford turning up.

Gradually the place began to look more like an office, too. The first weekend, Jessica brought in some building workers to redecorate the premises. Out went the dusty picture-rails and the dirty cast-iron fireplaces, to be replaced with smoothly papered walls and gas fires. The smokeless zone[6] already declared for the City was bound to be extended to the West End soon and then the fireplaces would be useless. It was a pity to see them go, but worth it since it meant the air would always be clean in the future[7].

In the bathroom, the men had to break up the huge, claw-footed Edwardian tub with sledgehammers to get it down the stairs. The gas-ring, the meat-safe and the chipped butler-sink in the kitchen went and modern appliances with Formica worktops were brought in. Jessica made sure that the refrigerator was the self-same Kelvinator from Gamages where she and Jim had met up. The bedroom remained unaltered, except for a brass plate marked **PRIVATE** which Jessica had attached to the door.

The builders could only work at weekends. They were on other contracts that required them to work for various councils during the week. This was fine, because as well as allowing her to be alone with Jim on weekday mornings it meant that there was no shortage of cheap, otherwise scarce, building materials.

She did not tell Jim about the building workers, sensing that he would not approve. He had a clearly defined sense of morality — whereas he would think nothing of leading a strike on a trumped-up excuse he made a point of putting the plug in the basin when he washed his hands, in order to save water. Water, he said, was an example of what everything would be like under communism. Anything you could possibly need would be available in super-abundance. There would enough of everything for everyone, free of charge. People wouldn't waste things just because they didn't have to pay, he said. It was just like now: you didn't leave the taps running when you didn't want a bath, even though no one charged you for the extra water.

Jessica did not enjoy talking about eventual communism nearly as much as decrying the present state of things. The Suez crisis filled both her and Jim with anger.

He said VE Day[8] had fallen just two days after his 21st birthday, but he had not been allowed to take part in the second world war. He said he'd tried to join up but he kept being rejected for service — he had always supposed that they didn't want too many Young

Communists in the ranks. As it was, people had often assumed he must have been a conscientious objector[9]. Now that the war bugles were again sounding, but for a far less deserving cause, he would welcome the chance of being labelled an objector, if anyone would listen. He said he'd rather fight for the Egyptians than for Mr Eden, at least they were on the right side in the war against capitalism.

As the months passed and the British armed forces began their astonishingly ponderous build-up, Jim went in to the *Tribune* each day to take part in what he saw as the production process for the British propaganda machine. His union colleagues showed little concern as they churned out papers with headlines such as: **SUEZ CANAL CONFERENCE TELLS NASSER: HANDS OFF!** or **MENZIES GROUP MEETS NASSER ON SUEZ**[10], or **NASSER TELLS MENZIES: MIND YOUR OWN BUSINESS**, or **U.N. GANGS UP ON BRITAIN OVER SUEZ**, then **DULLES CHICKENS OUT: U.S. WON'T FIGHT NASSER**[11]**, and ISRAELIS INVADE**[12], followed by **BRITAIN GOES TO WAR** and **EGYPTIAN AIRFIELDS BOMBED**. Six days after that headline, on Wednesday, 31st October, the comps made up the front page with **BRITAIN AND FRANCE INVADE: NASSER ON THE RUN**.

Many of the other papers were considerably more rabid in their attacks: the *Daily Sketch* disgraced itself on the 14th September with **GAITSKELL THE NASSER-HELPER**[13].

That the *Tribune* was not more gung-ho than it was about the build-up to war may have been due in part to the efforts of Jessica, forced as she was to live at home with the paper's proprietor.

Jim was insistent on this. He told Jessica of how he went home each night to his Bromley council house where, as often as not he met the cold-eyed "certain person," with her doctrinal rigidity and constant complaints about his bourgeois-deviationist tendency;

how she was always just about to move out so he could get back his own bedroom; and how she never quite did. He said he varied his morning route in to see Jessica for fear of being spotted, as he knew full well that if their liaison became known about he would lose his job. If by some miracle he was not sacked by the *Tribune* for having an affair with the boss's daughter, it was certain the men would no longer accept him as Imperial Father and he would find himself back as a stereotyper in the foundry. (In response to Jessica's frown he corrected his words to "being in love with the boss's adopted daughter".)

Besides, he said, if she managed to bring herself to be polite to the proprietor, she would be very likely to inherit the newspaper. Just think what she would be able to do with it. It might not be doing too well at the moment, but just imagine the millions of copies it would sell if it started telling the truth. If, instead of this Tory tripe, a paper started to speak to the working class in their own language. The *Daily Herald*[14] was hidebound and tame, trapped by the right wing of the Labour Party and the dead hand of the class-collaborationists on the TUC leadership, while the *Daily Worker* was handicapped by lack of money and resources. Jim said that if she was in charge, the *Tribune* could turn the Tories out of Britain forever.

Jessica accepted all of that as the formal reasons she could give herself for passing the nights under the same roof as the proprietor, but she enjoyed the deception as well. She would look over the breakfast table at the proprietor while thinking of what naughtiness she was going to get up to later on with his senior union official. She enjoyed thrilling herself by giving slight hints of what she was up to, such as "I expect to have a hard day at the office," or "things are getting a bit on top of me these days".

With her secret, she no longer felt such a strong need to be particularly unpleasant to the proprietor, and confined her attacks on him to the *Tribune*'s coverage of the Suez crisis.

"Look," he told her on one occasion, "I really don't know what you've got to complain about. You can't imagine anyone from my background comparing Nasser with Hitler. I think the *Tribune* has been fairly straight on the whole affair. Your complaint isn't with the paper, it's with the news it's reporting. I don't even write the paper myself, I set the general policy and let other people do the writing as often as not. What goes in is up to Artemus Jones, after all. Why, just the other day he had a signed article by Hugh Gaitskell and I didn't even complain."

"That's another thing," said Jessica. "I thought you were going to sack him. He's an odious creep and I want him to go."

"I've changed my mind," said the proprietor. "I've decided he can stay on for a little while longer — but I haven't told him, of course. I want to keep him on his toes."

"But you promised!" said Jessica.

"Did I really?" said the proprietor. "Oh well. Doesn't matter — there's someone else I'm looking at anyway. Perhaps I'll give them both the job. That will really make them work hard."

If Jessica was particularly concerned with Suez over these months, seeing the stupid British class system at work in all its puny arrogance, Jim was getting worked up about another topic as well. He was reading as much as he could in the papers, and decoding the reports in the *Daily Worker*, to find out about the exciting events in Poland and Hungary and in the Soviet Union itself.

As he explained to Jessica, he was no hard-line Stalin-lover. He had joined the Young Communist League in 1941 when he was just 17 because the Russians appeared to be the only people who were doing anything against Hitler. He didn't think communism mean repression; for him it meant freedom. He was so pleased when he heard about Khrushchev's secret speech[15] to the congress of the Communist Party of the Soviet Union denouncing Stalin's distortion of Party principles and Party democracy.

For many of the newspapers, Russia was not so much the birthplace of tyranny as the home of two other news phenomena: the Bolshoi ballet[16] which was so exciting Londoners and of the discus-thrower Nina Ponomareva[17], holed up in the Soviet embassy to avoid theft charges involving five 32s 11d hats missing from C&A[18].

In October, while Jessica watched the United Nations dithering over Suez, Jim was trying to find out about the new, liberal-minded, open policies of the Polish United Workers' Party and their acceptance by the Soviet leadership.

The *Daily Worker* was surprisingly straight in its reporting, using the same Western news agencies as the other papers, but the reports were never prominent and were frequently days late. He had to turn to Sefton Delmer in the *Daily Express* for the fullest accounts. From late October, even the *Daily Sketch* took time off from its coverage of the rock 'n roll riots[19], dance-hall troubles and the "petting problem"[20] to look with glee at the rapidly moving events in Poland and Hungary. After Khrushchev decided not to use troops in Poland, the Hungarian rebels were apparently surprised when their own army turned on them. It all appeared to be over, though, after Imre Nagy's new Communist government quit the Warsaw Pact[21] and told the Russians to go home, enabling the *Sketch* to report triumphantly **COMMUNIST RULE ENDS IN HUNGARY.**

On that day, as British and French troops massed in Cyprus for their imperial adventure in Suez, the Soviet Union denounced their actions as "a crude violation". Jim in turn marvelled at the Hungarian workers taking government into their own hands.

"See," he told Jessica, "that's one in the eye for all those people who say Communists aren't democrats."

By now, though, Jessica was receiving different opinions on the matter, and wasn't so sure. She knew she was in love with Jim, but she would have preferred him to be a little tougher.

10

Saturday 3rd & Sunday 4th September 1956

A month into his latest sexual adventure, Jim was still in a period of heightened excitement where he was prepared to put his time with Jessica before most of the other things he was supposed to be doing. He knew his union work was suffering, although he believed the members had not begun to notice.

The mornings he would previously have spent writing reports or filing were now more enjoyably occupied. Party activity generally slackened off during August, but Jim had not even been carrying out the minimal requirements, such as selling the *Daily Worker*. The only time he had for this work was on Saturdays now, when there was no *Tribune* to produce and when Jessica had the builders in. He usually had his own house to himself, as Sheilagh was frequently off with Sørensen, who generally managed to find some urgent Party crisis away from London at weekends.

He was often unable to concentrate and, instead of attending to union or Party business, went off and joined the queue at the golf course. He recognised that he was not setting a fine example of devotion to the cause, but couldn't help it. He was in love, in a quite illogical and dangerous way. The danger was an intrinsic and exquisite part of it, linked with the feeling of subverting the ruling class from the inside.

This particular Saturday was the first time since their meeting beside the Kelvinator that the two had been out of doors together. Jim would have loved to be able to display Jessica, to be seen hand in hand in hand with her in the streets of London, but felt he had to settle for some town where neither of them was known. They decided to go to the coast. They felt safe with Deal because no one either of them knew had ever mentioned going there. It was not the Southend beloved of East End printers on a day out nor the Brighton favoured by the sleazy section of the moneyed class.

Jim arrived at the flat at 9am by motor cycle. He did not let himself with his new key but waited outside for Jessica to arrive and brief the builders. She was wearing Jim's favourite dress, the brilliant white one with the tight bodice and voluminous skirt that she had worn to the television studios. It was gloriously impractical for a motor cycle. For the first couple of hours of the journey, to avoid a chance recognition, she had to sit in the sidecar, the bulky skirt crushed in around her. In the sidecar, enclosed by mica windows, there was next to no view as she bumped up and down. The rain held off for them and, after Jim had driven through the London traffic and along the Dover Road to Canterbury, he stopped to let Jessica on to the pillion for the final few miles. A scarf protected her hair from the wind, but she had to hold her skirt tightly to her legs to avoid it blowing over her head. Jim was wearing a sports jacket, his waterproofs staying unused in the sidecar behind Jessica's seat. She clung on to Jim's waist fiercely.

In Deal they found a charming town untouched by the modern age. There were certainly no rioting Teddy-boys driven mad by the crude, animal strains of rock 'n roll. There was a busy market, but in the narrow main street the shops were preparing to roll up the awnings for Saturday early-closing[1]. A haberdashery stood nextdoor to a gentlemen's outfitter, each of them with window displays protected by yellow Cellophane blinds.

At the ancient town hall, which doubled as the register office, Jessica made Jim pause to watch a couple coming out on to the steps to be photographed. Jim considered making a joke about the wedding they had intruded on, but thought better of it. In fact, the spectacle did not repulse him as he felt it probably should, if he had a correct understanding of bourgeois morality. Jessica looked at Jim with a grin, and he kissed her. Under his jacket, Jessica squeezed his testicles.

In the grand but seedy Royal Hotel, Jessica and Jim ate what the menu described as luncheon, in a dining room built out over the lapping shore. The edges of the carpet were bound with white-painted leather, in the style of the stairs leading to the cheap seats in a theatre. There was no one else in the room apart from them and an elderly waiter, and the echoing emptiness embarrassed them into talking in whispers. They looked out at the fishermen repairing their nets by the car-park. On their plates the fish was stale.

In the afternoon, they drove around looking for the coal mines for which the area was known. They did not see anyone who was obviously a miner, but when they rode round the tidy pit-village of Aylesham Jessica kept nudging Jim with her thighs, pointing and saying into his ear: "Do you think he might be one?"

They stopped for their tea at a shop near Canterbury Cathedral and tried to egg each other into staying the night in a guest house. In the end, Jessica admitted that she had told the proprietor she would be back as usual that evening. That made Jim say: "A promise is a promise."

As the sky darkened, they took the road back, Jessica again in the draughty sidecar.

Jim drew to a stop in the road beside Regent's Park, just a short walk for Jessica to the proprietorial home. Jim helped her out of the sidecar and she stood on the pavement near a streetlight. The harsh, blue-tinged mercury-vapour light exaggerated her features and transfigured her dress into a glowing azure icon, the atmosphere fog-free because of the recent rain. Jim took a step toward her and she told him: "I want you to marry me."

He kissed her, told her he loved her and, in a fright, rode off into the darkness.

On the long, cold ride back to Bromley, he wondered whether he had as much courage as Jessica. Neither of them could possibly afford to get married. There would as like as not be no inheritance for her as well as no job for him. Matters such as that did not appear to bother her as they did him.

As he parked the machine, he noticed that he had not turned off the bedroom light and wondered at his carelessness. That was what being in love did for you.

Inside, Sheilagh met him. She was standing on the bottom stair and was wearing his dressing-gown. "I've been neglecting you," she said. He continued on into the kitchen. Sheilagh followed him.

He had adopted the manner with her of being coldly correct. "I thought you were off with Sørensen this weekend," he said.

"No," she said. "The Central Committee's running a big campaign over Suez," as if that was any explanation.

Jim poured himself a glass of milk.

"You look cold," Sheilagh said, moving close to him. "Let me warm you up." She dropped the dressing gown to the floor. With her left hand she took the glass out of Jim's hand and put it on the table, and then pulled his head down to the level of her breasts. With the other hand she parted his jacket, entered his fly and gently squeezed his testicles.

"You mustn't feel jealous of Sørensen," she said. "Take me to bed. Jealousy is just the figleaf for bourgeois hypocrisy."

Jim straightened his tie, looking for something cutting to say, while nonetheless finding it impossible to hide his sexual arousal.

"Don't play the bashful bride with me," said Sheilagh. "Are you going to have me or aren't you?" She did not wait for a verbal answer but drew him immediately upstairs to bed.

Jim admitted to himself that he enjoyed the feeling of guilt he had from betraying Jessica, but did not want the chance of it being repeated too often.

"That was good," said Sheilagh, later. "I think we must both have been learning something. Just what have you been up to?"

She did not get a reply. She then said: "Sørensen is worried about you."

This provoked Jim into replying: "He finds a strange way of showing it."

Sheilagh snorted. "You've got a lot to learn about women, Jim. I'm not your personal property, and I'm not his either. Sørensen thinks you're the most promising comrade we've got in the print unions and you've got far to go in the movement. He's thinking of putting you forward for membership of the Central Committee and not bothering about trying you out for a period on the District Committee first."

"I'm supposed to be flattered?" said Jim.

"It's not flattery. It's knowing a good comrade when he sees one," said Sheilagh. "It's just that he's noticed that your work-rate has been dropping off a lot of late and he wants to know what's wrong."

"I'll tell you what — and this is something I've felt before I even knew about you and Sørensen — I can't stand the little tests of loyalty he sets for people. Like when he made me try to the *Daily Worker* chapel into blacklegging on their own dispute."

"But he tells me you did very well on that," said Sheilagh. "That's what strengthened his thoughts about having you on the Central Committee. Besides, we've all got our tests of revolutionary discipline. Mine is to find out what's going wrong with you and try to get you back on course."

"So that was what tonight was in aid of," said Jim. He got out of bed and went downstairs to the couch.

In the morning, he got up promptly, to avoid seeing Sheilagh. He had started keeping some clothes downstairs; the wardrobe was largely full of Sheilagh's things anyway, and she showed no sign of deciding to move them out.

As it was Sunday, he was deprived of his usual morning with Jessica so, to get out of the house and to be able to think a few things over on his own, he joined the crowded scene at the golf-course, although he usually avoided Sundays because of the extensive wait involved. As he paid his fee he was spotted by Eric Durkin, greengrocer and alderman, who was about to tee off. Trust him to be at the front of any queue. The alderman, who was with two companions, called him over. "What about you join us, Anstruther?" he said, loudly, so that it was really a question to his two companions. "We politicians should stick together."

The etiquette of the game required Jim to accede to the request, which he was anyway willing to do to avoid the wait. Jim never did find out who the two other players were, the alderman and greengrocer deliberately introducing them by name only. During the round, in which Jim did not excel himself, owing to having several matters on his mind, Durkin made a point of being particularly friendly. "Remember what I said last time we met?" he remarked when the two were coincidentally caught in the rough. "The Masons could do well for you, my boy. We know you're not a Communist really. Your heart's in the right place."

"That's very good of you, Durkin, but I don't think I want to join the Masons," Jim said, trying to balance distaste with politeness.

He realised he should not have used such niceties with Durkin. The man had no sensitivity to such matters and was not even embarrassed when caught mixing stones with the potatoes in his greengrocer's shop. Durkin said: "Don't come all coy with me, lad, it doesn't suit you. I know you better than you know yourself, and — there's no point saying you don't want to join, because you haven't been asked. When you *are* asked, you'll jump at the chance. No one's ever been known to say No to the Masons."

Jim was glad when the two strangers won, even more so when he saw Durkin having to pay them money.

On his return to dump off the clubs and change clothes before going off to the *Tribune*, Sheilagh was still there.

"Where have you been?" she asked.

He indicated his bulky bag of clubs. "Where do you think?"

"It was just that I'd hoped you might have been off doing something useful, such as canvassing or sticking up flyposters."

Jim changed his clothes in silence. During his train ride to work, Jim failed to read the newspapers he had brought with him, instead pondering on his predicament. He admitted to himself something he had not shown at the time: that he had felt a similar thrill to the one Jessica had communicated when they watched the wedding. It was just that he was a more practical person, he felt. He would give much to be able to set up home with Jessica, with whom he was love. (It might even help him get rid of the intrusive Sheilagh.) He wasn't even certain whether Jessica would pretend to have forgotten her impulsive marriage proposal. He wasn't even sure he wanted her to.

He told himself he was obviously not in love just because of Jessica's family money, but knew that that was not the whole truth. Her social position fascinated him, and a marriage to her would be his own victory over the ruling classes. The whole idea was quite impossible, though. He would never work again.

He made up his mind to put it to Jessica straight: I know you would like a wedding, and so would I. But it can't be. If we can't accept that, perhaps it would be better for us to part before we hurt ourselves even more than we have already.

11

Monday 10th September 1956

Sheilagh managed to wake half an hour earlier than usual, without using the alarm-clock. She did it just by forcefully telling herself the night before that she would. If you were determined to do something you could often make it happen.

She had avoided using the alarm in case it woke Jim, even though he had taken to spurning the various comforts of their bed to sleep downstairs on the sofa.

She dressed, in a blouse and tweed skirt-suit, and put on a pair of lace-up shoes with low heels. It was as well to be sensible as she did not know where she might end up that day.

She tiptoed down the stairs, avoiding the steps she knew would creak. She put on her soft leather gloves and a turban-style hat, collected her raincoat from the peg, and picked up her handbag. On the doormat was the *Daily Herald*, with a cheeky note from the newsagent: "No *Worker* today. Try this instead (and save ½d)." She picked up the paper and took it with her. She did not want its right-wing Labour politics to infect Jim.

The headline read: **NASSER STICKS TO HIS GUNS: TELLS MENZIES WHERE TO GO**. What an example to us all that man was!

She opened the front door as quietly as she could, went outside and let the lock click behind her. She walked past Jim's motor cycle and sidecar and went up the road. At the top and just around the corner, Sørensen was just where he had said he would be, behind the wheel of his black pre-war Austin 7 saloon[1]. He was wearing a snap-brim Fedora. The car was causing a slight traffic obstruction, but there was nowhere else he could have parked for a good view of the junction without being seen from it. The engine was ticking over.

Sheilagh opened the passenger door and got in. The springs of the passenger seat had collapsed through age, and Sheilagh had to sit so low that she could only just see out through the windscreen.

"I like looking at you in the mornings. It's a pity we couldn't have woken up together," said Sørensen, putting a hand on her thigh. "Is he still there?"

"Not since Saturday night," said Sheilagh, deliberately misunderstanding.

"Any hints of what he's getting up to in the mornings?"

"No," said Sheilagh, "but sometimes he implies he's going in to the *Tribune*."

"Yes, but we know he doesn't get there till afternoon, don't we?"

The two stared out in front for a long time, waiting for Jim to emerge on his motor cycle. Sørensen continued to feel Sheilagh's upper thigh. After a while, he said: "I really enjoy this work. Checking up on the membership."

He used his right hand to undo his fly buttons, releasing his shiny, tumescent member to point toward the car steering wheel, at a right-angle to the gear-lever. "Did you know that I'm going to head the British KGB[2] when the revolution comes?"

"Do you mean checking up on *him* — or on me?" said Sheilagh, taking hold of Sørensen's stiff organ in her gloved hand and slowly but firmly manipulating it.

"Yes, yes, that's it, don't stop," Sørensen kept saying. Suddenly, without any warning, he shouted "there he goes" and pushed the gear-lever into first. At the same time he let out the Austin's notoriously vicious clutch. The car jerked and bounded up the road in a series of orgasmic lurches in pursuit of Jim, who had just emerged on to the main road.

The vehicle came close to hitting Jim's sidecar, but he gave no indication of recognising the man behind the wheel or the woman peering out of the lower part of the windscreen.

"Bugger," said Sørensen. "I wasn't expecting him to come out just at that moment."

As they drove along, Sheilagh wiped her glove on piece of Kleenex[3] from a box she found in the car. "I don't like you swearing," she said. "It's the habit of a bourgeois pretending to be proletarian. Real working-class people don't swear."

"Fat lot you'd know," said Sørensen.

"Hurry up, you'll lose sight of him," said Sheilagh as the motor cycle and sidecar swept up the steep hill of Plaistow Lane.

"The car won't go any faster," said Sørensen. "In any case, I daren't exceed the speed limit. The Special Branch[4] are out to get me — any little transgression will do."

Sheilagh guessed that Jim was going to Bromley North station, so they drove there. They saw the combination parked outside, with the dim parking light already clipped to the side, and Jim disappearing into the ticket hall.

"Here, use these," said Sørensen, offering Sheilagh a pair of dark glasses.

"Don't be ridiculous. If he sees me, he'll recognise me. I'll just have to think of some excuse."

Sheilagh made Sørensen promise to ring her work, claim to be her father, and say she was ill in bed. "Now remember," she said, "it's got to be my father, because Jim always pretends to be my brother. They're not supposed to know I'm living with someone without being married."

She went in and bought a ticket. She didn't know where Jim was going to, so bought a single to Holborn Viaduct, and joined the train, just managing to get through before the barrier was shut. The last compartment before the engine was particularly crowded, largely with men on the way to the City. A young woman, particularly one with a copy of the *Daily Herald*, was most unusual there. There was no prospect of a seat, for which Sheilagh was grateful as she had to try to peer out of the smudged-brown window at each stop in case Jim got off early, which he did, at Peckham Rye. Sheilagh managed to jump out just before the train started to move off again and she followed Jim discreetly to another platform. She waited just behind the corner, rushing out at the last moment when Jim caught another train. When the train arrived at Victoria, Jessica stayed on board until Jim passed her window. There was a slight altercation at the ticket barrier when the collector complained about Sheilagh having the wrong ticket, but Jim, who had no reason to suspect he was being followed, did not turn round. To begin with Sheilagh could not understand why he had not caught the train straight to Victoria from the other Bromley station, or even from Bickley, until she worked out that he would need to return from Blackfriars after the night's work at the newspaper.

With Sheilagh in distant pursuit, Jim set out on a long and strenuous walk, behind the walled gardens of Buckingham Palace, skirting Hyde Park Corner, across one corner of Green Park and through the back streets of Mayfair. It was not a part of London that Sheilagh was familiar with and, from its look of self-satisfied wealth, not one she wished to learn any more of. When Jim turned into an area which appeared to specialise in prostitution, Sheilagh was quite surprised, and slightly offended. In one street, seedier than the rest, Jim let himself in at a door between two shopfronts.

She went close, to look at the door's polished brass plaque. **The Fund for the Abolition of Boxing. MAYfair 8989. Visitors by appointment only.** It was rather an elaborate piece of deception for a call-girl, surely.

"Every day, he goes there. Except weekends, that is." It was a brightly painted youngish woman speaking to her. Sheilagh was not quite sure what was happening, or why she was being spoken to, or whether the speaker was something to do with Jim's new life. She turned and gave a half-smile.

"You're not one of us, are you love?" said the young woman. "Are you a divorce detective, then?"

It seemed a reasonable enough thing to admit to in the circumstances, so Sheilagh said: "Something like that. What's this Fund thing about?"

"Search me," said the young woman. "There's comings and goings at all hours. You'll have to wait till dinner-time before this one goes, though. He's regular as clockwork."

Sheilagh thanked her and went to sit in the Italian café from where she could wait, at the price of several highly expensive cups of coffee, to see when Jim left. When he eventually did so, he appeared to be more than usually preoccupied, with a worried or stern look on his face. He looked at his watch and hurried away. Sheilagh did not bother to follow him, but instead went to find a public telephone to call the Fund.

"I'm interested in social and political research and I'd like to know more about your organisation," she said when Jessica answered. "I'm just round the corner — when can I visit? What about now?"

The young woman who answered sounded as if she might have been crying, but there were no suggestive remarks and no apparent surprise at being called by a woman — if this was indeed a front for prostitution, it was a most elaborate and convincing one. The woman said "come any time you want" in a way that Sheilagh took to mean that she didn't care what happened.

But she had work to do, and, unrepelled, knocked on the door. It was eventually opened by a particularly attractive and very young-looking woman, wearing a loose blouse and dark, tailored skirt-suit with a tightly-belted waist that emphasised her figure. It was tasteful, but still the outfit of a woman who was dressing for a man. Its wearer had permed, dark hair and an open welcoming smile. She appeared to have overcome whatever it was that had been upsetting her. Perhaps she just wasn't used to talking on the telephone. She made a gesture implying that Sheilagh should follow her. As Sheilagh tailed her upstairs, she said: "I'm thinking of getting one of those gadgets that lets you open the door from the office but, then again, it might appear impersonal."

By comparison with this glamorous-looking but vacuous-sounding young vamp, Sheilagh felt slightly frumpy, in her tweed suit and turban. The feeling, together with her nervousness about her mission, sharpened up her response. Even on straightforward occasions she liked to be thought direct in her speech. She said: "Do you think a lot about appearances?"

She was expecting a giggle, followed by an evasive answer, or perhaps a cold reproach. Instead, she was told: "I think this area tends to unsettle a lot of people. Does it worry you? I must say, I find it quite stimulating. I think it helps remind people that they shouldn't always go by appearances. First impressions can be misleading."

By now, they had crossed the landing, with its four doors, and had entered a room that wasn't quite an office but wasn't a sitting room either. Sheilagh was happily impressed by the forthright response to her brutal opening. She sat down on the part of the sofa indicated to her, while the young woman continued speaking.

"I'm Miss Ross. I run the Fund for the Abolition of Boxing. I'm the general secretary, or perhaps the chairman, I haven't decided which, yet. Which job title sounds best to you?"

Sheilagh decided she should take a little while longer before deciding what she thought about the girl. She opted to listen to what Miss Ross had to say about the organisation before asking about what Jim had been up to. He had never said anything to her about boxing, either for or against. It seemed reasonable to assume he was a visitor to the office more for the sake of its organiser than for its programme, whatever that might be. But this Miss Ross didn't seem the type of girl to be interested in a 32-year-old printing worker who was a known Communist, even if a rather slack one.

"My name is Naomi Murchison," said Sheilagh. "I'm particularly interested in the emergence of new organisations, and yours is one that I haven't heard of before. Perhaps you'd be able to tell me what you do?"

The name had come to her on the spur of the moment. It was only after Miss Ross introduced herself that Sheilagh realised that she could not give her real name, for fear that Jim might have mentioned it. The real Naomi Murchison had been in the class beneath her at school, a thorough little butter-wouldn't-melt-in-her-mouth madam, but someone whom Sheilagh and the whole school had envied for her golden curls and china-doll features. Sheilagh couldn't think why it was her name rather than anyone else's which came to her that moment.

Miss Ross, by now Jessica, showed off her scrapbooks of press cuttings, her pile of letters of support, the signed copy of Dr Summerskill's new book and her half-dozen attempts at a statement of aims and constitution for the Fund. She was proud of her visitors' book, autographed by people from Members of Parliament to boxers, and now by one Naomi Murchison. Sheilagh looked carefully at each of the names but did not find Jim's there, unless he was passing himself off as a member of the House of Lords. Before making her own entry, Sheilagh wondered how the real Naomi might have signed her name, and as a private joke decided on an affected style in recognition of Sørensen's name: Naømi Murchisøn. When it came to the address she almost put down Tylney Road, Bromley, before realising the danger and deciding to give Sørensen's East London address.

Jessica looked at the book and seemed as pleased of the visitor from Bow as she was with those from the House of Lords. She asked Sheilagh, as a professed student of such organisations, for advice on the best structure to adopt for the Fund. Sheilagh was noncommittal. It depended on the real purpose of the organisation, she said. If you wanted to get something done, you didn't waste time with setting up lots of checks and balances. On the other hand, if you wanted to get a lot of people involved in the organisation for its own sake, you set up lots of committees, discussion groups and the like. You only had to look at the so-called Communist front organisations to realise that.

What, Jessica wanted to know, was a Communist front organisation. It sounded exciting.

There was no such thing, said Sheilagh. That was just what the red-baters called any solidarity group, progressive campaign or working-people's organisation that could be denounced as being set up or infiltrated by Communists or so-called fellow travellers.

"Do you think the Fund could be called a Communist front, then?" asked Jessica, sounding enthusiastic.

"Something with a capitalist word like 'Fund' in it is not the sort of name an organisation wants," said Sheilagh. "Especially if it really is run by the Party. But then, you're not a Communist, after all."

"I could be for all you know," said Jessica, a touch indignantly. "As it happens, I'm not yet, but I'm thinking of joining."

Sheilagh wondered how on earth had Jim managed to find such an unlikely potential recruit. She considered whether the organisation was just what the young lady said it was, and whether there was no sexual purpose behind Jim's visit or visits. Perhaps he was even working for the Party, at the behest of some organiser other than Sørensen. Unlikely, though. She felt she was little nearer solving the mystery. It was now well into the afternoon and there had been no telephone calls to the office and no sign that Jessica had anything more to do than talk to her visitor.

Neither of them had had anything to eat since breakfast, Jessica because she had been in bed with Jim and Sheilagh because she had not been. Jessica took Sheilagh into the newly equipped kitchen and took a packet of sandwiches out of the Kelvinator. "Have some of these," she said. "They always make too many for me."

"Who is 'they'?" asked Sheilagh, as, back in the office the two of them sat side by side on the sofa, eating the sandwiches.

Jessica told Sheilagh of Mrs Burgess, the proprietor, and of her own feelings of isolation. Sheilagh was fascinated to hear the footling complaints of the poor little rich girl. The *Tribune* link with Jim was obvious, but she could not work out how the two could have met on the basis of sufficient equality for Jim even to have been able to speak to her, let alone visit her office.

"I don't see what you've got to complain about. You might not be very happy, but that could be because you've not got enough to do," said Sheilagh. "I've got reason enough for unhappiness myself. I was born in County Tyrone — that's in the *North* of Ireland — and my mother had eight other children, two of whom died before

I was born. We never even had enough to eat before we came to this country. My father's an educated man, but the only work he can get is digging up the roads."

Sheilagh was still bristling about Jim's taunt that it was easy for someone from a middle-class background who had never soiled her hands and had never known poverty to romanticise the working class she knew nothing about. So the past she invented for herself was not exactly true in all its details — far from being a road navvy, her own father was in fact a Technical College[5] lecturer. Sheilagh was nevertheless so used to the hyperbole that she had become almost to believe all of the tale herself. After telling Jessica the story of her life in stark and exaggerated simplicity as she was used to when required to recite her class credentials, Sheilagh delivered what she believed was the moral of the tale: "Now do you still feel sorry for yourself?"

Apparently, Jessica still did. "I should have known better than to talk like that to you," she said. "The truth is, I've never learnt how to get on with people. I've never had the chance. I was taken away from my real mother when I was only two weeks old, and adopted."

Sheilagh offered a few words of encouragement every now and then as Jessica poured forth her tale.

"I can still remember my pretend mother, but they packed me away to America when war broke out. I was only five, and out of school and in the vacations[6] I had to stay in an apartment in New York with her parents. They tried to be nice to me, but I think they'd forgotten how to deal with children. After six years of that they told me one day that my mother, that's my pretend mother, had died. I was 11."

"You don't sound like a Yank," said Sheilagh.

"No," said Jessica. "That's another part of the trouble. I don't fit in anywhere. Just after my pretend mother died they sent me back to London. The war was over, but the proprietor sent me to school in Switzerland. It was different to anything I knew. They all spoke French and I never managed to catch up. I didn't even make any friends — all the girls knew each other before I'd arrived and they all chattered away in French about me. In the holidays I came back to London but I didn't know anyone here either. The proprietor was always busy off making money out of people. When he was at home he was carrying on with his housekeeper. She has the same first name as my pretend mother, which I think is pretty sick.

"At the end of all that I didn't know what to do. I couldn't go to university. The proprietor said I was too stupid.

"Do *you* think I'm stupid, Naomi?"

"No, of course not," said Sheilagh. She could hardly say anything else. She was beginning to doubt whether Jessica would be such a good catch for the Communist Party after all. She had sounded most rational while explaining the Fund, but now she was on to personal matters there was a distraught tone to her voice, and Sheilagh felt that hysteria might be very close. Still, it sounded as if there was a lot of money available in her organisation, which it would be useful to control. She asked: "So what happened next?"

"He sent me back to Switzerland to something called a 'finishing school'. It almost finished me, I can say. This time they spoke English, but I'd learnt to think in French by then.

"I've been back in London for more than six months. It was horrible at first. I had to stay with the proprietor, there was nothing to do and no real people. No wonder I was miserable."

Jessica spoke of how the proprietor had spies all over the world who trailed her and reported back but how they had not managed to find out about her big secret. (Sheilagh, who wondered whether the big secret was Jim, was discomfited by Jessica's attack on people who followed you in the street.)

For a few weeks, Sheilagh heard, Jessica had felt that she might at last be in control of her future, and might have found the perfect weapon of revenge on the proprietor for all the evil he had done her. Now, Jessica said, she was no longer so sure.

"I'm a Communist, you know," said Sheilagh. "Do you have anyone you see regularly with whom you can discuss politics?"

"Yes," said Jessica, breaking into loud tears.

"I mean No," she said, gulpingly, between sobs. "Perhaps there used to be, I don't know any more. I can't talk about that.

"I've never had any friends. Now I'm back in England everyone has been brought up to know each other and I can't speak to them because I don't know what to say. All they can talk about is horses and dogs or parties and dresses and I see them having fun and I don't know the people they are gossiping about. All the other girls have fun together but I don't like any of them, and I don't think they like me. I'm different, you see."

By now, the tears had started to course down Jessica's face. Possibly to conceal the sight, she collapsed her head into Sheilagh's lap. "I don't know why I'm telling you all this, Naomi," she said, as Sheilagh stroked her fingers softly through Jessica's hair.

Sheilagh bent her head down, kissed Jessica on her cheek and whispered in her ear: "There's a man, isn't there?"

"Yes," said Jessica, catching hold of Sheilagh's jacket to pull herself upright. "Or perhaps No, but I can't tell anyone about it. He'd kill him!"

"Who would he kill?" asked Sheilagh, trying not to sound disbelieving. If the man in question was Jim, as she suspected, the thought of him killing anyone sounded most unlikely, in spite of the claims about the death of Gudger.

"The proprietor would kill him, and kill me too probably. That's why he says we can never marry."

Poor Jim, thought Sheilagh. The mad girl wants to marry him. That would serve him right!

She wrapped her arms around Jessica, who seemed to welcome the attention, and said: "My poor girl. All men are bastards. They lead you on, and then it ends in tears. Don't I know it! What you need is a real friend, someone you can trust and who can listen to your troubles." She looked closely and sympathetically into Jessica's eyes, very slowly brushed her lips against hers, and said: "That's what I need too."

They held each other tightly for a minute, until Jessica said: "Are you sure what we are doing is all right?"

Sheilagh already regretted deceiving her with the false name, but felt that it was the wrong moment to explain. She told Jessica firmly: "Communists must learn to discard all bourgeois inhibitions. Anything else is hypocrisy. Society can only develop when people start to be honest with themselves — that's part of the theory of scientific socialism. It's how you become free."

Jessica was silent for a few moments, before taking off her blouse and saying: "I think I'm going to like being a Communist."

12

Monday 22nd October 1956

After another boring Sunday, spent mooching about the proprietorial house, reading the papers, listening to the wireless and watching television, Jessica was looking forward to getting back to Mayfair. There would be Jim in the morning, work in the afternoon and probably Naomi in the evening. There was only breakfast to get through first, and even that was not so much of an ordeal as it used to be.

The proprietor was at the table already, with a pile of his rivals' newspapers in front of him.

"Good morning, Jessica," he said, looking up from the *Express*. "I'd like you to read this."

Leading the paper was a despatch from Warsaw. The headline was **TROOPS JOIN IN POLISH REVOLT.** It started: "Poland struck out again for freedom tonight." The piece went on to detail how the Polish United Workers' Party had adopted a new liberalised set of policies against the wishes of certain Kremlin hardliners — and how the Russians had allowed them to get away with it. The anonymous correspondent wrote: "Factory workers are in the vanguard of the smash-hit campaign that demands Poland for the Poles."

Jessica read the piece carefully. She didn't really know what to think about it, especially as she knew never to trust the *Daily Express*. Was this the death of Communism or a fresh start for a new age?

"Yes," she said. "So what?"

"I've been watching you over the past few months, ever since you've started this Fund," said the proprietor. Jessica felt a few seconds of terror, in case he was going to tell her that his spies knew what she was up to. But his attack was not quite so direct.

"I don't know who you've been seeing, who's been egging you on or putting you up to it, but I'm getting a bit concerned about your politics. You've never actually said so to me, but I suspect you're getting too close to the Reds for my liking. I just showed this piece to you to demonstrate how unpopular they are whenever they do get control.

"You might not feel part of the British people. After all, I have tried to give you a broad outlook on life by protecting you from some of the narrow-minded attitudes of the English. But you've got to realise that they're an extraordinarily down-to-earth and practical bunch of folk and they won't stand for any of this Red nonsense."

"What makes you think I'm a Communist?" asked Jessica, feeling wary but sounding provocative.

The proprietor did not answer directly. He said: "You're perfectly entitled to say anything you want to me about the *Tribune*. I even sympathise with some of the things you've said to me about Suez, but you mustn't lecture people or they'll turn against you. Why do you think they would keep voting Tory if they didn't like Tory Governments? They know what the alternative is." He picked up the folded *Express* and gestured with it.

"I know what it's like to live in a country where there are riots and blood in the streets. They had a Communist state in Hungary after the break-up of the empire. That was broken up by the monarchists and then another group threw them out in turn. It's that sort of thing I escaped from and I don't want to see it here."

By now Jessica realised that the proprietor had no firm evidence against her. He was just sounding off on his favourite subject again. She still didn't know what to think about the Poles, though, and so decided not to take the argument further.

"I'm sure you're right," she said, as the proprietor got up from the table.

"That's the spirit," he said.

Later that morning, sitting with him on the sofa in Mayfair, she asked Jim what he thought about Poland.

They had been through a bad patch after Jim's refusal to marry her. Jessica understood all his arguments. She even possibly agreed with them. He was so level-headed and so much in control. That made him attractive and desirable, but it also made him unattainable and infuriating. Jessica had been hoping that he would eventually change his mind, and every now and then dropped hints to remind him about what she wanted.

As far as Poland went, he'd have left the Communists years ago if he had thought they were not democrats, he said. The Polish Party was able to ease up a bit now that the threat from the West was reduced. The capitalist countries were tearing themselves apart — you only had to look at the Suez crisis to realise that — and all over the world the working class was coming into its own.

But that, he said, was not the matter particularly on his mind.

"You did believe me when I said why we couldn't get married?" he asked.

Jessica guardedly said that she did.

"Well," he said. "Would you agree to get married if we could do it in a way no one would be likely to find out?"

"Is that a proposal?"

"I think I've found the way," said Jim. "Neither of us would want a church, of course. Even if we did, that would be the way to be found out; ministers[1] are nosey people.

"But we'd be just as likely to be found out if we used your local register office, or mine, come to that. We *could* go to Scotland, but that would mean several nights away from London, which would give the game away. I've been looking into what happens, and although you have to use the local register office near the home of either the man or the woman, the registrar doesn't check that you actually live there."

"So?"

"That means you can choose anywhere in the country as long as one of you claims to live there."

"That's all very well, Jim," said Jessica, "but I don't want to marry you just to get a piece of paper. I want to be with you."

It was not just the idea of revenge against the proprietor motivating Jessica. She felt that marrying Jim might give her the first emotional security she had had in her life. She was sure that he still thought of her as a member of the upper class, but she no longer thought of him as a member of any class at all. She was still the poor orphan and he was someone with such a normal family background that he rarely bothered even to think about it.

"But you're with me now," he said. "You know why we can't risk anything else. I thought I'd found a way of getting married, like we both want, without throwing us both on the dole[2]. If you don't want to, though . . ."

Jessica decided to stop arguing. She'd get the marriage done first, and then work on the living together — aware that it in these post-war years many daring couples considered living together before getting round to the marriage bit. She moved closer to Jim, started undoing his trousers, and said: "If we can get married anywhere, why don't we go to Deal? I liked it there."

"I was thinking that, too," said Jim. He stood up, one hand holding on to his trousers, and took Jessica by the hand into her mirrored bedroom.

All that afternoon, Jessica could hardly work. She was longing for Naomi to come to visit that evening as she had said she might. Although she could not share her news, she wanted to share her happiness.

There was something uncanny about Naomi. It might have been obvious to anyone that Jessica was seeing a man, but none of her other visitors had talked with her about it. Even though Jessica never even hinted at Jim's identity, Naomi seemed to know as much about him as Jessica did herself. Perhaps such experience came with age.

Naomi called several times a week, always in the evenings after work, and generally talked politics. This, she admitted, was how you got taken over to become a Front Organisation (not that such a thing really existed, of course). It was all so terribly cloak-and-dagger, romantic and exciting.

Quite often, they ended up in bed together. That was part of scientific socialism too, Naomi assured her.

Jessica had not worked out which was naughtiest, going to bed with Jim, or with Naomi. Which would anger the proprietor the most? Which gave the strongest sense of being secure and being wanted?

She would have liked to see Naomi at a weekend sometimes, but Naomi said she was involved with a married man with whom she frequently travelled at weekends. Naomi said that she herself was never jealous: it was a bourgeois emotion unworthy of a class fighter like Jessica. But Jessica couldn't give it up; she even felt jealous on the occasions when Jim mentioned the "certain person" who had taken over his bedroom and wouldn't move out, forcing him to sleep in the sitting room.

By half-past six, Jessica had almost given up on her visitor, but then she heard Naomi's knock. From time to time Naomi said that she ought to have her own key, but Jessica was reluctant to give her one. She had promised Jim that no one else would have a key.

"You're looking ridiculously happy," Sheilagh greeted her.

"That's because I'm feeling happy," said Jessica, still on the doorstep. "There's something I want to tell you about."

"Sometimes I despair of you, Jessica," said Sheilagh. "Haven't you been reading the papers? Don't you know what's been happening?"

Jessica went upstairs, leaving Sheilagh to follow. The greeting perplexed her. She had been thinking more of her intended secret wedding than of international politics; besides, Jim had strongly welcomed what was happening in Poland. In that he even agreed, more or less, with the proprietor.

"Haven't I told you not to be taken in by the newspapers?" said Sheilagh, when she sat down beside Jessica. "You of all people should know that. Remember the test. Ask who stands to benefit from something happening and there you have the probable perpetrator.

"Believe me, this counter-revolution isn't in the interests of the working class. I see the hand of the Americans at work. Or British Intelligence, come to that. Probably both, not to mention the Roman Catholic church. The backward elements in Poland are notoriously superstitious."

She leaned forward and stared, with concern, into Jessica's eyes, and said: "Has that no-good man of yours been guilty of false consciousness? You're picking up bad thoughts, you know."

Jessica felt abashed. She didn't know what "false consciousness" was, but evidently Naomi didn't agree with it. Perhaps she should try to get Jim to meet Naomi to explain.

"Ah well, that's enough of that," said Sheilagh. "Now, tell me what your good news is."

"Another time," said Jessica. "It can wait."

13

Saturday 27th October 1956

Jim collected Jessica early. She was waiting in the autumn chill outside the closed gates of Regent's Park zoo, watching the giraffes through a gap in the fence.

She took her accustomed seat in the sidecar, bundling in the voluminous folds of her pleated skirt. The ride through Kent was uneventful and was much the same as before, except the greens had turned to brown and the greys of the scrubland and mudflats had less blue in them.

Jessica transferred to the pillion at Canterbury for the final uncomfortable ride into Deal. They rode around the outskirts of the town looking for a likely road to give as an address to the registrar. Anything would do, except the type of middle-class area where the registrar might by chance know the names of the genuine occupants. Jessica said she'd like to choose a miner's address, but there wasn't any way of telling from the outside who lived in any of the houses. Miners, it transpired, lived no differently from garage mechanics or billiard-hall attendants.

In the end, Jessica decided on 57 Park Avenue. It would be an extraordinarily grand address in New York, she said, but was more run-of-the-mill in Deal.

"If you're happy with it, that's fine by me," said Jim.

"What do you mean by that?" said Jessica. "I thought it was the bridegroom who applied for the marriage licence."

"It's normally the responsibility of the bride's mother," said Jim, hoping to sound authoritative.

Jim rehearsed her. "You do know what to say, don't you?"

Jessica looked nervous, but nodded. Jim kissed her and she made her hesitant way into the town hall just as a wedding party emerged on to the steps for a photograph.

She was gone for quarter of an hour, while Jim paced up and down the road, sometimes glancing in shop windows but always keeping an eye on his motor cycle and sidecar, parked at the roadside. When Jessica came out of the town hall she looked close to tears. Jim rushed up and held her. "What's wrong?"

"They won't let us get married," said Jessica, in such a loud wail that Jim felt sure they were being stared at by passers-by.

"Get on the bike and we'll go somewhere so you can tell me what happened," said Jim.

Presently, on a bench overlooking the sea, Jessica had recovered enough to explain what had gone wrong.

"He was horrible to me," she said. "First of all, he said he didn't have time to arrange weddings on a Saturday; he was too busy marrying people. So I just stood there and waited. In the end he must have taken pity on me, because he took out a pile of forms and started asking me questions.

"I'd gone all to pieces and when he asked if I lived within his jurisdiction, I didn't really understand what he meant and I said No. He didn't wait to let me that you lived at Park Avenue — he just starting shouting. He went on and on. About people thinking he had nothing better to do than waste his time with silly girls who fancied a seaside wedding just because they like the look of the place. I just ran away."

After that, she burst into tears again and said: "It's all ruined. I knew it wouldn't work. I'll have to live with the proprietor for ever."

"This chap sounds a nasty bit of work," said Jim. "I'll go and sort him out."

Jessica instantly stopped crying and sat up. "Are you going to hit him?" She sounded most enthusiastic.

"I wasn't planning to," said Jim. "You stay there and mind the bike. I'll be back soon."

He walked into town and up the step of the town hall, finding the superintendent registrar's office at the end of a series of corridors, lined with framed photographs of past mayors. Jim knocked, heard no reply, so went in. The linoleum ran out at the door and there was no carpet on the polished wood floor. There was a large man sitting at a table writing a letter with a fountain-pen. He did not look up, even though he must have been aware of the noise Jim made knocking on the door and walking across the hard floor.

Jim stood and looked at the top of the man's head. Eventually, still without looking up, and while still writing, the man said: "Well?"

"I want to get married," said Jim.

"Come back on a weekday," said the man. "I only do burial certificates and conduct wedding ceremonies on Saturdays. Births, wedding certificates and licences on weekdays."

"But I can't come during the week; I've got to go to work," said Jim, doing his best to sound reasonable and suppress anger from his voice.

At last the man looked up. He looked as irascible as Jessica had described him. "Can't understand any man wanting to get married. You'll think better of it after a few years, my boy. But that's your own funeral."

Jim thought it best to make a polite chuckle at the registrar's heavy-handed joke before saying: "I was thinking about next Saturday."

"Got some girl in the family way have we?" Jim began to realise what it was about the man's attitude that made Jessica want him beaten up.

When the superintendent registrar did not receive an answer, he sighed, and opened his desk diary. He lifted his head up to look straight into Jim's eyes, and said: "Do you reside within my jurisdiction?"

"I live in Deal, if that's what you mean. Number 57, Park Avenue."

"Huh!" the registrar snorted. "I suppose you're a miner. That will explain your funny accent."

Jim had actually intended to please Jessica by giving miner as his occupation, but to confound the registrar's prejudices, said: "No, I'm a stereotyper."

"What sort of occupation is that?" said the registrar, the sneer still in his voice.

"I'd explain, but you might not understand."

"Try me, laddie," said the registrar. "Remember, I haven't told you if I've got any spaces left for next Saturday. You don't want to wait so long that the bride gives birth on the register office steps, now do you?"

"It's an essential part of the letterpress process, where the image to be printed is transferred from a matrix to cast printing plates in relief form."

"I shouldn't imagine there's much call for that sort of thing in Deal," said the registrar. Jim cursed himself for not having agreed to be a miner. He was wondering what further explanation to give, when the registrar started speaking again.

"You've no idea how many people come in here trying to pull the wool over my eyes," he said. "People come here on day trips from London, fall in love with the town and think that justifies them in trying to get married here. Why, just before you came in I had some brainless flibbertigibbet in here asking to get married even though she didn't live here. Some people!"

Jim was indeed just about to hit the man, when the registrar said: "Yes, I can do next Saturday, after all. Eleven o'clock. There must have been a cancellation. See, some men have got the right idea."

Just at the last moment Jim realised that the whole plan would come unstuck when the registrar recognised Jessica. Further, he doubted whether he could stand being married by such a person. Jim found himself being made so angry that he feared he might indeed lash out, so he decided to escape.

"I look forward to seeing you again next Saturday," he said, turning toward the door.

Just as Jim was starting to move away, the registrar said: "Don't think you can get the services of the Superintendent Registrar just like that! You'll get one of my assistants instead."

Jim turned back toward the desk. He filled in the forms in the way he was directed, giving Jessica's address as Tylney Road, Bromley, so that no sharp local reporter would spot who she was from reading the notices of forthcoming weddings. As he finished, he was told: "That will be 1s. 6d. now, for the entry of notice. Next Saturday you will pay a further 1s. 6d. for the Superintendent Registrar's certificate, £2 5s. for the Superintendent Registrar's licence and 15s for the attendance of the registrar of marriages. That's three guineas in total. If you want a marriage certificate, that will be an extra 3s. 9d. It has to be cash, we don't take cheques."

"Is that all?" asked Jim, meaning it to be a request about the formalities.

The superintendent registrar deliberately misconstrued his remark and replied: "If you think that that's a lot of money, I can tell you: it's only the beginning of the bills you will face throughout your married life. The very best of luck to you!"

Back sitting by the sea with Jessica, Jim agreed that Deal's Superintendent Registrar was an unpleasant gentleman.

They had a meal of fish and chips, which they were amused to see came wrapped in a month-old *Tribune*. In the afternoon they found a jeweller's shop still open and bought an engagement ring and a wedding ring.

Jessica agreed to wear them on the customary finger only when she was with Jim, taking them off or switching them to other fingers at other times.[1]

14

Saturday 3rd November 1956

Jessica was so excited that she could not possibly have slept in. At half past six she was up and trying on her wedding dress. She spent time over her make-up and on tidying her newly permed hair.[1] She then inspected herself in the dressing-table mirror. For once, the mirrored walls of the Shepherd Market would have had a practical value, had she been there rather than in the proprietorial residence.

It was a lovely dress, by someone called Mary Black. She had found it at Marshall & Snelgrove. It was strapless, in tiers of black lace falling to just below the knee. She had a costume-diamond clasp at the waist. There was a chiffon bolero, and she wore it with very long black suede gloves and a jet-black fox stole. She had black Wolsey stockings and a fold-over clutch-bag in black doeskin and, from Bally of Switzerland, a pair of tiny shoes of black elasticated suede supporting a gilt and rhinestone buckle. Underneath, she had a new girdle. Everything was black: Jessica felt that white would not have been appropriate for this wedding.

The whole outfit, with the exception of the fur, which was hired, had cost an unbelievable £59 19s 5d. The Fund for The Abolition of Boxing paid. There had not been time to get anything made, but this was the best creation Jessica could find in the time and without anyone to ask for advice; *Vogue* had featured it in its latest issue.

She took the dress off, and with great care folded it into a suitcase, along with the handbag, high-heeled shoes, things for an overnight stay and Jim's favourite white dress for the next day.

Before putting on her travelling dress she pulled on beige pedal-pushers and a tight, black polo-neck jersey to go downstairs. She wanted to find some rolls to put in a paper bag for the journey.

It was still very early and normally on a Saturday the proprietor would have a lie-in. He was already up, though, and the two met in the hall.

He told her: "Come into the library, Jessica, I have something to say to you."

"Can't it wait? I'm in a hurry," said Jessica.

"No, it can't wait," said the proprietor, grabbing her arm. "Do as I tell you."

Jessica, firmly in the proprietor's grasp, had little choice. "It had better not take long," she said.

"It will take as long as I want it to take," said the proprietor, leading her into the room and finding a deep armchair.

The proprietor pushed her into it, sat down on the arm, bent towards her and said: "It's bad news, I'm afraid. It came through on the wires late last night so I decided not to wake you, but I'm afraid it's Lear Farnsworth. He's been killed in action[2]."

Jessica began to stand up, saying: "Can I go now?"

The proprietor forced her back into the seat, and said: "No you can't. The only place you will go is up to your room. You will clean your face of that ridiculous make-up, you will put on a black dress that covers your arms, and you will come with me to offer our condolences to the Farnsworths."

"Oh no I won't," said Jessica. "I've other more important things I'm doing today. If Lear Farnsworth chose to go out to try to prop up the British imperialist presence in Suez, he can pay the penalty."

The proprietor drew back his right hand and then hit Jessica firmly in the face. He drew back, appearing shocked, and said: "I didn't mean to do that. I'm sorry."

His tone changed from the instructional to the wheedling. He said: "What can possibly be more important than paying our respects to the family of your young man?"

"I'm going to a wedding," Jessica said.

"You mean you *were* going to a wedding. You'll just have to send your regrets. There's always so many people at a wedding that no one will miss you if you don't turn up. Is it anyone I know?"

"I hope not," said Jessica, pulling herself out of the armchair, slowly, so as to avoid another blow.

"If I don't know them, it can't be very important," said the proprietor. "Now you run along upstairs and change. There's a good girl. And . . . I'm sorry about hitting you."

Jessica ran from the room, rushed upstairs and grabbed her suitcase. Without taking the time to change into her travelling dress she ran downstairs. The proprietor was in the hall as she ran through. He reached out to grab her as she passed, but she managed to dodge his outstretched arm and reach the front door. The proprietor ran after her down the driveway and out on to the road. Jessica ran down towards Regent's Park hoping to hail a passing cab before the proprietor caught up. The suitcase was not heavy but its bulk hindered her run.

"Stop! Where are you going? Come back!" yelled the proprietor. He was managing to maintain the distance between them, but was not catching up. As he ran his yells grew more desperate but less loud. The last words she heard from him were: "Are you trying to kill me?"

Eventually, Jessica managed to hail a taxi. As it drew up, she turned and shouted at the proprietor: "Don't expect me to come back. Not tonight. Not ever."

At the station, Jessica ate a hurried sandwich in the cafeteria. She bought a *Daily Worker* and a *Daily Herald* to read on the train, in case Jim hadn't brought anything. She didn't really like either of the papers, although she felt that she ought to. Just before the train left she went back to the bookstall for the latest *Homes & Gardens*[3], a necessary preparation for married life.

She found a compartment to herself. After the train moved off, Jessica took out her powder compact and dusted on an extra layer, to try to disguise the red weal on her face. She settled down to read the papers, skipping quickly through *Homes & Gardens* and then the *Herald*. She hoped to have finished it and to be reading the *Worker* by the time Jim found her. The *Herald* led on **NOON CRISIS FOR EDEN**, on the first Saturday sitting of the Commons since 1949. The leader read: "At this grave moment, Eden[4] weakens the power of peace. He turns his back on the United Nations and reasserts the right of States to use violence to secure their interests.

"Every word of his argument can be thrown back at him by the Russians. It is a world disaster. The end cannot be foreseen. The country must get rid of this deluded leader. He has done us damage enough."

She read the news of the Anglo-French bombing attacks and the Israeli ground advance, hoping to see some reference to the action in which Lear had died. In fact, there was little about the fighting, the papers devoting far more space to the politics. The *Worker* led with calls for a general strike and commented: "We, who condemned the fascist bombing of Abyssinia, Guernica, Warsaw and Rotterdam, and who ourselves experienced the horrors of the blitz[5], are asked by the Tories to stay silent while they commit this crime in our name. The reply of the British people is: 'Never!' This is the meaning of the growing number of demands from important working-class organisations for the use of industrial power[6] to bring the Tories to their sense."

There was a report on the abandonment by the BBC Home Service of a live edition of *Any Questions?*[7] when the panellists ignored the 14-day rule and started to discuss the Suez crisis. But there was nothing about the death of Lear, or even about his regiment. Jessica did feel mildly sorry about his death, even if he was part of the imperialist warmongering machine. His last words to her had been: "If I died without your having said 'goodbye', then you'd reproach yourself." The boy was trying to make her feel guilty from beyond the grave, but she did not intend to let him. He had been a harmless enough fellow although it was thoughtless of him to die at such a time, threatening to disrupt her wedding plans. Doubtless he hadn't meant to.

She wondered what Jim would have to say about it all. She gave up waiting for him to find her and went walking up and down the train's swaying corridors looking into each compartment. He was not there. He would still be in time if he caught the later train, but it still made Jessica nervous. If anyone had a right to be late it was the bride, not the bridegroom. She spent much of the journey worrying about what to do if he did not turn up.

He was there, though, at Dover, wearing a new suit and polished shoes. Jessica disguised her relief at not being jilted with a display of peevishness. "I couldn't find you on the train. I looked everywhere. Where were you, Jim? You shouldn't have done it to me."

"I went First Class," he said. "For the first time in my life. I thought I was entitled to, on my wedding day. I looked for you there. I thought people like you went First Class all the time."

Jessica told him: "I'm beginning to realise that you understand almost nothing about me, Jim Anstruther."

They walked in huffy silence to the waiting taxis. In the back, Jim said he was sorry.

"Let's do the usual thing and wait until after we are married before we start having rows," he said.

Jessica said she was sorry too. She said her nerves were still on edge from the earlier row with the proprietor and the death of Lear.

They went to the same hotel as they had visited previously, wishing to create an instant tradition. The elderly man who had earlier acted as waiter asked them to sign the visitor's book before showing them to their room. Jim signed as Mr and Mrs Anstruther. The waiter, who doubled as the manager, looked closely at them, and said: "Are you sure you're married?"

"We will be by this afternoon," said Jessica.

The man's grumpy manner changed. He smiled. He said he hoped they'd both be very happy. He slid back the window behind the registration desk and called out: "Jill! We've got a honeymoon couple."

Jill and the elderly waiter/manager, who turned out to be called Collins, bustled around and promised to make the stay of Mr and Mrs Anstruther as memorable as possible. The hotel was almost full with a golfing party, they learnt, but that would be no trouble. Collins would move some of the guests around so the Anstruthers could have the best room available. In the meantime, he hoped they would not mind using another room for changing clothes. When he heard the words "golfing party" Jim remembered that there were five golf courses near Deal, including Royal St George's, venue for the first Open championship played out of Scotland, in 1894. He had an awful premonition that they might run into Eric Durkin, the golfing alderman, but he did not communicate his fears to Jessica. As it was, though, their nemesis was to take a different form.

When Jessica came downstairs freshly made-up and with her startling black outfit replacing the sweater and pedal-pushers, Collins asked: "Is there anything else, and I mean anything, that we can do for you?"

He appeared to be so genuine in his request that Jessica summoned up the courage to say: "Well, there *is* something . . ."

"Of course! What is it?" said Collins.

So he agreed to leave someone else in charge of the hotel and to come to the town hall to be witness to their wedding. Collins said that on the way to the town hall they were bound to bump into some friend of his whom they could ask to act as the second witness.

As it was, the couple getting married after them had arrived early, with a photographer, who agreed to act as a witness in exchange for a commission to take a picture.

The registrar was a pleasant lady and the ceremony was soon over, after Jim paid £3 5s 3d. It was surprisingly quick and there was no repetition of the grilling she and Jim had been subjected to the previous week. They did not even have to perjure themselves again, the registrar merely copying out on the certificate the information previously given. Jessica was surprised to see that, despite what Jim had told her about the row with the superintendent, his occupation was listed as Miner.

Walking away with Jim afterwards, with the autumn leaves swirling about their feet and with Collins blethering away behind them, Jessica tried to recall what it was that they both been made to promise in the brief ceremony. She hoped that her inability to remember was not a bad omen. Jim said he was similarly affected. He was so overwhelmed he was having difficulty in remembering even his name, he said.

Back at the hotel, Collins said: "We've got just the thing for you. While they're getting your room ready, I hope you will accept this as our wedding present."

He produced two glasses and a bottle of chilled champagne. He steered the newly married couple toward the empty dining room, past the open bar, where a party of men in sports clothes were noisily enjoying themselves.

Jessica sat down opposite Jim at a small table overlooking the sea. It was the same table as they had used on their earlier visit. Collins opened the bottle, filled the two glasses, and left the couple alone for the first time.

They raised their glasses to each other, and Jim said: "I think we've done the right thing, Jessica."

Then he said: "What do you think I should call you now we're married?"

Being Mrs Someone, even Mrs Anstruther, and even in private only, as it would have to be, didn't sound naughty enough. She was just about to say: "Let's get upstairs as soon as we can," when the doors to the dining room swung open. In strode a man with a beer glass in his hand. He shouted out: "I thought I recognised you! It's Jessica Ross, isn't it?"

Jessica looked at him with shock. She had seen him somewhere before but could not put a name to him. Being recognised was the worst thing that could have happened. It was what Jim had been dreading all along. She turned back to her new husband, who was sitting opposite her, his glass still in the air. He looked thunderstruck. After a second, he gradually turned his head so that its back was toward the newcomer. "Get that man out of here quickly," he muttered.

The man with the beerglass walked up to their table, picking up a spare chair with his left hand as he approached. He spun it around in his hand and put it down at the table, its back touching the starched linen of the tablecloth, its seat facing out toward the room. The man sat down, leaning on the chairback and facing Jessica. He put his glass of beer on the table, saying breezily: "I hope you don't mind if I join you?"

Jessica stared at him, her mouth open but with no words coming out.

The man spoke the words for her: "Of course not, Talbot!"

He looked at her, beaming. "You don't know who I am, do you?" he asked.

Jessica glumly shook her head. "Funny that; I thought everybody knew me! You should do — you were on my show, my programme. I'm Talbot Posner!"

Jessica still said nothing. She couldn't. She had no idea how to save anything of her collapsing world. She was even more worried for Jim, who had gloomily foretold such a happening.

"I'm glad I've bumped into you like this," said Posner. "I must say I was pretty mad at you at first after you wrecked my show like that, but I just want to say thank you for putting in a good word for me. Thanks for your help!"

Jessica looked blankly back.

"You haven't heard?" It was Talbot Posner's turn to look perplexed. "Don't you know? I'm to be the new editor of the *Tribune*. Your father wants me to start tomorrow."

If there had been any chance of escape, this news had put paid to it. Jessica started to feel sick.

Talbot Posner grinned with self-satisfaction. "That's enough about me for the moment, though," he said with a hint of reluctance. "Tell me about yourself. What are you doing down in this neck of the woods? Strange place for a girl who gets herself into the Society columns all the time, isn't it?"

He leant over and in a conspiratorial tone said: "Who's your young man? Is this life's young love I see before me? Come on, you can tell me! Your secret's safe with Talbot Posner! I won't tell a soul!"

Here was a possible lifeline. He was probably lying — who could possibly trust a journalist — but there was no other chance of escape. Jessica started: "Actually . . ."

Posner immediately interrupted her and looked at Jim, who was still turned away, looking out of the window. Posner tapped him on the shoulder and said: "Don't I know you from somewhere? Where was it? No, don't tell me . . . let it come to me . . ."

Jim suddenly stood up and said: "Please leave Miss Ross alone. Can't you see she's in a state of shock?"

He went round the back of the table and, using his left hand, helped Jessica to her feet.

"She has just heard that her fiancé has been killed in action. I'm her personal physician and I'm giving her treatment for nervous collapse," he said, lifting the champagne bottle from its bucket in his left hand and walking slowly to the door, supporting Jessica by the waist. As he walked, Jim kept his face turned away from Posner. At the door, Jim said to him loudly, still without turning his head: "Remember what you promised about keeping a secret: no one must ever get to hear about this."

It took a minute or two to locate their reallocated bedroom. When they did, and were inside, Jessica said: "You were marvellous!"

"We can't stay here," said Jim. "There's just a tiny chance that we might get away with this."

Their clothes had been taken out of their suitcases and hung in the wardrobe. As they packed up again, Jim appeared to have changed his mind about their chances. He said: "You know what people are like. If he doesn't remember who I am, he will when he sees me in a corridor at the *Tribune*. Even if he doesn't find out about our wedding from Collins he's bound to tell the proprietor about seeing you."

They drank the champagne out of the toothmugs they found in the room, then took their hastily stuffed suitcases downstairs to the hotel lobby. Through the window to the bar, Talbot Posner could be seen with his golfing cronies. Jim got Collins to telephone for a cab. Jessica could see him paying the bill from a roll of £1 and 10s notes and a few of the doomed white fivers. With Jim on one side and Collins on the other, she was helped out of the door and into a taxi. Collins said, over her head, to Jim: "We're all sorry to see you leave like this, sir. I had absolutely no idea she was expecting. You'd never have told from the look of her."

"Corsets," said Jim.

Sitting together in an otherwise unoccupied First Class compartment in the train back to London, Jessica was prepared for a bitter reaction, but Jim appeared to have accepted the disaster with resignation. There was no point worrying themselves by brooding on what might happen, he said. Instead, he suggested, they should take a tip from the *Worker* — when the Communist Party lost an election, it was described as a victory, when it was almost wiped out it was called a setback and when it was annihilated it was described as an opportunity to reassess strategy.

This was ponderous, gallows humour; and it wasn't the first time Jim had made anti-Communist remarks lately.

"I wasn't brooding," said Jessica. "I think I might even be glad we've been found out. I'm proud of you, Jim. I want people to know we're married."

The three months of deceit had been a bit of a strain. Being naughty without being found out had lost its delicious romance.

"The only thing that upsets me is that I'll miss seeing the proprietor's face when Talbot Posner spills the beans," said Jessica.

"Are you absolutely certain he's going to?" asked Jim, apparently hoping against hope that things might carry on as they were.

"I'm fed up with living a lie," said Jessica. "I think I'll have to go and own up to the proprietor, to his face. I can't imagine what he'll say!"

"Fed up with living a lie? We've only been married a few hours!" said Jim, looking as though he'd been slapped around the face with one of the Royal Hotel's stale fish.

"Actually, I *can* imagine what he'll say, and it isn't very nice. He's bound to hit me again. But I needn't worry any more, because I've got you," said Jessica, nuzzling her bruised face against Jim.

"I hope you don't intend to tell him immediately," said Jim, beginning to sound seriously worried rather than merely morose.

"Perhaps not quite yet," said Jessica. "But I ought to get to him before Posner does. I can't miss out on giving him a piece of news like that."

"I think you'd better come home with me. My own house should be empty this weekend. We'll spend our honeymoon night there," said Jim. "I don't want you near a telephone in the state you're in. I beg you at least to think the whole thing through before you do anything rash."

"Spoilsport," teased Jessica.

"No. I'm serious. If there's anything rash going to be done, *I'll* do it. It's *my* job that's at stake. If I create a really big strike, they'll not be able to sack me — that would be a case of victimisation."

"That's why I like you," said Jessica. She drew down the blinds of their compartment, wedged the door closed and took off her wedding gown.

"This will be my first time with a married man," she said.

15

Sunday 4th November 1956

Jim woke with his bride beside him in the cold, mirror-less bedroom. They had not had very much to drink after the hurried bottle of champagne, so at first he could not explain the painful banging and the ringing in his head. He turned over, away from Jessica, but the noise did not stop.

Then Jessica woke. "You'd better answer the door," she said.

Jim twisted round under the bedclothes, groaned, and put his feet to the bedside mat. He stood up, and covered his nakedness with the dressing gown from the back of the door. The coarseness of the felt made his skin uncomfortable.

He walked down the stairs. "Stop that noise," he shouted.

The banging and intermittent ringing stopped for long enough for a male voice to shout back: "If you open the door, I'll stop knocking on it."

It couldn't be the Betterwear salesman[1] on a Sunday, and it wasn't likely to be Mormons[2]; they were generally more polite.

Jim opened the door to find Sørensen on the doorstep. The man was totally insensitive to how normal folk conducted their lives, Jim believed. He told him: "If you've come to see Sheilagh, you're out of luck. Besides, I thought she went gallivanting off with you at the weekends."

"No. It's you I've come to see," said Sørensen, stepping inside. "You don't mind me coming in."

"Is that a request or a statement?" said Jim.

Sørensen walked into the kitchen. He seemed to know his way about; he must have been there before, Jim realised. It did not make him any more kindly disposed toward him.

"Sheilagh's in the car outside," said Sørensen. "What I've got to say to you is entirely a matter between ourselves."

"Don't think you can come here and stir up nastiness about that," said Jim. "As far as I'm concerned, I never want to see her again. So you can collect her things and get out."

"You misunderstand," said Sørensen, sitting down at the kitchen table. "Sheilagh has told me all about your bourgeois views, so I'm not surprised. This visit is nothing about her, though. It's altogether far more serious than mere personal relations."

"What can be more important than that?" said Jim. It wasn't something he believed, but he wanted to prick the pomposity of the Party official.

"I think you'd better make me a cup of tea while I explain," said Sørensen. "What I'm going to ask you to do is the biggest service the Party has ever called on you for."

Jim did not like being told to make the tea, but nevertheless put water in the kettle, placed it on the stove and lit the gas[3]. As he did so, he realised that he had already started obeying Sørensen's instructions. "To be quite frank, I'm sick of your little tests," he said.

"I will give you your instructions," said Sørensen. "As you will know if you've been listening to the news, armed forces from the Soviet Union have this morning crossed into Hungary, at the request of the new Hungarian Socialist Workers' Party, to seal off the Austrian border, end the strikes and put down the counter-revolutionary insurrection."

"Oh no!" said Jim, slumping into the chair opposite Sørensen.

"Don't be so melodramatic," said Sørensen. "You knew what was going on. You must have seen it coming."

"I've been busy on a personal matter," said Jim, lamely. "I think I feel sick, though."

"I thought that might be your reaction," said Sørensen. "There are a lot of people in the Party here who are rather taken aback."

"Taken aback? I'm shocked," said Jim. You didn't react with equanimity when your whole political hopes were destroyed at one blow. But there was nothing he could actually do about it.

The kettle was beginning to boil. He had to get up to lift it off the stove and fill the teapot. He put a bottle of milk on the table. As he was getting out the cups and saucers, he wondered whether to ask Jessica to come downstairs so he could introduce her to the man he had talked to her of only as "a senior Party official".

He put down two cups and saucers and a sugar bowl — and decided it would be better if Jessica remained where she was. Sørensen's cold-fish outlook was not something to be inflicted on someone you loved.

"Your reaction is that you need time to think about it," said Sørensen. He was wrong. Jim knew exactly what he thought about it.

"Why are you telling all this to me, Sørensen? And on a Sunday morning, too. Is the whole Executive on holiday?"

"I'll lay all my cards on the table," said Sørensen, pouring himself a cup of tea and adding milk and three spoonfuls of sugar. He left Jim to pour his own. "The whole Party is bound to be at sixes and sevens about this until the correct policy emerges. We have a counter-revolutionary element of our own, it would appear. Some of them have been building up a nest of opposition. I have reason to believe that some of them have been meeting in the offices of the *Worker* itself. You have doubtless seen some of their fascist-inspired outpourings disguised as news reports from

Hungary. One editorial even claimed that the Nagy government kept a *Daily Worker* journalist in prison for seven years without charge or trial."

"And you've got that place well taped," said Jim, remembering his own experience of being listened to with the industrial organiser's Soviet-built equipment.

"Precisely — as you know. We also know that in the event of Soviet forces being invited in to restore revolutionary discipline in Hungary, some of these elements planned to use the columns of the *Worker* itself to build up this anti-Party attack."

Sørensen took a few carbon-copy sheets of Telex[4] printing out of a pocket and handed them to Jim: "This is the editorial matter issued by Moscow for printing in the *Worker*, but there are so many dubious elements at that paper that I expect they will try to substitute their own material."

Jim only glanced at the words. He prompted Sørensen: "So?"

"This is where you come in," Sørensen told him, sipping his tea. "We will have great difficulty stopping them, before the Central Committee meets to announce the new Party line. We mustn't have the Party washing its dirty linen in public — so the *Worker* must be stopped. We can't have it stopped by Party instructions, that wouldn't be democratic. It has to be stopped by its own staff."

"You'll have difficulty there," said Jim, with a bit of a chuckle for the first time that morning. "You know as well as I do that half the print workers hate Communists and Communism. They won't go on strike just to suit you, you know."

Sørensen leant across the table and said: "I know that. That's why they're going to go on strike for *you*. You're going to foment a dispute at the *Tribune* and it's going to spread around Fleet Street. I leave you to choose the reason for the strike, there must be hundreds."

"That's preposterous! I can't go around causing strikes just like that!" said Jim.

He was trapped in a way that Sørensen could not realise. He had worked out that he had to bring about a serious stoppage at the *Tribune* before the new editor managed to speak to the proprietor. That way, they wouldn't dare sack him as the unions would see it as a clear case of victimisation. On the other hand, if he did stir up a strike at just that time, he might look as if he were just a Party pawn. Even before that morning's shock news he was increasingly worried about the Party. He was even thinking of leaving it and certainly did not want to help it cover up this Hungarian outrage. Still, if it was a question of his political principles or his job . . .

"Of course you can stir up a strike whenever you want to. You always used to. What's changed?" said Sørensen.

Jim felt that at least a show of reluctance was called for. "What's changed is that I think these so-called counter-revolutionaries should be listened to, not shot. They can't all be American spies. If their ideas are wrong they will be defeated by argument. If they are right the people will back them."

"You could well be right," reasoned Sørensen. "Although I think the argument has moved on from who is right and wrong. The Party in Britain needs time to think. It needs that time or it will tear itself apart. Only you can give it that time. We must stop the *Worker* coming out with an ill-considered view on the matter.

"Who knows: it could be that the Party, given time, will condemn today's events. I will stand by it, whatever it decides, because I'm a Party man through and through."

"Since you put it like that . . ." Jim started, deciding that now was the time to appear to give in to reasoned argument.

"Yes . . ." prompted Sørensen, eagerly.

"I think there might be a few issues the union should be looking into at the *Tribune*," said Jim, cursing himself for not having enough moral strength to throw the man out.

"Marvellous! I knew you'd be with us," said Sørensen. "Sheilagh wasn't so sure. She said I'd have to threaten you with exposure over the affair you're having with the boss's daughter, but I knew you'd respond to reason and an appeal to comradeship."

At one time, the revelation that the Party indeed knew all and would stop at nothing would have made Jim feel proud. Now it made him feel sick. It infuriated him that a man such as Sørensen, and the unspeakable Sheilagh, could think he'd be persuaded by such unpleasant tactics. "I think you'd better go now, before that sort of muck makes me change my mind," he said. "Go — before I hit you."

As Sørensen passed through the passageway on his way out, Jim could see Jessica, with a sheet wrapped around her, watching him from the top of the stairs.

"Who was that?" she asked, as the door closed behind the organiser. "Why don't I ever get to see you hitting someone?"

"That was the 'senior Party official' I told you about."

"Oh. Had he come to collect the clothes of 'a certain person' that I can see lying around?"

"No," said Jim. "He'd come to tell me the Party had changed since I joined it. Did you know they've invaded Hungary?"

"Ooh, No!" she said. "Who's invaded? Them, or us?"

"The Russians," said Jim.

"Oh! Us," said Jessica. "That's marvellous. It'll send the proprietor mad. He just can't stand the Russians."

"That's one way of looking at it, I suppose," said Jim, as he went upstairs, still in his dressing gown.

The two sat on Jim's bed and discussed the foreseeable future — the period until that evening. Jim had to go to work at the

Tribune. Since he intended stirring up trouble, there was no saying when his day would finish. Meanwhile, Jessica was to go to Shepherd Market, even if the builders were still there, and wait until she was sure the proprietor had gone to the office. Then she was to go to Avenue Road to pick up her belongings. She said she understood why Jim wanted her to delay telling the proprietor about their happy news until the newspaper strike was underway.

Did she want a lift to the station or did she want to wait and risk a meeting with the "certain person" who believed she still had a right to live there?

She went with him. They sat next to each other on the train, respectability and the beatnik[5], Jim in his suit and tie but without a hat, and Jessica shivering in jeans and a sweater. They shared Jim's overcoat. Before Jessica had to change trains, Jim told her about Sørensen's wish for a strike at the *Tribune* to give the Party to make up its mind about Hungary. "He sounds a brilliant man, this Sørensen," she said.

Together they read the words in the Telex provided by Sørensen which the Soviet government required to be printed in the *Worker*:

> At the request of the Revolutionary Workers' and Peasants' Government, the Soviet Army held out a helping hand to the working people of Hungary by defending them against terror and routing the gangs which were carrying out the putsch.
>
> Their request reached us at a time when the rebels had already killed thousands of Hungarian patriots, and the Hungarian workers and peasants supported by the Soviet Army had

themselves put an end to the outrages committed by the fascist murderers.

The working people of Hungary were justified in calling for the removal of shortcomings in the field of economic development, for the raising of the material standards of the population and for the elimination of bureaucratic unwieldiness in the machinery of government.

Yet, this movement for overcoming the existing shortcomings was from the very outset joined by the forces of reaction and counter-revolution which for long had been hard at work underground preparing to abolish the system of people's democracy in Hungary to overthrow the rule of the workers and peasants, to restore landlordism and capitalism, and to bring fascism back to life.

The reactionary forces and enemies of the Hungarian people brought armed gangs into the country to launch a reign of bloody terror and kill Hungarian patriots wholesale.

Jessica folded the despatch and put it in her handbag. Jim said: "No wonder my visitor doubted the *Worker* would publish that. It's drivel."

Jessica said: "Jim, how could you possibly attack the Soviet Army!"

Before Jim could think of how to reply, the train drew up at Peckham, where Jessica had to get out. So he responded with a kiss on the cheek and the words: "I love you."

Arriving presently at the *Tribune* building as he had done so many times before, Jim wondered whether this time would be his last. He entered via the empty despatch bay, making a mental note to visit there later as the men came on shift to see what their grievances might be. He moved on into the press hall, looking for Fred Dawlish.

"How are things doing?" Jim said.

"Same as ever," said Dawlish.

"No problems, then? The reel-store problem hasn't come back has it?" Jim asked.

"Nothing like that," said Dawlish.

"No bits of rotting human flesh attracting the rats?" wondered Jim.

"We rarely find journalists attracted to the press hall, rotting flesh or not," said Dawlish.

"That's a good one," said Jim, reluctantly moving on in his quest for exploitable grievances. He walked through the other departments, even including the proof-readers, in spite of the likelihood of getting involved in a lengthy conversation about prospects for the forthcoming cricket tour of South Africa.

Bill Enright had a complaint about a blocked lavatory and about the never-changing canteen menu, but there wasn't any great burning issue there awaiting exploitation.

When he met Francis Josling he did not get a good reception. "You desert us for months when we have had any number of complaints," said Josling. "So much so that some people were saying management must have bought you off. Now you come over all solicitous about our wellbeing. Something funny's going on. What is it?"

"Nothing at all, Francis," said Jim in a shocked tone. "I certainly don't want people thinking I'm in the bosses' pocket."

He leant closer to the man. "That's why I'm anxious to have a short, sharp strike every now and then — just to remind management who really runs this place."

"So, it's not Communist Party instructions that's making you act like this," said Josling.

"To tell the truth," said Jim, still in a low tone. "I'm getting a little worried about the Communist Party myself."

"Glad to hear it," said Josling. "Can I interest you in the Socialist Review Group[6]? What with the collapse of your type of Communism in Eastern Europe, we think the workers are just about to turn to us in a big way."

Jim politely silenced Josling in the way he normally reserved for Jehovah's Witnesses[7], and moved off, no nearer to finding the cause of his strike. The issue presented itself just as Jim ended his tour and went to his cubby hole in the corridor. The telephone on his desk was ringing. He picked it up.

"Is that you, Anstruther? O'Brien here. "Can you come to the meeting room right away? Something rather urgent has just come up."

Jim went back to the proof-readers' department, collected Francis Josling, and went with him to find out what the Printer wanted to talk about. O'Brien was there with Colonel Cumberledge. Jim and his companion sat down at the table in the positions indicated. The Colonel said: "As this isn't part of our regular series of meetings, I'd rather not have an argument about who should take the chair. So, can we leave the seat at the end of the table vacant?"

"I'd like to record our protest at the short notice given for this meeting and to the breach of procedures and disregard of custom and practice involved," said Jim. He was clutching at straws.

"Noted," said the Colonel. "Now, I'll come straight to the point: you tell him, O'Brien."

O'Brien leant over the table, his usual unflappability missing. He said: "It's like this. We've got instructions to double the run. Printing is to start two hours early and continue flat out till dawn."

The Colonel added: "It seems the proprietor says that what with the invasion of Hungary and the ultimatum to Britain and France to get out of Egypt, we'll sell all the papers we can print."

Jim didn't need to search for an issue any more. Here it was on a plate. He said: "This is preposterous. You can't double the print order using the same number of people. And another thing: the Colonel might not know this but you do, O'Brien — the building will shake to pieces if you try to put that sort of strain on it. I can't have people risking their lives just to boost the proprietor's profit."

He stopped, and added a thought that had just occurred to him: "Where's the extra paper coming from? The Newsprint Rationing Committee[8] would never let you add pages or double the print-run without weeks of discussion. If we let you go ahead, they'd withdraw your paper ration and then we'd all be out of a job."

"I don't think it's anything to do with money," said the Colonel, sounding as if he couldn't understand what was going on, either. "I think it's some point of principle. He's given orders that any copies that can't be sold are to be given away in the streets. I'm told the whole front page has been written by him, and it's all about Hungary. The whole Suez business is relegated to the inside pages.

"I can't figure it out, myself, but those are our orders. That's why he's the proprietor and we are only employees. I'm appealing to you, Anstruther, for God's sake, help us."

"Not a chance," said Jim, looking for confirmation from Josling. "Not a chance."

The Colonel replied, in an unnatural tone, as if reading from a script: "As you realise, this is an issue of the utmost importance. I know it will destroy our negotiating position, but I have been instructed to ask you what you would accept in order to give us a full, uninterrupted run. Name your price and we'll pay it."

Jim spoke quickly before Josling could stop him. "I told you — nothing doing. It's not a question of money. It's a matter of procedures, of staffing and of safety. You haven't given enough notice. We couldn't find the extra hands in time and the whole building could fall in and kill us all. Nothing doing."

"That's unreasonable — how could we have given notice of an invasion?" said O'Brien.

"Indeed," said the Colonel. "But there's something else. My private offer to you still stands. We need a new night manager, Anstruther. You can have the job any time you want, if we get tonight's issue out."

Josling turned angrily to Jim. "You bloody sell-out! You never told me about this."

Before Jim could defend himself by saying that he had obviously not accepted, the Colonel said: "That offer can include your deputy. There's a senior management position waiting for him, too."

"I think I will have to leave this meeting and see the FoCs of all the unions," said Jim. "Attempted corruption of chapel officials is something they will take most seriously. You'll not get any production tonight, that's for sure."

With Josling nodding vigorously at his side, Jim stood up to go. Before they even started moving toward it, the door opened. The proprietor himself marched in.

Jim had not seen him close-up before. He was of medium height, with dark hair greying at the temples. His facial features were large and his mouth loose. He looked exceptionally stern, but was attempting to smile.

"Don't stand up on my behalf," he said, coming over to Jim, his hand outstretched. "You must be Mr Anstruther. I've heard a lot about you."

Jim, caught standing up at the wrong moment, subsided into his seat. Reluctantly, he shook hands with the great man, who then leant past him and shook Josling's hand too. The great man nodded to the Colonel and to O'Brien and sat down at the head of the table. "Thank you for keeping my seat vacant," he said.

He turned to Jim and said: "They tried to tell me not to meet you myself. Said it wouldn't help at all; would give quite the wrong message. They said you'd see it as a weakness and would exploit it for all you were worth. Well, I'm quite prepared for that, and I'm here to throw myself on your mercy."

"You don't need mercy," said Jim. "We do. Just as you arrived, we were about to walk out in protest against your plans to kill our members."

"I don't remember giving any instructions about killing," said the proprietor, looking in mock consternation at O'Brien and Cumberledge. "Did I tell you to kill anyone, Colonel?"

"Definitely not, Sir," said Cumberledge.

"I thought not," said the proprietor, turning back to Jim. "So let us conduct our talks without making wild accusations. Perhaps we ought to start again . . .

"My name is Otto Ross, and I own this newspaper. I understand your name is Mr Anstruther."

"Yes," said Jim. "As you also know, I'm the Imperial Father of the Combined Chapels of the Printing Unions at this newspaper. We are in charge of production. If you don't get our agreement, you don't get a newspaper."

"That's being pretty straightforward, Mr Anstruther. I'm glad to see you talk in the same language as I do."

Jim noted that the proprietor had barely a shade of a foreign accent.

The proprietor continued: "I saw you on television, Mr Anstruther. You managed to make mincemeat of one of my editors. It was interesting to watch."

Jim wondered whether the remark was intended to tell him that the proprietor knew what he was up to with Jessica, but the proprietor said: "I wonder: what are your ambitions?"

"I'm not so sure I have any," said Jim. "Perhaps I'd like to get rid of this Tory Government. But if you mean 'what would I like as a bribe,' I've already given your minions the answer — nothing doing."

"I wasn't being so crass," said the proprietor, as the Colonel winced. "Although I think the management here would be improved if someone of your obvious intelligence and abilities joined." The Colonel winced again. "No, it wasn't that. I am trying to work out what kind of a man you are."

"I don't have to stay and listen to this," said Jim.

"I don't suppose you do," said the proprietor, leaning back in his chair. "But I bet you will. You're fascinated. You want to see what I'm going to say next."

This was true.

"Tell me about your life," said the proprietor.

"I don't see why I should," said Jim. "And I don't see how it will help you print newspapers — but I don't see that I've anything to lose. In fact my life has been dominated by my birthdays: I was born on the 5th May, on Karl Marx's birthday. Lenin had just died. My second birthday took place during the General Strike[9]."

The proprietor was leaning toward him, with a look of rapt attention. "Go on," he said. "What happened to you then?"

"My father was thrown out of work in Dundee and we came to London, and he got a job sweeping up at the *Daily Mail*. I started my indentures there myself when I was 14. A year later, war was declared — so, instead of the six-year apprenticeship, my training was compressed. By 16 I was fully skilled. VE day was two days after my 21st birthday, when I became a local councillor in a bye-election, but that didn't last long."

Jim stopped himself, embarrassed. He was talking far too much, which was quite obviously the proprietor's intention. Although how it was going to help him get a paper printed, Jim could not work out. "I'm sorry," he said. "I didn't mean to go on like that, but you did ask."

"Don't apologise," said the proprietor. "You are quite right, I did ask. And I'm glad you've told me. Is it true you're a Communist?"

Jim was surprised by the bluntness of the question, and must have appeared so. The proprietor glanced at the Colonel and O'Brien and said to them: "Go off somewhere and make yourself busy."

He then looked at Josling and said: "This is just a private talk. I promise we'll ask you back when we start negotiating."

Josling bridled. "The chapel committee will hear about this," he said to Jim.

There was an air of such intensity about the proprietor that Jim found himself transfixed, powerless. He knew he was acting totally in contradiction to his intentions, but could not stop himself. He said to Josling: "That's OK Francis. I'll speak to you afterwards."

As the three men left the room, the proprietor said: "Well? Is it true you're a Communist?"

"Yes, I am," said Jim. "What's the matter? Have you never met one before?"

"Indeed I have," said the proprietor, ruefully. "I have indeed. Many of them. There was a Communist republic[10] set up in my country after the war, you know. The first world war."

He said it with an air of awful significance, as if announcing the end of the world. (For someone who frequently described himself as British, it had been a slip to call Hungary "my country".)

"You were kind enough to tell me something about yourself," he said. "So permit me to lay my own life bare in front of you . . .

"When that Communist state was set up around Budapest it was in a putsch you know. There was turmoil for years, street fighting all the time between them and the monarchists and others. My father had a printing business, but he was killed in the war by the Russians. There was just me to feed my invalid mother. Nobody helped us, not the monarchists and not the Communists. All they were interested in was winning power for themselves.

"I've seen these people in action before. I know what to expect."

The proprietor was fixing him so strongly with his eyes that Jim was beginning to feel uncomfortable. He regretted allowing Josling to be sent away, and began to understand how Jessica could be so obsessed.

"That wasn't the end of my troubles," said the proprietor, edging his chair closer. "Oh no. After my mother died, I travelled throughout Europe before eventually finding a haven in this country. I was grateful that at last I had found somewhere that people could be free from persecution and allowed to get on with their own lives in whatever way they wished. I got married to a young American widow here and we settled down. It was her money from her first marriage as much as mine that helped me set up our printing business. I suppose I was trying to copy my own father."

Jim was trying to edge away, but the proprietor leant toward him and grabbed his arm while continuing to talk. The man's not sane, thought Jim.

"You think I was doing well? So did I. But then the despots caught up with me again. That was the second world war. My wife couldn't have children after what she'd been through but we'd managed to adopt a daughter. We sent her off to America to be safe. I should have gone myself, because there came that knock on the door. I was a naturalised British subject and my wife had a British passport from her first marriage, but they still arrested me and interned me on the Isle of Man."

Then with the inspired question of the obsessive, the proprietor said: "I'm not boring you, am I? It's just that it is absolutely imperative that you understand why this paper is so important to me."

Jim was certainly not bored, but was almost frightened by the proprietor's emotional intensity. He did not reply. No response was looked for, as the proprietor continued: "My wife helped the business to survive all the time I was away, because I joined British Intelligence as soon as they let me out of the camp. She died too, in the closing stages of the war; she fell downstairs in the blackout. Everyone I love seems to die.

"It was just after the war ended that I managed to get hold of the *Tribune* — but you know that, don't you?

"That's why you must know how important it is to me: its campaigns, its honesty, its truth. I owe a lot to this country, and the *Tribune* is my way of trying to pay back some of that debt . . ."

The proprietor was beginning to calm down, he was leaning forward less aggressively, and was starting to pant from the emotion exertion which he had just displayed. But he had not finished. He pushed the chair back and stood up, only then letting go his grip on Jim's arm. He moved round the side of the table to stand beside Jim, brusquely pushing Josling's empty chair out of the way with his foot. He took from a jacket pocket a series of large tracing-paper drawings and unfolded them in a pile in front of Jim on the table.

"This is my paper for tomorrow," he said. "It's my tribute to my father, my debt to my wife, my duty to this country, and my tryst with our readers. It's the biggest thing I've done in my life — because what is happening today is the worst horror in my lifetime."

He had worked himself back up into a frenzy, and was jabbing with his right finger at the front-page dummy. "Read it! Read it!" he yelled. "That's what you're trying to stop! The Russians invade my birthplace and put children to the slaughter and you try to prevent our readers from seeing the truth."

There on the front page was a photograph of terrified refugees crossing the Austrian border in a snowstorm, and the huge, black headline, echoing Radio Hungary's final, unheeded cry: **WE DO NOT FORGET YOU!**

Jim looked at the layout. The juxtaposition of the words and the picture of the refugees certainly looked poignant.

Underneath the picture of the tank was the final page of last Hungarian News Agency transmission:

> *good bye we do not forget you*
> *bye, the russians are too near*
> *we shall leave our post*
> *good bye friends, save our souls*

In a separate panel were the final words of the Freedom radio station "We fight to the last drop of blood," before it went off the air with a woman's voice screaming "Help Hungary . . . Help . . . Help."

The proprietor turned to Jim and said: "That's not all. In their brief few days of freedom I had a phone call from my own little brother, who's still there. I don't know now whether he's alive or dead. I took down his words. He said: 'There was one thing above all else we just couldn't bear. That we had to praise them. Misery, near-starvation, going about in rags, and all sorts of humiliation were not enough; on top of it we were forced to express our everlasting gratitude to our own masters and the glorious Soviet Union, day in day out. I hated that more than anything else.'"

Jim wondered what he was doing preventing the man saying something he felt so strongly about. The proprietor was so obviously sincere that he would give anything for this one edition that Jim began to doubt himself. Perhaps he should allow the man his increased production. He was so obviously willing to give anything in return. A possibility crossed his mind, whimsically. This might be the time to ask the proprietor for Jessica's hand in marriage. He let out a slight chuckle at the thought.

The proprietor immediately responded to the change in mood. "I see that you're at least thinking about it. Let me call my new editor in to show you the words. I wrote them myself, and I hope to God the readers are not denied the chance to see them."

He picked up a telephone and waited for the operator to answer, which took as long for him as it frequently did for Jim. Without bothering to introduce himself, he said: "Tell Posner to come here immediately," and replaced the handset.

Within seconds, the door of the conference room opened. It was not Posner who came in, but Jessica. She closed the door firmly behind her.

She was wearing the white dirndl dress again and carrying a white leather handbag. The proprietor looked overjoyed to see her.

"Jessica! Come in," he said. "What brings you here? I've been trying to get you to come to the office but you never do. I'm glad you've changed your mind."

"You won't be," Jessica said. She looked at the table with its page plans and at Jim, who was almost as surprised to see her as the proprietor but not quite so happy. He foresaw trouble.

Jessica then said: "What are you two up to? It doesn't look good to me."

The proprietor did not respond to her negative manner but ushered her over to look at the pages. She walked to the table and stood between the proprietor and Jim, in a way that let her rub up against him unseen. The proprietor showed her the pencilled words and the drawing of the tank with pride, the manic enthusiasm returning to his voice.

"This is the greatest issue of the *Tribune* there has ever been or ever will be. What tears me apart is that there had to be such a tragedy to bring it about. They are turning my birthplace into a cemetery. The streets of my childhood once again ring to the sound of Russian tanks. It cannot be Hungary's destiny to be the perpetual victim of the bloodthirsty Russ."

"Absolute piffle," said Jessica. "Drivel . . . balderdash . . . tripe, and you know it."

"What do you mean by that?" said the proprietor in a warning tone, turning toward her and raising a threatening hand to her.

"I mean that, if you were a true friend to Hungary, you would welcome its liberation from a bunch of CIA-sponsored counter-revolutionary cut-throats. The Red Army is the best guarantee anyone could have against the fascists. It's not good to see you in support of the same people who brought in the gas chambers."

The proprietor yelled: "Don't you ever dare to say anything like that to me again."

He brought his raised hand smashing across into her face in a blow that made her fall on to the table. The proprietor stood back, breathing heavily.

After a moment he lifted her gently back to her feet and smothered her in his arms. "My angel," he said. "I don't mean to hit you, you know that. I love you more than I can say. I know you only say things like to annoy me — that you don't mean them, really."

"Don't you bloody believe it!" said Jessica.

"You ask *him*," she said, nodding her head backward toward where Jim was sitting.

"What's he got to do with it? You don't even know him," said the proprietor. "He's the local union man, and I think I was beginning to persuade him about Hungary, too."

"You'll never persuade him," said Jessica, fighting herself free from the proprietor's smothering embrace. "He's more of a man than you'll ever be."

She took two steps back, paused for effect, and then said, coldly and carefully: "That's why I married him."

The proprietor, breathing even more heavily, grasped the back of the chair Jim was sitting in, and gasped: "You can't mean that!"

"Oh no?" said Jessica opening her handbag. She grabbed a piece of paper from it and let the bag fall to the floor. With both hands, she unfolded the piece of paper and thrust it in the proprietor's gasping face.

"What's this then? Is it a marriage certificate or is it a dog licence[11]?"

The proprietor did not read the paper. His face drained of colour. He let go his hold on Jim's chair, clutched at his stomach, gave a loud but diminishing groan, and fell to the floor.

Jessica kicked him, furiously. "Get up, you bastard! Get up!"

He made no move.

Jim turned slowly to Jessica, in awe at her ferocity. He said: "We'd better call a doctor, quickly. I think he's had a heart attack, or perhaps it's a stroke."

Jessica stepped over the twitching body. With a heave, she pulled Jim's chair in a part circle, away from the table. She smoothed down her skirt and sat on Jim's lap.

"Don't bother about him, he's just play-acting," she said, slipping her hand inside Jim's shirt. "He's always going on about his heart, just to gather sympathy. It doesn't work with me. Mark my words; in a few minutes he'll be back on his feet, ranting and raving as if nothing had happened."

She opened her mouth for a long and deep kiss. After a few minutes she got down from Jim's lap and looked at the proprietor's still form. She nudged it with a toe and it did not move. She said: "I don't think a doctor would be any use. We'd better call an undertaker."

There was a knock at the door and, without waiting, Talbot Posner bounced in, carrying a sheaf of galley proofs. He said: "I've got the front page here, guv. Is it a goer?"

Coming up to the table, he registered the presence of Jessica and Jim with surprise but without comment. He looked around for the proprietor. He followed Jim's gaze and registered the presence of the body on the floor.

"Blimey!" he said. "I've had a drink or two in my time, but nothing quite as serious as that."

"You'd better call a doctor," said Jim, lifting the telephone handset and offering it to Posner. "I think you'd also better find the proprietor's obituary. He has it permanently set up in type and updates it every few months. It takes up several pages."

Posner took the telephone and told the operator to get an ambulance. As he was speaking, Jessica took the proofs from his hand and started tearing them into pieces.

Posner turned to her and said: "I never told him, you know. I said I wouldn't, so I didn't."

Jessica carried on tearing up the proofs. "You won't be needing these. There won't be any edition tonight. The printers have gone on strike."

She turned to Jim for confirmation: "Isn't that right, Jim?"

Jim bit his lip and said: "I'm not so sure about that. Circumstances have changed in the last few minutes."

He looked at the body on the floor and said: "The old boy was pretty much set on having a big sale."

Jessica looked at him, shocked. "But remember," she said. "The Party needs time to sort out its ranks. Remember your ideals."

She took the Soviet government despatch out of her handbag and started reading it.

"Damn the Party," said Jim. "Think of the Hungarians." He looked at the body on the floor and said: "Think of your father."

Jessica looked from Jim to the body on the floor and back again.

She turned to Posner and said: "They're both the bloody same."[12]

Endnotes

Chapter 1

1. Lady Farnsworth was a member of the London and Provincial Anti-Vivisection Society (LPAVS), which was in the final stages of merger negotiations with the National Anti-Vivisection Society, which itself traced its history back to 1875. Lady Farnsworth was strongly influenced by her friendship with Norah Elam, a prominent member of the LPAVS and of the British Union of Fascists, which had been proscribed by the Government in 1940.

2. All sons and daughters of Barons and Viscounts, as well as the younger sons of Earls, take the courtesy title "the Honourable" — usually abbreviated to "the Hon". Lear Farnsworth's father was Baron Farnsworth.

3. According to the Army Dress Regulations: "Like the British constitution, the field of uniforms and insignia has unwritten conventions without which such things become meaningless and, at the very least, lose their prestige." One of the conventions was that soldiers should not wear uniform when they were not on duty and in a civilian setting.

4. "National Service" was the system of compulsory male conscription into the armed services. It was unusual, but not unknown, for members of the upper classes to join at officer level. Service lasted for 18 months, followed by four years in the Reserves, who could be called up again in an emergency. The system was gradually unwound from 1957 and was abolished in 1960.

5. The Marshall & Snelgrove department store in Oxford Street was regarded as stylish, although it was in fact owned by the rather more mass-market store Debenhams.

6. Subaltern: a military term for any junior officer below the rank of Major.

7. The English cricket team won by an innings and 170 runs

8. *Stompin' at the Savoy* was not named after the Savoy Hotel, London, where this ball was being held, but after the Savoy Ballroom in New York City. The 1933 jazz standard had just been re-released by Benny Goodman.

9. The Rhodesia Castle was a 17.041 gross ton luxury liner built by Harland & Wolff in Belfast in 1951 for Union Castle's "Round Africa" service.

10. According to a parliamentary answer by the then Chancellor of the Exchequer, Harold Macmillan, given in February, the earnings of men aged 21 and over in manufacturing and certain other industries covered by the regular Ministry of Labour inquiries were £10 17s. 5d (ten pounds, seven shillings and fivepence) a week in April 1955 "the latest date for which figures are available". This equates to £565 a year.

11. The Canadian James J. Parker (aged 29) was almost 5 inches taller than his American opponent Archie Moore (aged 42), and his reach was 2 inches longer. The much-anticipated fight was in Toronto, in front of Parker's home crowd. What could go wrong?

12. Even money – the betting odds offered an equal chance of his winning or losing. Gambling for cash was illegal, except at a racecourse, in Britain until 1960. Illegal betting was widespread.

13. *No Mean City* was the title of a best-selling pulp fiction novel, first published in 1935 but still widely read. It depicted, with brutal candour, life among the "hard men" and razor gangs of Glasgow. The book was much hated among the upright citizens of the largest town in Scotland, who preferred to name the place

Second City of the Empire – although that title was by then more properly held by Hong Kong, which had a population of 2.5 million to Glasgow's 1.78 million.

14. Half a crown, or half crown. A coin valued at 2 shillings and sixpence, one-eighth of a pound (usually shown as 2s 6d, and equivalent to 12½p in the decimal currency which came in in 1971). The largest of the standard silver coins, at 32mm diameter. By this date, the coins were not actually silver, but cupro-nickel. It was enough to buy two packets of 20 cigarettes.

15. Tenements. These were a type of building shared by multiple dwellings, typically with small flats on each floor and with shared entrance stairway access. The smallest of these flats, a "single end", had just one room. Two-room flats were known as a "through and through". There was running water in each flat, but the toilets were usually shared facilities outside on the ground floor level.

16. Razor gangs took their name from their weapon of choice – the open, or cut-throat razor, known in the US as a straight razor — at the time still used for its official purpose in barber shops. The razor gangs were most at home in the East End and South Side of Glasgow.

17. *The One o'clock Jump*, a jazz standard written in 1937 by Count Basie, had recently been re-released in a 45rpm vinyl single, rather than the original 78rpm shellac record.

18. 79 degrees on the Fahrenheit scale is 26 degrees on the Celsius scale, which the official Meteorological Office started using in 1961.

Chapter 2

1. Young ladies of the upper classes were often sent to an expensive finishing school, frequently in Switzerland, to round off their education, with classes on deportment, etiquette, and — most importantly — how to acquire a suitable husband.

2. The strike, at British Motor Corporation plants, notably the Morris and Austin factory at Cowley, in Oxford, and Longbridge, in Birmingham, was caused by the dismissal of 6,000 workers as automation became more widespread.

3. A guinea was £1 and 1 shilling, so a thousand guineas would be £1,050.

4. "Gentleman" was a class indicator. It was defined in Chambers's Dictionary as "a man of good birth; one who without a title wears a coat of arms; more generally, every man above the rank of yeoman, including the nobility; one above the trading classes; a man of refined manners."

5. Colloquially, in 1956 "BF" had not come to mean boyfriend but was supposed to mean, at best, "bloody fool", or depending on who was speaking, something more obscene.

6. Hoo-ha. British slang, meaning a state or condition of excitement, agitation, or disturbance.

7. Local four-digit telephone numbers were always preceded by the name of the exchange, with the first three letters capitalised to indicate the number to be used for self-dialled calls. Thus HAMpstead 3404 could be dialled as 426 3404. Not all local telephone exchanges were automated by this time, which is why the exchange required a name as well as a number.

8. Swann & Edgar's was a mid-market department store at that time owned by Harrod's. It was situated on Piccadilly Circus, which made it a popular meeting place as it could be accessed both from street level and directly from the Piccadilly Underground station.

9. Point duty. Many traffic junctions were not controlled by traffic lights but instead at busy times had a policeman standing in the centre to direct traffic. There was a system of hand signals used which   drivers had to learn in order to pass the Driving Test.

10. The Beaverbrook group of newspapers, including the world's largest selling paper, the *Daily Express*, as well as the London *Evening Standard*, was owned and controlled by Lord Beaverbrook, a wily, Canadian-born Conservative politician.

11. Phone calls still cost twopence, so perhaps the proprietor was expecting Fibbins to have to make more than one call.

12. Charing Cross Hospital was still in the Charing Cross area of London, in Agar Street, north of the Strand, conveniently close to the Savoy Hotel as well as Charing Cross railway station.

13. The proprietor has mis-named King Edward VII's Hospital, doubtless remembering its wartime role. The private hospital is located in Beaumont Street, Marylebone, London.

14. Royal Masonic Hospital. This private hospital, in Hammersmith, West London, was supposed to treat only Freemasons, which implies that Otto Ross may have been a member of that order.

15. The phrase "on the square" was and is a discreet reference to membership of the Freemasons.

Chapter 3

1. All printing workers belonged to the union relevant to their particular trade. The membership body organising each union was called a "chapel", a word dating back to the early days of printing and possibly even earlier, to the days when monks controlled the production of books. The elected head of each chapel – the post which in other industries would be a "shop steward" - was called "Father of the Chapel", or "FoC". In a procedure laid down by the Printing and Kindred Trades Federation, the various unions co-ordinated their activities by sending representatives to a "combined chapels committee", which appointed one of their number to represent them, who took the title "Imperial Father of the Federated Unions".

2. δ

3. Each union carefully guarded its rights to a particular job. Thus, changing a lightbulb would be a job for an electrician.

4. "William Hickey" was the pseudonymous byline for the *Express's* gossip column, taking its name from the rather better written 18th century diarist.

5. The case room was where the newspaper was set up in metal type and the pages assembled.

6. Linotypes were the line-casting machines which, like giant typewriters, spewed out "slugs" or cast lines of type instead of having to cast each letter individually as had been previously done. The set copy was then brought to the "collecting random" where it was put in order and placed on a metal tray known as a galley.

7. The foundry was where papier-mâché imprints of each page – called "stereos" – were converted into semi-cylindrical printing plates for running on the huge letterpress printing machines. The people who worked there were called "stereotypers".

8. Blackfriars station was the terminus for the London, Chatham and Dover line. The early editions destined for Dover were for the few copies sent for sale across the English Channel. Readers in Dover itself and other towns in Kent would receive a later edition sent on a later train.

9. The change was made on 3rd June 1956.

10. British Railways continued the railway tradition of using the otherwise archaic spelling "shew" rather than the more current "show" on its notices.

11. A "motor cycle combination" was a motor cycle with permanently attached sidecar, usually for passengers.

12. Most motor cycles did not have locks or electrically operated starter motors, so could be easily stolen unless immobilised by the removal of a vital part, in this case a sparking plug. (The American usage of "spark plug" had not yet crossed the Atlantic.)

13. It was still a legal requirement that vehicles parked in the road be lit after dark. If left on for extended periods, a vehicle's sidelights would drain the battery, so most users used a separate low-powered light which nevertheless complied with the law.

14. This was a twin-cylinder model, but nevertheless, removal of only one sparking plug was sufficient to disable it.

15. Marge was a colloquial name for margarine.

16. This was an affectation. Keiller's marmalade was more expensive than Robertson's, but it was made in Jim's home town, Dundee. Robertson's was also made in Scotland, but in Paisley.

17. Formica was the brand name of an American melamine laminate just becoming popular for inexpensive table tops.

18. The Communist Party of Great Britain was organised as the British section of the Third International, and was thus theoretically subservient to its Soviet sponsors. It maintained the doctrine that it should consist of revolutionary cadres and not be open to all applicants. It followed the principle of "democratic centralism" whereby once a policy was decided on by a higher body it could not be questioned. The central power was held by the National Executive (known at that stage as the "Central Committee") and day-to-day operations were overseen by District Committees.

19. Josef Stalin, general secretary of the Communist Party of the Soviet Union and effective dictator of that country.

20. The labour theory of value states that the value of a commodity is to be measured by the labour hours necessary to produce it. In a capitalist society, most of this value is taken by people who have expended none of their own labour its production.

21. At its peak just after the war, the CPGB's membership stood at about 60,000 adults. It gradually declined over the years and by the end of 1956 was down to about 30,000.

22. Karl and Sophie Liebknecht were founders of the Communist Party of Germany. Karl was murdered in 1919 after the failure of

the Spartacist Uprising. Sophie was still alive, dying at the age of 80 in Moscow in 1964.

23. *The Daily Worker* was set up in 1930 as the Communist Party's newspaper, and was re-established in 1941 when the Soviet Union entered the second world war after a period when the paper had been banned. The paper was not a member of the Audit Bureau of Circulations, so its sales figures are disputed: the highest estimates of the *Worker's* circulation were 500,000 copies a day.

24. The Biro ballpoint pens had only recently become available, and Jim had to pay 55 shillings for his — £2 15 shillings, equivalent in value to more than £73 in 2022. By contrast, a fountain pen could be bought for 1s 6d.

25. Mashie – equivalent to a 5 iron, used in thisF case to reach the green in a fairly short hole.

26. Niblick – equivalent to a 9 iron, useful for playing out of the rough.

27. The Dunlop 65 golf ball was introduced not in 1965 but in 1934, the "65" relating to a score registered by Henry Cotton in winning the Open Championship that year.

28. Alderman. These were senior councillors, not directly elected but appointed by the council itself (including the outgoing aldermen), for a term of six years. Thus political control could be maintained even if a party lost at the polls.

29. Elections to local councils were still dominated by supposed Independents, not formally affiliated to any party, which is how Jim Anstruther had himself managed to be elected – officially Independent although in fact a Communist. Similarly, many actual Conservatives described themselves as Progressives. At the time, the borough of Bromley was in Kent rather than London. The Conservatives were already planning to abolish the Labour-dominated London Council, creating the Greater London Council in its place by including various outer London boroughs

such as Bromley so that the Conservative Party would be more likely to take control.

30. Even then, the word "Scotch" was not acceptable in referring to Scots people.

31. Hugh Gaitskell was leader of the opposition Labour Party

32. Anthony Eden, leader of the Conservative Party, was Prime Minister, having taken over from Winston Churchill the previous year.

33. Colonel Gamal Abdel Nasser had been president of Egypt since 1954, having led the 1952 overthrow of the British-backed King Farouk.

34. It was not until 1965 when the death penalty for murder in Great Britain was at last abolished. The 1956 attempt was a Private Member's Bill sponsored by Labour MP Sidney Silverman, and was opposed by the Tory Government. The 1965 Bill, also a Private Member's Bill sponsored by Silverman, was not opposed by the then Labour Government.

35. The union's name was usually abbreviated to the acronym Natsopa.

36. The main meal was usually taken at the middle of the day and was called dinner, followed by an evening meal called tea or supper.

37. The Ashes are a series of "Test" cricket matches between England and Australia played in England or Australia every four years or so since 1882. The 1956 series – which England won – was marked by Australian accusations that the grass had been shaved off the Old Trafford wicket in Lancashire to help the English spin bowlers.

38. Carbon copy. Before the widespread use of photocopying machines, duplicates of typewritten material could be created by the typist inserting sheets of graphite-impregnated carbon paper between multiple sheets of paper on the typewriter platen. Up to

five or so copies could be made at one time, each one fainter than the previous copy. The tradition lives on in the "cc" — representing "carbon copy" — in emails.

39. The paulo-post-future tense of the passive voice of Ancient Greek verbs, chiefly used to indicate that an event would take place immediately.

40. The first Battle of the Somme took place in 1916 near the French river of that name between armies of Britain and France on one side and of Germany on the other. "The conditions are almost unbelievable," wrote Australian soldier Edward Lynch. "We live in a world of Somme mud. We sleep in it, work in it, fight in it, wade in it and many of us die in it. We see   it, feel it, eat it and curse it, but we can't escape it, not even by dying." More than a million men were killed or wounded there.

41. Foolscap — a paper size often used in typewriters. Its width is roughly similar to that of A4 but its depth is 1¼ inch (33mm) longer. The system of organising paper sizes by such measures as A4 did not start until 1975 and the adoption of ISO 216. This is now used worldwide, except in North America.

42. Parker suffered a humiliating defeat, with the referee stopping the unequal fight in the ninth round.

43. R. Hoe and Crabtree was a joint venture between R Hoe & Company of New York and R. W. Crabtree & Sons of Huddersfield. It made printing presses in a factory in Borough Road, London – conveniently close to Fleet Street, where most of the national newspapers were produced.

44. Chewing gum really took off during the second world war when American GIs living in Britain had Wrigleys gum in their ration packs. Gum was then viewed as a glamorous, luxury item during the era of wartime austerity and rationing. When rationing ended in the early 1950s, gum was one of the confectionery products people flocked to buy.

45. Union negotiators had learned that many times in stalled talks there was a deal to be made behind the scenes through informal talks in the men's washrooms.

46. Historical inevitability. Marx and Engels thought socialism was inevitable, not whatever people might do, but because of what people, being rational, were bound, predictably, to do.

47. The Newspaper Proprietors' Association, which was a trade association of employers in which all major national newspapers were represented, indeed had a policy of not undermining each other during a strike. The association later renamed itself the Newspaper Publishers' Association.

Chapter 4

1. The proprietor's car was the four-door limousine version of the Humber Pullman. Without the partition between the front and back seats it was sold to owner-drivers as the Humber Imperial. At 212 inches (5.387 metres) it was the same length as the Rolls-Royce Silver Cloud.

2. Jessica had seen the 1935 version, directed by Alfred Hitchcock, regarded as one of the cinema classics. The 1959 version featuring Kenneth More and Sidney James, was in colour but was otherwise undistinguished.

3. *Reach for the Sky*, just released, starred Kenneth More as the RAF Group Captain Douglas Bader who, after losing both legs in an air crash, returned to flying, becoming a fighter ace. Later in the same year, Bader caused great offence when he responded to public statements by African Commonwealth leaders about the Suez crisis by saying they could "bloody well climb back up their trees".

4. It is not clear when Jessica might have seen *The Cloister and the Hearth*, which was a 1913 British silent film.

5. The racy looking, aluminium-bodied Paramount brand ceased production in 1956 as the £1,009 price proved uncompetitive. There was no connection between the British car company and the American one of the same name.

6. Casual anti-Semitism was still widespread in British society, notwithstanding the horrors of the second world war. It may be assumed that Otto Ross was himself Jewish, although probably non-practising. The name Ross was frequently chosen by immigrants who had been born with names like Rosen or Rosenberg.

7. The Bentley car marque, even though by then owned by Rolls-Royce, still carried the glamour of the pre-war "Bentley Boy" car racers.

8. The Curzon cinema, then as now, specialised in showing films not on general release.

9. See Chapter 1, note 14.

10. Farnsworth is being uncharacteristically prescient here. "Restoring order" was indeed one of the pretexts later used by Britain and France for their joint invasion of the Canal Zone.

11. The Olympic games were due to be held in Melbourne, from 22nd November to 8th December, during the Australian summer.

12. The black and white film, released in 1955 but being shown for the first time in Britain, was officially *L'Amant de Lady Chatterley*.

13. Cinema programmes usually included, as well as the main film, a secondary and shorter feature, as well as a travel documentary, trailers for future shows, a newsreel, and advertisements. *Look at Life* was the running title of the travelogue series, which this time featured Sarawak, which was experiencing its short life as a British Crown Colony between 1946 and independence as part of Malaysia in 1963. Sarawak had previously been the property of the White Rajahs, the Brooke family.

14. The Italian liner Andrea Doria sank on 25th July off Nantucket, after a collision with the liner Stockholm. Forty-six passengers and crew of the two vessels died.

15. Premium Bonds, in which monthly cash prizes were to be given to holders, were announced in the Budget in April. The winning numbers were to picked by a proto-computer called ERNIE, standing for Electronic Random Number Indicator Equipment.

16. The Royal Military Academy, Sandhurst, was where British Army officers were trained. Lear Farnsworth would have attended. Princess Margaret was the younger sister of the Queen.

17. Until 1956 Bank of England five-pound notes were printed in black and white on one side of a large piece of white paper. They were held to be too easy to forge.

18. The end of each cinema performance was marked by the playing of the National Anthem, *God Save the Queen*, during which patrons were expected to stand in silence. The practice gradually ended in the 1960s.

19. The English-language service Radio Luxembourg was a Medium Wave station. Broadcasting from the European Grand Duchy, it circumvented the BBC monopoly of broadcasting on British territory, using what was said to be the world's most powerful privately owned transmitter. Unlike the BBC, it broadcast mostly popular music and was financed by advertising.

20. Younger people spoke of "the radio", whereas earlier generations stuck to "the wireless" — a phrase which had its origins in days of Morse Code and "wireless telegraphy".

21. Fenwick's department store in Bond Street, in the West End of London, specialising in ladies' clothing.

22. Simpson's of Piccadilly was Britain's largest clothing store in floor area. Although most known for its gentlemen's tailoring it also sold ladieswear.

23. The Shaftesbury Memorial Fountain, which stood in the centre of Piccadilly Centre, was topped by a winged statue of Anteros, popularly but incorrectly known as Eros, the Ancient Greek god of love and sex. Because of its central position, it also featured alongside the front-page title, on the masthead, and above the Londoner's Diary gossip column of the London *Evening Standard*.

24. One of London's oldest hotels, marked by quiet luxury, and popular with visiting Americans.

25. Crawford was from Dundee, as was his father. One of the city's largest employers was D. C. Thomson, publisher of Scotland's best-selling paper, the *Sunday Post*, as well as the daily *Dundee Courier* and a host of children's comics, including *The Beano* and *The Dandy*. The company was vehemently Conservative and refused to employ Catholics or members of trade unions.

26. Savile Row – a street with many expensive bespoke tailors.

27. Copper coins were the farthing (¼d), which was fast disappearing, the ha'penny (½d) and the penny. The minimum fare for a journey of any distance on the Underground was 4d.

28. "Sheriff's officer" is a Scotticism. The equivalent in England was a Bailiff.

29. Trolley buses were like trams in that they were long, double-decker vehicles powered from overhead electric lines, but like buses in that they did not run on rails and were steered by their driver. The last one ran in 1962.

30. The pubs, which had shut after the lunchtime trade, were not permitted to open again until 5.30pm.

31. Florin – a two-shilling coin.

32. To clype. Another Scotticism – to tell tales out of school, to gossip, to inform against someone.

33. Excerpts from the Authorized Version of the Bible, the gospel according to Mark, chapter 14, verses 18 to 43.

Chapter 5

1. Capital, volume 3, chapter 48.

2. The baker's boy still delivered to homes several times a week, although the service had almost totally stopped by the late 1960s. Daily doorstep deliveries of milk took longer to die out. In the area Anstruther lived in there were rival milk roundsmen, representing United Dairies and the Co-op. Naturally, Jim used the Co-op service.

3. Tinned Spam from the US was first introduced to Britain in 1941, largely edging out the tinned corned beef previously imported from Argentina. It remained popular in the 1950s, even after the advent of domestic refrigerators.

4. The Communist Parties of France, Britain, the US and other countries had been active in recruiting men to fight in the International Brigades in the Spanish Civil War, from 1936 until 1938. More than 2,000 came from Britain, 500 of them from Scotland alone. In the International Brigades as a whole, 15,000 died in combat against the Fascist rebels, in what was later seen as a dress rehearsal for the second world war.

5. Moss Bros, known for its trade in hiring out gentlemen's evening wear, had its main store directly opposite the Communist Party offices. After 150 years at the same address, it closed in 2016, whereas the Communists shut up shop in 1976.

6. The PKTF was the co-ordinating body set up in 1890 to bring together the various trade unions involved in printing. It closed in 1973.

7. The Imperial Father of the Tribune print unions did not count as a full-time official, even though he carried out union work full time, since his wages were paid by the company he nominally worked for as a stereotyper in the foundry as a member of SLADE,

the Society of Lithographic Artists, Designers, Engravers and Process Workers.

8. Fray Bentos steak and kidney pies came in a flat metal tin which was notoriously difficult to open, especially with a blunt can opener.

9. Charles Fourier, 1772-1837, was a French utopian socialist. Fourier believed that the second most corrupting force in civilized society after capitalism was monogamous marriage. He decried marriage as slavery for women and a sexual prison for husband and wife, against which both partners constantly rebelled by lies and deceptions. By contrast, Marx, and particularly Engels, who wrote extensively on the family and private property, saw themselves as scientific rather than utopian socialists.

10. The Young Communist League was the youth section of the Communist Party and was seen as a recruiting school for activists in the adult party. The age of members was officially from 12 to 29, although in practice most members in their 20s either joined the adult party or left.

11. Intertype was a copy of the Linotype machine, which was possible since the Linotype patents had expired.

Chapter 6

1. The ITA was set up to oversee Independent Television – ITV – Britain's first commercial television network, set up by the Conservative Government to counter the advertising-free BBC. The authority was supposed to enforce "public service" obligations on the broadcasting companies, meaning that – like the BBC – the network had to "educate and inform" as well as entertain. The first ITV company to start broadcasting was London's Associated-Rediffusion, which went on air in September 1955, thus at the time of this meeting the business had been operating for just under a year.

2. Jawaharlal Nehru – then sometimes known as Pandit Nehru, "Pandit" being an honorific – was the first Prime Minister of Independent India, from 1947 to 1964.

3. Instructions had been issued for the Royal Film Performance in June. In the event, none of the three busty actresses obeyed the instruction, Marilyn Monroe and Brigitte Bardot being presented in full décolletage, while Anita Ekberg wore a torpedo-shaped bra under a corset dress.

4. The Government agreed in December to suspend this rule for six months – and never reinstated it afterwards.

5. Linoleum was a floor covering made from solidified linseed oil on a canvas backing. It was superseded by vinyl flooring in the 1960s.

6. Draughts – known in the US as checkers.

7. A tabloid newspaper owned by Associated Newspapers, which also ran the *Daily Mail*. It was Conservative in outlook and never managed to compete with the *Daily Mirror*.

8. The BBC's *Highlight* evening current affairs programme did beat *As It Happens* to an interview with Brigitte Bardot on the day following the *Royal Film Performance*, in which the 22-year-old French actress was indeed dressed in a twin-set buttoned up to the neck. She spoke of her love for animals.

9. Cliff Michelmore, presenter of *Highlight*, continued presenting television shows for the BBC until 2007. He died in 2016, at the age of 96.

10. Vox-pops – short for "vox populi", Latin for "voice of the people" - meaning short interviews with members of the public, generally carried out in the street.

11. Kingsway, the road near Fleet Street where the Associated-Rediffusion television company was located.

12. A kipper was a smoked herring and could not, as such, be caught.

13. The BSA Bantam, a two-stroke 125cc motor cycle based on the German DKW RT125, had largely replaced the BSA 250cc C10 by 1956.

14. The television licence, required for each household with an active television set, cost £3, which included the right to listen to the radio. A radio-only licence cost £1.

15. Not to be confused with an earlier Artemus Jones, the subject of a noted libel trial in 1910. *The Sunday Chronicle*'s Paris correspondent wrote a supposedly fictional account of an Artemus Jones, a Peckham church warden who had gone to Dieppe in northern France with a woman who was not his wife. A real Artemus Jones, who had once worked for the *Sunday Chronicle* and was now a prominent barrister, sued for libel and was awarded £1,750 in damages. The case led to the defence of unintentional defamation in 1952.

16. The August edition of "the British fashion Bible" was already on sale.

17. Norman Hartnell was known as a fashion designer favoured by the Royal Family. He also produced a series of perfumes, of which Jessica preferred the scent "In Love".

18. A brand of filterless cigarette produced by Gallaher. The name refers to the Royal Navy, and the packet featured a drawing of a sailing ship. Smoking had traditionally been associated with the Navy, which cigarette manufacturers sought to reference with the names of brands such as Senior Service, Player's Navy Cut, and Capstan.

19. Nikita Khrushchev was First Secretary of the Communist Party of the Soviet Union. He and Nikolai Bulganin, Premier of the Soviet Union, had made an official visit to Britain from 19th to 27th April that year, during which they were given a warmer welcome by the public than by their governmental hosts. The

propaganda success of the visit led to Khrushchev's decision to visit the US in 1959, which proved even more triumphant.

20. Each of the cameras would be set up with its own white balance and an excessively white part of the picture would be likely to unbalance the shot.

21. John Profumo was later promoted to Secretary of State for War, effectively the Minister responsible for the Army, a post from which he felt required to resign, along with his Parliamentary seat, after admitting that he had lied to the House of Commons regarding a sexual affair with a young woman, Christine Keeler, who was simultaneously in a sexual relationship with a senior naval attaché at the Soviet Embassy.

22. The Universal film *Dracula* had its premiere in 1931.

23. The Cominform, the official central organization of the International Communist movement had actually been disbanded in April that year, following Khruschev's "secret speech" about the excesses of the Stalin era.

24. A Private Member's Bill was a way of introducing legislation without official Government backing. In practice, few of such Bills are actually passed into law, but the system is still widely used as a way of generating publicity.

25. Cockney was the working-class London dialect, which was gradually softening and giving way to the "Estuarial English" accent.

26. The words "We don't want to fight; but, by Jingo, if we do, we've got the ships, we've got the men, we've got the money too" come from a patriotic song written by George "Jingo" Hunt in 1877 in advance of the Crimean War with Russia.

27. German general Erwin Rommel's army was defeated in 1942 at the battle of El Alamein. The British victory, along with the Germans' subsequent defeat at the Battle of Stalingrad, was a turning point in the second world war.

28. The Gurkhas were mercenary soldiers from Nepal serving in the British Army. At the peak of the second world war there were 10 Gurkha regiments, and even in 1956 there was a full Gurkha division in Malaya where it was supposed to train for a potential wartime role in the Middle East.

29. Army slang for "pretty damn quick" but apparently a phrase that originated in the US in the 1870s.

30. A saloon car made by the Standard Motor Company in Coventry. The Standard company was not part of the British Motor Corporation so was not affected by that firm's strike.

31. Jowett stopped making cars and vans in 1953. During the second world war several thousand cars and vans had been converted to run on coal gas stored in large bags on their roofs, thus avoiding the strict petrol rationing. Petrol rationing was reintroduced in December 1956 in response to the Suez crisis.

32. As the name implied, Player's Weights cigarettes had originally been sold by weight rather than number, although by the post-war years they were available in packets of five, 10 or 20. They were priced lower than Player's main brand, and to capitalise on the move towards tipped cigarettes a new sub-brand, Tipped Weights, had just been introduced. Advertising of cigarettes on television continued until 1965, after which cigarette advertising was still permitted on cinema screens and advertising of cigars continued on television.

33. Gibbs SR, a brand of toothpaste made by Unilever, was the first product to be promoted on UK television, on 22nd September 1955.

34. Anadin tablets were basically aspirin plus caffeine. Aspirin had been a trade name owned by the Bayer company of Germany but their trademark rights had not been properly enforced and had hence lapsed.

35. Richard Dimbleby, even by then regarded as veteran broadcaster, had been used by the BBC to voice the television commentary for the Queen's Coronation at Westminster Abbey in 1953.

36. Gamages was a large department store in Holborn, conveniently close to Fleet Street. It had an extensive hardware and kitchen appliances department.

37. Quarto was a size of writing paper, the same width as foolscap but shorter in length.

38. "Bolshevik" was a term of abuse directed at Communists or their sympathisers.

Chapter 7

1. The telephone system was run as a monopoly by the Post Office Telegraph and Telephone Service until 1969, when it became the Post Office Corporation (Telecommunications division). The system was privatised as British Telecom in 1981.

2. The Gieves & Hawkes men's tailoring company at 1 Savile Row had long specialised in military and naval uniforms.

3. Catterick, near Richmond in Yorkshire — a huge British Army camp and training centre.

4. In the call boxes of the time, one inserted two pennies for a local call and dialled the number. When the phone was answered the caller could hear the other party but could be heard until Button A was pressed. If it was a wrong number – as was frequently the case – the caller could press Button B to have the 2d returned.

5. Waveney was the Co-op's own brand, owned by the Co-operative Wholesale Society. The Anstruther household, as a matter of socialist principle, tried to buy from the Co-op whenever they could. Their local Co-op was run by the South Suburban Co-operative Society.

6. These were followers of Leon Trotsky, the revolutionary who had fallen out with Stalin and opposed the Communist Party

from the Left. Trotskyites had formed a plethora of tiny, rival organisations in Britain, many of which spent most of their time arguing with other Trotskyite grouplets.

7. The Polish United Workers' Party was the name of the governing Communist Party in that country. Contrary to the spirit of democratic centralism, the party was seriously divided in 1956. In June, following a series of strikes, the party chose a new leader, Władysław Gomułka, who proceeded to introduce "a Polish way socialism" rather than the more rigid and doctrinaire policies of his predecessor. The initial "Gomułka thaw" in 1956 and its acceptance by Moscow meant that Poland avoided the fate of Hungary.

Chapter 9

1. Drummond's bank, whose plush banking hall was grandly situated beside Admiralty Arch, was by then owned by the Royal Bank of Scotland. Jessica chose it because it was known to look after the funds of the Conservative Party. If the Tories trusted it with their money, it must be safe enough for normal people.

2. The prestigious Peter Jones department store on Sloane Square was and is part of the John Lewis employee-owned partnership.

3. A reference to the final words of the *Communist Manifesto*: "Let the ruling classes tremble at a Communistic revolution. The proletarians have nothing to lose but their chains. They have a world to win. Workingmen of all countries unite!"

4. *Boxing News*. Published weekly since 1909. Now a magazine, in 1956 it was in tabloid newspaper format.

5. That year Edith Summerskill, a medical doctor as well as a Labour Member of Parliament had already published her anti-boxing book *The Ignoble Art*, (Heinemann, London. ISIN B0006DB3OS). In 1960 she introduced in Parliament a Private Member's Bill to ban professional boxing. It was defeated by

120 votes to just 17. Elevated to the House of Lords as Baroness Summerskill she made a similar attempt in 1962, which was again defeated, but by a narrower margin, 29 votes to 22.

6. In response to London's notorious fogs, the worst of which, in 1952, was blamed for 6,000 deaths (although later research put the figure at about 12,000), the Government introduced the 1956 Clean Air Act, which allowed it to declare "smoke control areas" in which coal fires were prohibited – although "smokeless fuels" such as coke could still be burned. The City of London – which was free of any heavy coal-using industry – was the first such smokeless zone.

7. Jessica was being too hopeful. The next year, notwithstanding the Clean Air Act, in the London fog of 2nd to 5th December 1957 smoke and sulphur dioxide concentrations reached levels comparable to 1952 and there were at least 760 deaths.

8. VE Day – marking Victory in Europe, or the defeat of Nazi Germany – was on 8th May 1945, although the war continued in the Far East until 15th August. This makes Jim aged 32 to Jessica's 22.

9. In the second world war there were about 60,000 registered conscientious objectors in Britain, compared with just 20,000 or so in the first world war, presumably because the conditions attached were less stringent. There had been several "reserved occupations" regarded as essential to the war effort, among them miners and lighthouse keepers. Printing workers were not exempt from service in the armed forces. It was widely believed in Communist circles that members were deliberately excluded from the forces so they could not influence the political views of the soldiers, sailors and airmen.

10. A delegation led by Australian Prime Minister Robert Menzies was sent to Cairo to negotiate with the Egyptians over the Suez crisis. The attempt was an abject failure.

11. The US Secretary of State, John Foster Dulles, made it clear from the start of the Suez crisis that it was against any armed conflict.

12. It is now known that the Israeli invasion of Egypt had been secretly co-ordinated with Britain and France in order to provide a pretext for their own armed incursion, supposedly "to separate the combatants".

13. Hugh Gaitskell was leader of the Labour Party, which had bitterly opposed any use of British troops in Egypt, insisting that the crisis had to be solved by the United Nations. In fact, a UN plan to stop the conflict was vetoed by the British and French at the Security Council. Gaitskell argued the British and French action was a "transparent excuse to seize the Canal".

14. *The Daily Herald* was earlier the official newspaper of the TUC, the Trades Union Congress, but was now owned by Odhams Press although it still supported the Labour Party. The *Herald* was later sold to the International Publishing Corporation but continued to support Labour, even after it was renamed *The Sun* in 1964. It abruptly switched sides when it was bought by Rupert Murdoch's News Corporation in 1969.

15. Khruschev had delivered the "secret speech" on "The Cult of Personality and Its Consequences" to a closed session of the 20th Congress of the Communist Party of the Soviet Union on 25th February 1956. Khrushchev charged Stalin with having fostered a leadership cult of personality despite ostensibly maintaining support for the ideals of communism.

16. Following the visit of Khruschev and Bulganin, Moscow's Bolshoi Ballet was due to perform at the Royal Opera House, Covent Garden, in October.

17. After four days of bargaining, even involving the British ambassador to Moscow, Ponomareva left the embassy and appeared at Marlborough Street Magistrates' Court where she

was given an absolute discharge but was ordered to pay 3 guineas costs, immediately leaving on a ship back to the Soviet Union, the costs presumably unpaid.

18. C&A was a large, inexpensive clothing store, founded by Dutch textile traders Clemens and August Brenninkmeijer. The company had actively collaborated with the German Nazi occupiers of the Netherlands throughout the war, taking advantage of forced labour in order to expand the business. C&A closed its last British store in 2001.

19. After the film *Rock Around the Clock* was screened at the Trocadero in Piccadilly in London, police were called to quell a potential riot as teen-agers leaving the cinema acted boisterously and in an overly excited fashion. The distributors, the Rank Organisation, abandoned plans to show the film in other venues around Britain for fear of further disturbance.

20. The *Sketch*, in line with its policy of prurient moral outrage, claimed there was a "problem" with "petting" among young people – essentially non-penetrative sexual activity.

21. The Warsaw Pact, officially the Treaty of Friendship, Co-operation and Mutual Assistance, had been set up only 15 months previously, as a military agreement between the Soviet Union, Poland, Hungary and five other Eastern European socialist countries, in retaliation for the American-dominated military pact known as Nato, or the North Atlantic Treaty Organization, rearming West Germany and integrating it into full membership. The action by Imre Nagy's Hungarian government in withdrawing from the Warsaw Pact was seen as a deliberately provocative repudiation of the country's subservience to the Soviet Union.

Chapter 10

1. Shops generally closed at noon on Saturdays and did not open again until 9am on Monday, in addition to one day a week – the

"early-closing day" which varied from Wednesday to Thursday according to the rules set by each town – when the shops did not reopen after the midday closure.

Chapter 11

1. It was still difficult to buy cars in the years after the war, and there were many pre-war models still on the road. The mass-selling and inexpensive Austin 7 was one of these. Even the four-seater saloon models had only two doors, the front seats folding to allow access to the rear. Even when new, it was under-powered, with a 750cc engine delivering a theoretical maximum speed of 60mph (96km/h). One of its many other problems was a notoriously vicious clutch, engaging very sharply.

2. KGB was the short-form for the Soviet *Komitet Gosudarstvennoy Bezopasnosti*, the Committee for State Security, or secret police.

3. The tissues brand "Kleenex For Men" was introduced in 1956 and heavily advertised.

4. The Metropolitan Police "Special Branch" was founded in 1883 to monitor activities of the Irish Republican Brotherhood. In the 1950s it spent most of its time carrying out surveillance on what it regarded as subversive elements, including the Communist Party.

5. Technical Colleges provided further education between high school and university or polytechnic and also offered courses to provide qualifications for tradesmen. They should not be confused with the Technical Schools, which had been created under the 1944 Education Act as a half-way-house between the academic Grammar Schools and the mass-education Secondary Moderns. They were intended to teach pupils mechanical, scientific and engineering skills to serve industry and science, but very few such schools were ever actually set up.

6. Since Jessica was talking about her years in the US, she used the American term. Later on, in a different context, she reverts to "holidays".

Chapter 12

1. "Ministers", while not actually incorrect in an English context, is Scottish usage.

2. The dole. Alleviating financial distress caused by unemployment became part of the "cradle to the grave" welfare system set up by the Labour Government after the war. The Conservative Government made no major changes to the system.

Chapter 13

1. It was still unusual for men to wear wedding rings, and in any case Jim would not have been able to make such a public statement.

Chapter 14

1. Permanent waves, or "perms" had returned to fashion after the war, when "utility" hair styles had been dominant.

2. He was one of only 16 British armed services personnel known to have died in the Suez engagement.

3. The glossy monthly favoured by middle-class British housewives had been published monthly since 1919. It was priced at 2 shillings.

4. Anthony Eden did not last much longer as Prime Minister following his disastrous handling of the Suez crisis, resigning the next January, with "ill health" given as the reason.

5. *The Worker* was drawing parallels between British and French actions over Suez and those of the Nazis and other fascists in a mirror image of the way Anthony Eden and other Conservatives were trying to liken Colonel Nasser to Hitler. The horrors in Abyssinia had been carried out by Mussolini's Italy in 1935-76, the terror bombing of Guernica was carried out by Nazi German

aircraft in 1937 during the Spanish Civil War. There had been similar Nazi atrocities in Warsaw and Rotterdam, while London and other British cities had been attacked by the German air force during its Blitzkrieg, or "lightning war" in 1940-41.

6. A call for strike action.

7. *Any Questions?* — a weekly BBC radio discussion programme started in 1948.

Chapter 15

1. Betterwear salesmen went door-to-door offering brushes, household products and cleaning materials.

2. Mormons – from what was officially called the Church of Latter-Day Saints – started the missionary activities in Britain as early as 1879. After a pause for the war, their missionaries - polite and earnest young men, always dressed in suits and ties – went door-to-door seeking converts.

3. Electric kettles were available, but since the early models took as long to boil water as traditional kettles, they were not widely used until the coming of the Hotpoint Hi-speed Kettle in 1959.

4. Telex was the switched network of teleprinters similar to a telephone network, used for sending printed messages. Multiple copies of a Telex message could be made by the use of carbon-paper-interleaved rolls of printing paper.

5. Beatnik was a term of abuse used in the 1950s popular press to describe a young person with scruffy or unconventional clothes, or with an unusual lifestyle.

6. Socialist Review Group – one of the many Trotskyite sects active at the time. The SRG was based around the small-circulation magazine of that name. It renamed itself the International Socialists in 1962 and again renamed itself in 1977 as the Socialist Workers' Party.

7. A religious revivalist group using the same door-to-door preaching tactics as the Mormons.

8. The committee, together with official rationing of newsprint supplies, had in fact ended, but Jim was hoping that management would not be aware of the fact.

9. The 1926 General Strike lasted nine days, from 4th to 12th May 1926. It was called by the general council of the Trades Union Congress in support of the 1.2 million coal miners who had been locked out by their employers who wanted to enforce wage reductions and longer working hours. In response, the Government enlisted middle class volunteers to boost the police force, to publish a government-controlled newspaper, and to maintain what the Government saw as essential services. After discussions with the Government the TUC agreed to end the strike without even an undertaking that participants would not be punished.

10. It lasted 133 days.

11. The dog licence, which was priced at 7 shillings and sixpence per animal, was abolished in 1988.

12. Jessica's statement echoes the final sentence of George Orwell's Animal Farm (Secker & Warburg, 1945): "The creatures outside looked from pig to man, and from man to pig, and from pig to man again; but already it was impossible to say which was which."

Acknowledgements

The cover picture was taken by American photographer Tony Frissell (1907-1988) of Swedish model Lisa Fonssagrives in 1951, and is held in the US Library of Congress Toni Frissell Collection. On original publication in *Harper's Bazaar* 1951 the location was stated as Victoria Station, London, but it is now believed to have been taken at Paddington Station.

Thanks to my friend Suresh Menon, who took the picture of me on the back cover while I was at my desk at the *Business Times* in Singapore. I would like to thank Lesley Lodge, herself an acclaimed author, who read an early version of this work and encouraged me to continue.

The newspaper headlines quoted from the *London Evening Standard, Evening News, Evening Star, The Times, Daily Sketch, Daily Herald, Daily Worker* and *Daily Express* are taken from the editions of those newspapers held at the British Library Newspaper Collection at Colindale, North London, now relocated to Boston Spa, West Yorkshire.

My thanks to Peter Langdon for his painstaking work in creating the cover and the internal layout of this book in its ebook and printed form.

Despite the best endeavours of all concerned, there are bound still to be errors that have crept in; please send any corrections to me at clyne@europe.com.

Made in the USA
Las Vegas, NV
31 August 2022